MIDLIFE DAWN

DRUID HEIR BOOK 1

N. Z. NASSER

HANORA SKY PRESS

Midlife Dawn: Druid Heir Book 1
Copyright © N. Z. Nasser 2021
Published by Hanora Sky Press

All rights reserved.

No part of this book may be reproduced, stored in a retrieval system, or transmitted, in any form or by any electronic or mechanical means, without prior written permission from the author, except for the use of brief quotations in a book review.

This book is a work of fiction. All characters, organisations and events in this novel are products of the author's imagination. Any resemblance to real people, living or dead, or to real companies or occurrences is coincidental.

eBook ISBN 978-1-915151-00-1
Paperback ISBN 978-1-915151-01-8

THE PLAYERS

Alisha Verma - Druid Heir
Rosalie Verma - Alisha's mother
Joshi Verma - Alisha's father
Echo - Alisha's cat
Marina Ambrose - Alisha's best friend
Ezra Neuhoff - Alisha's half-werewolf, half-wizard mentor
Gaia - Mysterious old woman
Sahil Verma - Alisha's brother
Robert Jameson - Detective
Phinnaeous Shine - Shapeshifter, Prime Sorcerer
Orpheus Might - Vampire, Minister for History and the Today
Rayna Willowsun - Druid, Headmistress of Wildwoods School of the Wondrous
Helio Woodwink - Fairy, the Minister for the Bestiary
Lavinia Drach - Witch, Minister for Defence
Lavinia's coven - Ravynne, Elvira, Agatha, Isadora, Chandra, Morgan
Alisha's night class students - Fei Yen, Faeza, Nita, Marek, Tomás, Santiago, Farzad, Nagma, Ethan, Hassan
Alex Harrison - Alisha's ex-husband
Melissa Ramsay - Rosalie's colleague and friend

Kraglek - Magical octopus touched by the goddess Ganga
The girls who faced Kraglek - Mirabel, Gaylia, Maura, Nessa, Soleis
Julianne and Milo - Alisha's neighbour and her pet poodle
The electrician
The gravedigger

1

I stood under fluorescent lighting in the hallway of the community centre. I knew better than to take a call in the middle of teaching, but it wasn't every day a detective called to discuss the suspicious circumstances of your mum's death.

She was killed last week, on the eve of her retirement, and my heart had broken into a thousand pieces.

Stifled chatter came from the other side of the classroom door. My students had obviously decided to abandon the comprehension I'd tasked them with and snoop on me instead. You'd think they were of nursery school age, not adults attending a night class.

My phone burned hot against my ear as I processed the detective's words. "What do you mean her car had flowers growing from the metal? Flowers don't grow out of metal, Detective."

"It was as if they'd grown to cushion her. And the flowers aren't the only anomalies we've discovered," said the detective.

I blocked out the sound of the class as my pulse raced. "What kind of anomalies?"

"Your mother was driving at a perfectly respectable speed.

There were no other vehicles involved. It could be she saw a fox and made an evasive manoeuvre that went wrong. It wouldn't have been the first time. But the crime scene report showed an electrical fault. It raised question marks, given your mother's car had just been serviced."

They'd found her upside down, still dangling from her seatbelt. What I couldn't work out was how someone who drove at a snail's pace could crash on a quiet, lamp-lit road. "That's odd. I arranged the service myself. I trust the mechanic."

"Nothing to worry about, I'm sure, but I'd rather cover all angles." The sound of shuffling papers reached my ears through the phone line. "Was your mother worried about anything? Did her behaviour change prior to her death?"

I frowned, both at his questions and the ruckus still coming from the classroom. "She'd been working longer hours, I suppose. It's nothing she couldn't handle."

"You know she was reprimanded at work for releasing lab animals?"

"That's impossible." I opened the classroom door.

Four eavesdroppers fell out, righted themselves and gave me sheepish grins.

I shooed them back to their seats before retreating into the corridor again.

"In my line of work, you soon learn that nothing is impossible," said the detective. "Sometimes, we don't know the people we love best."

Wasn't that the truth?

It had only taken me over a decade to accept that my ex, Alex, was a prize jerk.

I didn't intend to end up in a dead-end marriage, but it just happened. Too many meals in front of the television, too few adventures together, too many differing expectations. The last straw was when the loan sharks came knocking. He'd gambled away our life savings, and I hadn't even known. I thought he'd said no to our dream house and travelling abroad because he was being sensible.

Turned out he really liked fruit machines. The arsehole.

"Detective Jameson, was it? Can we pick this up another time, please? I have to get back to my class."

"Not a problem, Mrs Verma. I'm sure we'll be talking again." He hung up.

"It's Ms Verma, actually," I muttered, making my way back into the classroom.

Pages fluttered as the ten students in my night class pretended to pore over the text I'd asked them to read.

I plastered on a smile and sneaked a look at the top drawer of my desk, tempted to grab another painkiller. I'd been swallowing them like sweets all day. After the week I'd had, nothing was going to take the edge off my headache except possibly a rewind button. For now, I pushed aside the discussion with the detective. "Right, you lot. I take it you know the text back to front now. I'll take eavesdropper number one first. You're up, Marek. When was the Great Fire of London?"

"1966?" said Marek with a glimmer of hope, although he was almost always wrong.

"No, afraid not. Scan the text and try again using a full sentence."

I taught English and survival skills to immigrants in godforsaken London, where the streets were mean and job opportunities were scarce. The council paid me a decent wage and didn't pay much attention to the curriculum. I focussed on a mix of English grammar, vocabulary and deciphering texts. I also included cultural norms, like introducing my students to the pub and sweaty gigs and a sprinkling of literature. The balcony scene of Romeo and Juliet could be a great icebreaker.

Mum had been a big reader too.

I didn't want to talk about Mum in the past tense. I wanted to hear her voice and watch her pottering in the garden during her retirement. It wasn't any consolation that she'd lived a full life. I mean, her work as a scientist changed lives, her marriage to Dad was a fairy tale, and her grown children had long flown the nest.

I just wanted her here with us. Were you ever old enough to lose your mother?

Forty-year-old me needed her still, what with my messy divorce and a stagnant career.

Instead, I found myself teaching my third night class of the week at a community centre in South London, pretending everything was okay, just like all the other middle-aged, multitasking women I knew.

Smiling on the outside. Screaming on the inside.

Of course, Mum's death had left me spinning, but I'd been a hot mess long before. Somewhere along the way from radiant fiancée to escapee from a combusting marriage, I'd lost my spark. That's not even including midlife woes like not being able to go braless and needing afternoon naps just to get through the day.

"Miss, Marek has got his hand up," said Tomás, one of my Portuguese students.

I grimaced. "Sorry, Marek, I didn't see you there."

"He's right in front of you," said Nita, my youngest student.

I gave my best encouraging smile and crossed my fingers behind my back. "Go ahead, Marek."

He scrunched up his brow in concentration. "The Great Fire of London is in 1669."

The class groaned. By now, most of them had worked out the answer.

"Not quite. The Great Fire of London *was* in 1666. You'll get there."

Fei Yen and Faeza, two middle-aged Chinese women, put their hands up, eerily in sync with each other as always. They spoke perfect English but enjoyed the social side of the night class.

"Yes, Fei Yen?"

"I think Marek would do better if we were reading about Princess Diana. Everyone likes to read about her."

"Or the Black Death," said Faeza.

"Or Jack the Ripper." Santiago's ruddy face betrayed the beer he'd consumed before class.

I shook my head. "Let's just focus on what we have in front of us. How about you next, Santiago?" I looked down at the page. "Sorry, I've lost my train of thought. Just give me a minute."

"Are you okay, miss?" said Nita.

"Of course, she's not okay. We read it in the cards," Fei Yen and Faeza said in unison. They ran a tea and occult shop called Shanghai Moon around the corner from my flat and were always spouting nonsense about horoscopes and tarot cards and whatnot.

"I'm fine." Except, I wasn't fine. I couldn't tell my class that, obviously. My job was to build them up and send them out into the world, not to burden them with my troubles. I could go home and eat chocolate instead. I'd been working out hard in the gym as an *up-yours* to Alex, but one giant bar of Cadburys wouldn't hurt. Not that my waistline would thank me.

There was no easy way to lose a loved one, but I'd royally messed things up. After forty years of being the *good* child—the one who accompanied my parents to the doctor, arranged for their car to be serviced and always came home for celebration days—I'd lost it with Mum on the day she died. Worse still, our last conversation had been about my ex-husband. Hell, if I could rewind to that day, I'd replace that conversation with anything but him: the time I had worms as a kid, saggy boobs, or the best drain cleaners for unclogging pipes. *Anything* would have been better than wasting our last conversation on him.

I'd already given Alex twelve years of my life. He didn't need to hijack my last conversation with Mum too.

For twelve long years, I was stuck in a rented house with his dirty pants and socks piling up on the floor. Like he'd ever lift a finger. Still, I'd thought he loved me. Why else would he insist we keep trying for a baby? I tried to enjoy Fridays and Sundays, I promise, but some days I had to think of Chris Hemsworth or Chris Pine to get through it. Any Chris would have done, really. I felt bad, of course.

Even after the divorce, he could have just driven off into the sunset and married the next gullible fool. Instead, he stuck around and tried to win custody of my cat—the beautiful Bengal cat, which had been mine since childhood.

What kind of man did that?

Someone who deserved a kick in the jingle bells, that's who.

Still, as soon as I hit forty, I decided to live my life for me and embrace my weirdness. If you're still contorting yourself for other people when you hit middle age, when will you learn to embrace your chin hairs and soar to new heights? I drew a line through my sorry relationship with Alex and moved into a new, smaller flat with my cat. Just your friendly neighbourhood cat lady, that's me. Thank my lucky stars I hadn't taken his name. I could just pretend he never existed.

Only Mum hadn't seen it that way.

Now she was gone, I couldn't tell her that it didn't matter about him. I would take on all the arseholes in the world if it meant one more day with her.

"Earth to Ms Verma," said Nita.

I tuned back into the class. "Right, class, copy down the questions from the board. Reread the text and answer the questions in full sentences. Use a dictionary. You've worked so hard tonight that we're finishing twenty minutes early."

Okay, so it was a lie. We'd not even hit a third of my lesson plan, but a small lie never hurt anyone. It was the whoppers that floored you.

Nita piped up. "But Ms Verma, we thought you could teach us the back kick again."

I shook my head. "Sorry, not tonight."

Adding kickboxing to my curriculum really helped with student motivation. I taught them a few moves if they impressed me with their learning. London was a city of strays. Its inhabitants needed to know how to be quick with their fists and boots to survive the streets.

"We'll practice next time, I promise. Don't forget to do your homework. No excuses." My body sagged with relief when my students scattered into the moonlit night.

I'd taken a big long hard look at myself when I turned forty and wasn't sure I liked what I saw. Sure, my body had weathered the years just fine. My long, dark hair was a little wild but as thick as it had been at university. My mixed-race skin had a glow that offset the incoming crow's feet. I might never have carried a baby in my belly, but I had more flexibility than your average forty-year-old. Still, I'd hardly changed the world. Not even my small corner of it, unless you counted conjugating verbs and teaching cockney rhyming slang to my students.

It was nearing ten o'clock by the time I tucked in the last chairs, switched off the lights and locked up the community centre. I zipped up my coat, pulled my hood up against silver arrows of rain and set off home through the grubby car park, passing high-rise blocks, chimney stacks and asphalt marked with chewing gum and dog mess. Reaching home took a good twenty-minute walk to my flat on the other side of Balham or a ten-minute jog across a couple of grimy estates. The sorts of places that stank of piss in dank corners and A-class drugs swapped hands under cover of darkness.

I kept my eyes open and my keys in my hand as a

weapon against any unwanted attention. Every Londoner worth their salt knew to keep their wits about them late at night. It was easy to underestimate a forty-year-old woman, but I could handle myself. Years of yoga and kickboxing had seen to that.

Mum had always insisted I be able to look after myself. London was a jungle compared to her native Brittany. The funny thing was, darting shadows and slinking shapes seemed a breath away since her death.

At the top of my road, something brushed my shoulder. Not a branch but a hand.

Without missing a beat, I held the palm in both hands, twisted under the arm and pushed my attacker into a kneeling position. I raised my leg to kick him in the face, but a gust of wind came from nowhere and knocked him off balance. He flew three feet and landed in a heap on the rain-slicked pavement.

Anger, hot and blazing. "Get lost, arsehole."

I had the upper hand, so I backed away, my fists ready to take him on. I hoped I didn't have to flip him again because my back was sore, but I had no doubt I could handle it. My flat was minutes away, but I didn't want a random knowing where I lived.

Grey eyes, longish hair, low-slung jeans. In any other setting, I'd have given him a second look, but he had no business creeping up on women late at night.

The man gritted his teeth in pain. He opened the palm of his hand. "You dropped your keys."

Embarrassment made my cheeks flush hot. My boss would have skinned me if I'd lost the community centre keys. "Oh, sorry about that. Can't be too careful."

He sprang to his feet, light-footed despite the rain, dusted himself off and tossed me the keys.

I caught them, stuffed them into my pocket and made a show of buttoning it shut.

"Quite the reflexes you have there." The cut of his jaw and the glint in his eyes told me he was dangerous.

I eyed him warily. "Yeah, well, thanks again."

"Don't mention it." He definitely had a wet bum, judging by his stiffness as he walked away.

I waited until he disappeared from sight before pushing on towards my tree-lined road, where headlights flashed over the yellow bricks and mortar of the buildings. I unlocked the door of my building and walked through the Victorian-tiled hallway to my ground-floor flat, half expecting to trip over the cat.

"Echo?" I called once inside, slipping my shoes and coat off.

Still no sign of him.

Usually, he was my shadow. He threaded through my legs when I came in the door and even followed me to bed. He was a mean fighting machine, but he'd been missing since Mum's funeral, and I was starting to get worried. I'd even put out scrambled eggs for him.

If Alex was behind Echo's disappearance, maybe I'd get a chance to kick him in the nuts after all.

I headed for the back bedroom, where I'd left the window open for him. It wasn't like I had anything to steal. The landlord didn't strictly allow pets, but turned a blind eye as long as the other tenants didn't complain.

I checked the living room, hoping to find Echo curled on the sofa. In the kitchen, the scrambled eggs had dried into a rubbery mess in his bowl. I scraped them into the bin and put out some kibble instead, not that the fusspot ate that willingly. My empty fridge hummed in the corner.

"Bed it is then." I downed a glass of water and made myself a hot water bottle. Then I padded to my bedroom and flicked on the light. "What on earth? You've got to be kidding me."

That was *not* how I'd left my flat that morning. An

enormous imprint flattened the centre of the bed as if a rhino had lain there. Patches of dirt marred the white cotton sheets. Even the freshly fluffed pillow had been compressed. I'd only just changed the sheets. The bed should have smelled of lavender, not muck.

Had Echo been back and brought a harem of cats with him? It wouldn't have been the first time.

"It's not my day. Actually, scrap that. I need a reset button for the past week." I dusted off the sheets and then burrowed under the duvet as storms swirled outside, wondering why Mum would release animals from her laboratory and how on earth flowers could grow from the chassis of a crushed car.

2

The next afternoon, I made my way to Balham tube under clouds as dark as iron filaments. I stuck missing cat flyers for Echo on trees, gritting my teeth at the sight of my phone number on display for all to see.

Since the divorce, all sorts of whackos had been calling to ask me out. Meddling Indian grannies at our temple had spread the rumour I was a free agent again. I knew because they texting me hair-raising pictures of their unattached offspring. I might have been flattered, but it was the swan song of my ovaries they were after, not me.

I rode the escalator down towards the platform.

Alex had claimed the car in the divorce, and I let him think he won that round. Car insurance cost an arm and a leg, and London's sprawling public transport system meant I could just as easily get around without one. A few minutes later, I was aboard the rattling northern line tube towards Elephant & Castle in a carriage with open windows, enjoying the gusts of underground breeze. My best friend Marina always said the air down here was grim—moist and full of germs—but I liked it. It blew away the cobwebs in my head.

I needed that today if I was going to be in any fit state at Mum's memorial.

I hopped off the tube and met Dad and my brother outside Mum's former workplace, a grey concrete high-rise with milky windows a stone's throw away from the monstrous roundabout at Elephant & Castle. They were dressed in suits. My brother's gave off distinct Saville Row vibes, which made Dad look even more of a mess in his moth-balled, crumpled offering. A smear of indigo paint sat just beneath Dad's chin like he'd missed the canvas with his paintbrush. When he was in the middle of a piece, no one else existed.

"You scrub up well." I hugged them and wiped the paint off Dad's face.

Dad's haunted eyes stared at me. He'd lost his soulmate, after all. "What would I do without you?"

"You'd be right as rain," I said, though I knew Mum had been the strong one.

"Has Echo turned up yet? I can help look for him."

"Let's just get through this first, shall we?" said my brother, Sahil. At two years my senior, he was a successful businessman with a portfolio of rental houses and a penthouse apartment next to St. Paul's that dripped in luxury.

"It's not a memorial if there are no prayers, is it?" said Dad. "It's not like they'll be praying for Rosalie's soul here. I should have stayed home and prayed at our shrine."

Mum had been Christian, but she hadn't been a churchgoer. She liked Christmas Eve carols and Norwegian Christmas trees, but that was about it. Dad only went to temple for the social side. I couldn't remember the last time he knelt at our Ganesha shrine. Hardly anyone prayed nowadays: Christian, Hindu, Muslim, you name it. These days, most people worshipped mobile phones or Netflix instead.

Sahil looked at his watch, his mouth in a grim line. "I have to hurry, sis. I have a meeting I have to get back for."

"I thought the plan was to go through Mum's things with Dad?"

He raised a well-groomed eyebrow. "News to me."

Fair to say, my brother wasn't my favourite person. He showed up on his terms and rarely softened unless it was for one of his boob tube-wearing or whiskey-drinking friends. Every time I decided to try to like him for the sake of our parents, he pushed my buttons again.

"Let's go." I propelled them towards the revolving door, feeling more like a jailer than a family member.

Inside the lobby, a receptionist in chopstick-thin heels handed out name labels to stick on our chests and ushered us past security. Together, we rode the elevator to the fourth floor and exited past laboratories where centrifuges whirred and employees huddled over microscopes and Petri dishes.

I swallowed the lump in my throat. How many times had Mum and Dad debated whether microscopes or telescopes were better? Whether the greater miracles were cells or stars?

"We've arranged for finger sandwiches, teas and coffees, and of course, the CEO will be here to say a few words." The receptionist led us into a conference room, where rows of chairs had been set out in front of a lectern.

With only a dozen people in attendance, most chairs stood empty.

The receptionist showed us to reserved seats in the front row. "Would you like me to introduce you to everyone?"

Dad and I exchanged looks.

"No, thank you," he said.

We sat down just as the big boss, Michael, entered the room, his bald head gleaming under the spotlights. A hush descended over those gathered as he strode over to us.

A bald head behind a vast desk, Mum had said.

"Joshi," he said to Dad. "How awful to see you in such circumstances. Please accept my condolences."

"Michael, thanks for arranging this." Dad shook his hand. "You really shouldn't have."

He nodded at us all. "What a tragic loss. Shall we get started?" He extricated himself and moved over to the lectern. "Thank you all for coming. We're here to commemorate the life of Dr Rosalie Verma, who was taken from us so suddenly last week. As many of you know, Rosalie may have been French, but she was also a Londoner through and through. She loved her city, and she loved EvolveTech. Why else would she have stayed here for almost two decades?"

The crowd murmured politely.

My mind flashed to the graveyard with the mound of fresh soil.

"Rosalie was a diligent, popular employee. She cared deeply about her work. She was also a wife and mother, and she leaves behind a grieving family and friends. Her work on Parkinson's, MS, dementia and, most recently, on cell regeneration can't be underestimated." The boss's eyes narrowed.

I followed his gaze to the back of the room.

There stood a woman with a cherubic face, though she must have been in her seventies. Her plump frame was wrapped in a green sari. Despite the rainy forecast, she wore flat, gold sandals, and her thick, black hair was plaited over one shoulder. Rosy cheeks, bright eyes and a soft mouth softened her wrinkly face. She was the most interesting person in the room by far—a spark of colour in a sea of black suits and white lab coats—flanked by two disgruntled security guards.

Michael tore his eyes away from the disruption and smiled at a friend of Mum's sitting in the congregation.

"Melissa, as Rosalie's closest friend here, perhaps you'd like to say a few words?"

He waited for her to reach him, then strode to the back of the room.

I gave Melissa an encouraging smile as she approached the lectern. Behind me, a scuffle erupted that made my sense of injustice prickle. I'd had just about enough of men pushing women around. Yes, I might have been a little sensitive after Alex and the loan sharks, but I wasn't going to sit back and watch a little old lady be manhandled.

"Where are you going?" whispered Dad as I slipped out of my seat.

"I'll be right back." I grabbed my jacket.

I arrived just as the security guards shoved the old lady back into the elevator, closely followed by Michael.

"We're not sure how she evaded security, sir," the ginger security guard huffed. "We caught her on CCTV in Dr Verma's lab. By the time we got there, she'd snuck into the memorial service."

"I'm quicker than you." The old lady grinned.

"This sounds like a police matter," said Michael. "Unless you want to tell us why you're here?"

"I came here to pay my respects," said the old lady. "It's not often that someone as old as me finds inspiration in mortals."

"She's off her trolley," said the ginger security guard.

I'd heard enough. I reached out, blocking the doors from shuddering shut and plucking the train of the old lady's sari from being swallowed by the doors. "No need for the police or to be so rough." I turned my back on the men. "Are you okay?"

Her eyes glinted. "Quite all right, dear. I'm tougher than I look."

"You knew my mother?"

"Oh, I knew her very well. She had courage and curiosity

in spades. When the night nears, those two qualities are more valuable than a hundred offerings."

Maybe she was a little weird, but in my experience, the best kind of people were weird. It was the ones who hid all their flaws that I had to worry about. My blouse had ridden up my arm in the mad dash over to her, exposing my scars.

The old lady's smile widened when she noticed.

I pulled down the sleeve of my blouse, self-conscious. The scars had tingled this past week as if they were fresh and not decades old. Mum had always encouraged me not to be conscious about scars. They told a story, she said. The thing is, these weren't any old scars: a circle of nine dots on the soft flesh of my left inner arm, white and raised as if they were braille. They drew attention. I needed them like I needed a bathtub on my head.

The lift doors pinged open on the ground floor.

I turned to Michael. "I need some air. Could you possibly tell my father I'll see him at his house?"

A cursory nod. "Of course."

I put my arm around the old lady. "Shall we?"

The old lady chuckled. "Fresh air sounds delightful."

She was off her rocker. Smog filled the London air, and clouds threatened rain. No surprise there. I was the third generation to live in South London, and I knew better than anyone how often the skies in London darkened. My paternal ancestors arrived from India back when this city was the crown of civilisation and air travel was cheap. With India booming these days, maybe my father's family should have stayed there. Only then we would have had monsoon to contend with.

"I didn't get your name," I said as we ended up in the same segment of the rotating door and shuffled forward.

Cunning eyes assessed me. "I've been known by many names through the years. The one I like best is Gaia."

"How did you know my mother?"

"Rosalie called me when her eyes opened. We had common interests."

"She called you on the telephone?"

Gaia cackled. "No, dear, I don't need one of those. She did it the old way, with an open heart and an offering."

I searched her cherubic face and saw no malice there. "What were you doing there today?"

"I was hoping to see how far your mother had reached on her project, but those silly sods had cleared everything away." Keen eyes on mine. "I don't suppose she told you anything about it? It was rather marvellous. Of course, it wasn't strictly an EvolveTech project, but I like a woman who bends the rules. Too often, we are constrained by them."

I frowned. It wasn't like Mum to work on personal projects on company time. "Mum and I didn't often talk about her work. I didn't always get the complexities."

Her eyes twinkled. "Never mind. One day your brain might catch up with hers. Genetically, it's not a sure bet, but you might be lucky. Don't worry. We'll find a way through together. Centuries of patience can't easily be undone."

She was weird, but I really liked her. After the week I'd had, a batty old woman with a zest for life was exactly the tonic I needed. "Tell me more. There's a café a few blocks away. Let me buy you a cuppa."

"This isn't my first adventure. I wish I could tell you my stories, but your ears may not be ready."

We'd not even made it halfway up the street. Gaia wasn't exactly racing-horse fit, and I'd slowed my pace to match hers. I stopped to put on my jacket, struggling to hear her over the boom of traffic.

"Ready for what?" I looked up, turning a full circle on the pavement, my brow furrowed.

There was no hint of her green sari among passers-by.

"Charming. She could have at least said goodbye."

I took the bus to Dad's. I'd shown my face at the memorial but preferred to grieve privately. Our family home, a three-storey red-bricked house with pretty sash windows and peeling shutters, overlooked Tooting Bec Common. The walls inside had been lined with books and Dad's paintings. It was miles too big for one person, but I couldn't bear the thought of Dad selling up.

I walked up their driveway and vaulted over the side gate. The ease of movement surprised even me—up and over as if I skated the breeze. I landed easily, feeling pretty cool.

Choosing more kickboxing classes over comfort eating post-divorce had paid off.

I located the back door key underneath the geranium planter, where all the woodlice liked to hide, and let myself into the back door. Inside, I turned on the lights and went straight past Dad's shrine to the living room sofa Mum had always chosen to sit on.

My soft voice pierced the quiet of the empty house. "I wish you were here. I wish you hadn't left us so soon."

How could it have only been a week since we'd been in the back garden, trying to get away from the stink of Dad's acrylic paint in the house? The sudden urge to look at old photos overwhelmed me. I made a beeline for the dining room to find the stash of family albums in the sideboard, scattered them on the floor and knelt beside them for a trip down memory lane. I picked up my parents' wedding album first and turned to the first page.

My heartbeat accelerated. I blinked, in case my eyes deceived me, then looked again, turning the pages of the album quicker and quicker.

Mum had faded from every frame as if the photographs had developed in reverse.

My fingers fumbled as I checked the baby albums, the

family holiday albums and the first-day-of-school ones. Mum's image had vanished from every photograph, leaving a void where she had been. As if she'd never existed.

I sobbed, startled as the key turned in the front door.

"Alisha? I'm home," said Dad. Footsteps came my way. He hovered in the doorframe, taking in the mess and my stricken face. "What's all this?"

"Mum's gone."

He sighed. "I know, love."

I shook my head, my voice sharp. "I mean, she's gone from all the photographs."

His eyes clouded over. "Whatever are you talking about, Alisha? Your mother's right there."

A sob threatened to turn into more. What the hell was going on?

I composed myself, not wanting to upset him. "I'll put the kettle on. A cup of tea will see us right."

He put a heavy hand on my shoulder. "Yes, it will, love. I'll just head up to change, and then we can have a natter."

I picked up their wedding album again. The one I'd looked at over and over as a teenager when I'd dreamed of white weddings and a man sweeping me off my feet. The one that made me want to find a relationship like theirs, with their lifetime of secret glances and hand-holding.

Dad was there in all his seventies' glory.

Mum, with her belted A-line dress and Brigitte Bardot eyeliner, had been erased.

3

I invited Marina over to my flat for dinner the next day. I didn't have much in. A perk of the divorce was not having to listen to Alex grumble about an empty fridge. The term hangry had his image next to it in the dictionary. I'd never known a man to be so ruled by his stomach.

Marina and I were like sisters. I didn't have to cook her an impressive meal. My best friend would have been happy with a bag of crisps, which was great because my cooking skills left a lot to be desired. We settled for cheese on toast and opened a bottle of Rioja between us, though I preferred Merlot, being half French. When the microwave pinged, I grabbed our plates. We ignored the small table in my kitchen and slumped on the living room floor to eat with our legs stretched out and cushions to pad our bums.

"I loved Rosalie." Marina's face was puffy, like she'd been crying. "Do you remember how, when I first started getting migraines, my mum would tell me just to get on with it? Your mum would let me come over, tuck us into bed together and nurse me with cocoa and hot water bottles. She was the best."

My throat scratched with unshed tears. "I thought so too,

but I didn't tell her enough. We fought about Alex the last time I saw her."

"What happened?"

"It was stupid. She said she missed cooking for Alex. She liked how he always licked his plate clean."

"Gross. Anyway, it's way too soon since the divorce to be saying anything nice about Alex. For the record, he's the absolute worst. You know Rosalie was on your side, right?"

"I know that now, but at that moment, it was like a red rag to a bull. I mean, I wanted her to name his faults to make me feel better, not compliment him. But Mum didn't let emotions get in the way of facts. Then she said it was a shame that money broke us up, and at least he hadn't slept with anyone else."

Marina winced. "Ouch. I'm sorry."

"So I told her Alex could rot in hell. Then I grabbed my bag and left without another word. The crash happened the next day, and we hadn't even patched it up."

"I reckon she just wanted you to have what she had with your dad. It just came out wrong. Do you remember how many times she picked me up when I was heartbroken? She believed in love, and she wanted that for you."

Marina and her parents had fallen out when she'd come out as bisexual as a teen. Her parents thought it was a fad until they caught her smooching both our school's star netball player and a chess club geek at the bottom of the garden. All hell broke loose, and Marina ended up staying at ours for weeks before the uneasy truce with her parents. Marina didn't fall in love with a person. She fell in love with personalities. It didn't matter a jot to her whether the person she loved was male, female or transgender.

She loved without boundaries. It made her formidable as a friend and also as a vet.

"Maybe you're right," I said.

"Alisha, I know I'm right. She loved you. A few cross

words won't change that." She hugged me. "I know what you need. A distraction! Before Rosalie died, I'd planned to take you out on the pull. Imagine. All that time in a meh marriage, and now you're free to explore. We could be each other's wing-women. Nothing like some hot stuff to perk up a woman."

I laughed in spite of myself.

"Too soon? I mean, you need to break in that new bed of yours."

"You're trouble, from your gothic nail varnish all the way up to your chemical hair."

"Yes, but you love me anyway. Still no sign of Echo?"

I shook my head mournfully. "Not even scrambled eggs tempted him home."

I was starting to worry in earnest. Usually, I couldn't even go to the toilet without Echo wanting to be with me. He scratched at the door, even if I wanted privacy and refused to sleep anywhere but my bed. His attachment to me meant Mum and Dad had let him come with me when I moved out. He'd been my family cat for as long as I could remember, which was odd because Bengal cats lived for about fifteen years. He had a penchant for salmon, though, and we'd never scrimped on his food and vitamins, so he was in good nick.

Another reason why I feared something had happened to him. Usually, nothing would keep him away from his food.

"Time to up the ante then. Forget about the kibble," said Marina. "Try some really strong canned meat. He'll be able to smell it a mile away. Or put some of his bedding outside the window. Just the thought of another beastie using it will tempt him back."

She was hands down the best vet south of the Thames. Although, it took a while for her clients to see past her cascades of pink, turquoise and purple hair and the plentiful tattoos on her always-bare arms. She was like Jessica Rabbit on acid: an explosion of buxom curves and rainbow colour.

Like I said, Marina Ambrose was a force to be reckoned with.

Almost all my most cherished memories involved her: flour fights in Mum's kitchen when we were small, skating as teens in the deep of winter, phone calls until the early hours, dancing until our feet hurt. We'd been friends since primary school. We'd mopped each other's tears, laughed until our sides ached and held back each other's hair when we vomited. I didn't trust anyone as much as I trusted her.

I filled her in on what the detective had told me and about Mum disappearing from the photo albums.

"There's got to be a sensible explanation. Have you checked the pictures of her in your phone gallery?"

I shook my head. "Why didn't I think of that?"

"Your mum just died, Alisha. I'm not surprised you're not fully functional. Did you know animals such as elephants, chimps and dolphins respond to grief? Give me your phone."

I took a gulp of wine and unlocked my phone. "No, I'll do it. Here goes."

I hadn't taken as many pictures of Mum as I should have. Our moments together had seemed so ordinary I rarely thought to capture them on film. I had to go a way back to find one of her.

But when I did, I sucked in my breath. "Look."

Mum's photos appeared as black squares of nothing.

"Give it here." Marina snatched the phone. Her fingers darted across the keys until she reached the monthly, then yearly overview. "Holy crap."

I flopped on the floor. "I'm losing my mind."

"I'm not surprised. That is some freaky shit."

She lay down too, and we leaned our heads together, just like we did when we stargazed as children.

I breathed out. "I'm glad you're here."

"Where else would I be?"

A thud sounded behind us, followed by a clang of fallen dishes. We clutched each other in fright.

"I think that was the kitchen. Stay here," I whispered, hauling myself up.

"Fat chance," she said. "I'm coming with you, but I'll stay behind you in case you go into warrior mode."

I looked around for a weapon, but pillows weren't going to cut it, and there was no way I would throw the cheesy plates as frisbees or ruin a bottle of good Rioja. I put my fists up, and we advanced slowly, rounding the corner barefoot.

A strange slurping sound met our ears.

"What on earth?" I gripped Marina.

The creature was a metre and a half long, maybe longer, stretched out with its forelegs on my counter and nibbling on the block of Marks and Spencer's mature cheddar I'd left out. It had strong legs, a powerful body, a long tail and a thick, golden coat of fur covered with exquisite rosettes.

I rubbed my eyes and looked again. "That's not… That's a fricking leopard in my kitchen!"

Marina's blue eyes widened. "That's not just any leopard. It's an Indian leopard. Don't move. Stay very still."

"You're the vet," I said. "Got any tranquilliser darts with you?"

She shook her head.

Of all the places Marina and I had been to rescue animals —up trees, in sewer drains, in rundown theatres—it would be in my kitchen that we were mauled to death. Maybe the neighbours would call the police. I thanked my lucky stars we were both dressed at least. Imagine being rescued when you're just in your knickers and bra. Or worse, braless. It's not like we were twenty anymore. At this rate, we'd be lucky to make it to forty-one.

We took an involuntary step back as the leopard swung around, taking in his wide muzzle, foot-long whiskers, jewel-like eyes and teeth that could tear meat from the bone. Even human meat.

Marina sprang to life, shouting, waving her arms and stamping her feet. "Don't run. It'll trigger the chase instinct. Make yourself big. Make noise!"

I followed her lead, clapping and jumping up and down, hoping to scare him off.

"How rude, ladies," the leopard said. "I've been away over a week, and you're acting like buffoons."

Marina and I looked at each other, aghast. We must have had a glass too many. There was no way the leopard was talking.

"What, all those fantasy movies you watch, and you've never seen a talking cat?" He shook his magnificent head and padded towards us, sending my kitchen chairs scattering. "Dear me, you've not figured it out yet, have you? And judging by your expression, Marina, it looks like you can hear me just as well as Alisha." He lifted his lip in mirth. "Which means you're a peculiar too."

Marina cowered behind me.

The leopard was so close now I could feel hot, cheesy breath on my face.

He tilted his head, licked his paw and raised it to his muzzle to bat away the remnants of cheddar. Green eyes rested on my face, and I discerned both gentleness and ferocity there. At the corner of one eye, a three-inch scar marred his striking head. A scar I'd known all my life.

Either I was going mad, or the world I thought existed was something else entirely.

I took a deep breath, my heartbeat a roar in my ears. "Hello, Echo. How about you start at the beginning and tell me exactly who you are and where you've been?"

4

Echo purred in satisfaction, although I wasn't sure how satisfied an Indian leopard squashed into the tiny kitchen of a London flat could be. I ignored the rapid drumbeat of my heart and prayed to Dad's gods and Mum's one God that I wasn't making a mistake. Hopefully, he wouldn't eat us as soon as our backs were turned.

I led the way back into the living room, pushing Marina ahead of me just to be safe, my body a buffer between her and the beast.

"Relax. I already feasted once today," said the leopard, and he didn't mean the cheese. He leapt onto my two-seater sofa, his golden, spotted fur contrasting with the navy fabric. "Although it would serve you right if I devoured you after that photograph of me on the missing poster. It's hard enough having a domestic cat as my face to the world without you publicising such a ridiculous picture."

Marina poked me in the ribs. "Can you hear him too?"

"Yep."

If she could also hear the leopard, then grief hadn't addled my brain. My instincts had taken a hit, but if I concentrated, the leopard sounded like I imagined Echo's personality to be. Having lived with my Echo all my life, I had a habit of talking to him all the time and knew him as well as I knew myself. My Echo was sharp-witted and mocking. I could tell by how he stared at me with disdain if I dropped a vase or said something he disagreed with. He had a thing for the ladies and preened like a peacock. The leopard had vanity in common with him.

Could it be so farfetched to believe what my eyes and ears told me? I'd even smelt the cheese on his breath. My fingers itched to touch his fur, but it was too soon to gauge our safety.

Marina and I took the armchair on the opposite side of the room.

"Maybe this is a new manifestation of migraine symptoms," she said.

"I don't get migraines."

"Was our food drugged?"

"Nope."

"Because that would explain this hallucination."

I leaned into her for reassurance. "Can you explain why we're hallucinating the same thing?"

"Sadly not." She shuddered. "A leopard can leap six metres. We'd be goners if he decides not to play nice."

The leopard grunted. "I'm not deaf. I can hear you. Humans can be so small-minded. Now, if you'll just let me fill you in, I'm sure we'll all feel much better."

"Go ahead," I said, visualising a kitchen knife. It's not that I wanted to stab the leopard if he really was Echo. I wanted to test whether he could read my mind. That would tell me if he was a hallucination after all. A hallucination wouldn't be that clever.

The leopard sat up, his face benign and utterly oblivious to my half-murderous thoughts.

I relaxed. Not a mind reader, then.

His voice was a low rumble in our ears. "I come from a galaxy far, far away."

"Really?" I almost fell off the perch of my armchair.

He gurned, his mouth widening and revealing sharp, jagged teeth, and a honking sound filled the kitchen. He was laughing. "No, not really. I come from the plains of India, and my family has been in service to your family for centuries. Although I don't care much for that idiot father of yours." His gaze softened. "Your grandmother, on the other hand, was magnificent. When she left India, I swam across oceans to follow her here, though she freed me of our ancestral oath. I left the land of my ancestors and followed her to this pigmy island because it is not my fate to be an oath breaker. I will die in service to this bloodline. It is my duty. Luckily, the internet did not exist then, so the evidence of my journey, though unfortunately captured on film, is buried in the BBC news archives."

Marina stared at him open-mouthed.

"Echo, can you possibly skip forward to the bit where you turn from my Bengal cat to an Indian leopard? That's the bit I'm struggling with," I said.

He growled, a gentle admonishment but enough for the hair on my neck to stand on edge. "Pah, have you listened to a word? It was the other way around, Alisha."

"My apologies. Please proceed."

"As I was saying, when I reached these shores, your grandmother Rajika arranged for a glamour so that humdrums would see me as an absurd Bengal cat. Rajika had warned me not to follow her, partly to save me from such humiliation. Having disobeyed her, I had no choice but to agree to the glamour."

"You're quite a showstopper in your cat form, actually," said Marina. "I should know. At least fifty moggies pass through the doors of my surgery each week."

The leopard inclined his head. "I thank you for not mocking me. It is a balm to know that some of my majesty also exists in my smaller form."

He *was* beautiful in both forms, but I was pretty sure Marina was using Animal 101: showing kindness to avoid becoming prey.

"What's a humdrum?" I said.

"A non-magical, of course. A person with ordinary eyes and no magical talents." His eyes glinted, glassy green pools of pleasure. "You two don't have to worry about being ordinary. You've never been that. Surely by now, you've noticed the otherness Rosalie's death unleashed?" He bowed his head, and I thought perhaps he mourned my mother. But when his head rose, all softness had disappeared. His body tensed, and his claws dug into the velvet of the sofa. "Darkness swirls around us."

Icicles of fear encased my heart. "What do you mean, Echo?"

"From the start of their relationship, your parents' heads were filled with humdrum dreams. Buying a house. Setting up home. Raising a family. Establishing their careers. After your grandmother's death, your father shunned his magic completely. He'd always hated the rules and demands of being part of the Otherworld. The artist in him is a free spirit. When the magic flowed between him and your grandmother, he was in his element, but he hated the constraints imposed on them. He didn't understand why his magic had to be supervised. New users of magic have to pass a trial, and his own trial was traumatic. Rajika was always being called away from the family. When she lost her life, it was too high a cost." Echo tilted his magnificent head. "Then came the day that unleashed Joshi's protective instincts and caused him to turn against the Otherworld. You were only four. You found a bird's nest in the garden and kept a careful watch over them. Do you remember that day?"

I nodded, and a shudder ran up my spine. "Three jade eggs with brown freckles all over."

It was my first real memory: the terror of the blackbirds carving my skin, the warm little bodies frantic against my little arm, the nightmarish blood and the bruises.

"You *do* remember. The mother bird tolerated you. When the eggs hatched, everything changed. I was asleep on the lawn, and I heard a screech. The birds flew at your little arm, their beaks drilling in a circle."

"I remember the blood. I remember Dad scooping me up."

"Your father went into a frenzy after that. He knew the baby birds were too young to fly. He knew magic was involved. Your magic had awakened. He decided to bind your magic. Your grandmother must have turned in her grave that day. If she had been alive, she would have persuaded him otherwise, but without her, there was no one to hold your father back."

I traced my scars. They throbbed beneath my finger. "What about my mother?"

"Rosalie wanted to slow down and think it through, but your father was adamant. His grief for Rajika was still so raw, and Rosalie didn't want to add to it. So when your father approached Rajika's old witch ally to bind your magic, she didn't intervene. A drop of blood each from the four of you and a quick spell, and it was done." He sighed. "And since I had vowed to protect your bloodline to the death, I was stuck, pretending to be a Bengal cat."

"Holy shit," said Marina.

The leopard nodded sagely. "Indeed."

I tried to wrap my head around the unfolding family history. "So all this time, Dad's been hiding this from us?" There was not a cat's chance in hell that my brother knew; Sahil would have boasted if he had been the first in the know.

"Your father's a damn fool," said the leopard, "but surprisingly good at giving ear scratches."

"And if I walk down the street with you, my neighbours won't scream?"

"They will not be able to see my majestic form. The glamour is effective against all humdrums, except in the moments directly before death when it is possible that humdrums gain true sight, according to the witch. If I am by your side, your neighbours will simply think I am a brainless cat acting like a dog."

Marina piped up, her voice small. "It's all very hard to take in. You're saying that we're both from magical lines?"

The leopard snorted. "I have no idea what you are, Marina Ambrose, whether stray or purebred, but Alisha is the granddaughter of Rajika Verma. She is most certainly of magical heritage."

"And what does that mean? Do we have hidden talents?"

Echo inclined his head. "Of that, I have no doubt. No peculiar I know of is ungifted, although the extent and form of magical talents vary greatly according to fate, birth, study and experience. It is for you and Alisha to find out what has been dormant in you, and I will stay by your side as you uncover your skills. At least, I will stay by Alisha's side, and if you happen to be here, I will do you the great courtesy of offering you my wisdom."

A question tugged in the recesses of my mind. "And my grandmother Rajika? I assumed she died of old age."

Echo's roar reverberated across the room, a sound wave that made us recoil. "A druid of Rajika's ability? You know not of what you speak. It is nigh on impossible for a woman of Rajika's stature to be felled by mere old age. No. Your grandmother died defending the Celestial Library. It was a battle for the ages. She fought bravely, as did I, but she kept the heathens from the door, loyal to the end." He indicated the deep scar running from the corner of his green eye. "Did you never wonder where I got this laceration? No mortal blade or lowly street moggie could do this to me."

Well, there went my kitchen knife theory.
I leaned forward. "Am I a druid, Echo?"
Emerald eyes glinted. "You are."

5

The city had extinguished its twinkling lights by the time Marina left my flat. I walked her to the door, leaving Echo alone in the living room, his hefty paws kneading the velvet of my sofa.

"Are you sure it's okay to leave you alone with him?" Worry etched her face. "I'm going to cancel my surgery."

"Don't you have a collie going under the knife first thing?"

She nodded. "Followed by a Siamese and a pet rat."

"That settles it. Go and get some sleep. You must be knackered."

"Actually, my head has never felt clearer. Even the residue of my last migraine has cleared. I should stay."

A firm shake of my head. "I've got this. Go."

"I could bring you some sedatives. I'll measure up just enough for his weight." She bit her lip while she calculated. "He must be pushing eighty kilos, maybe more. We should really call this in. What if he escapes and goes on a rampage?"

"Call who? A safari park? London Zoo?"

"Don't be ridiculous. The Royal Veterinary College or the RSPCA, of course. Or Tony, the big cat expert."

"And say what? Excuse me, madam, would you like to extract a talking leopard from my kitchen?"

"You have a point. It's just, he's got nine lives, but you've only got one..."

For an educated woman, Marina believed in a lot of hocus pocus. She refused to walk under ladders or open an umbrella indoors and took great care not to break mirrors. She picked up dropped pennies, hated the sight of crows and avoided leaving her house on Friday the thirteenth.

"Echo, do you have nine lives?" I called down the hallway.

His answer rumbled back. "Do I look like a witch's cat?"

I turned to Marina. "See? I'm safe. I promise I'll give as good as I get if he decides I'm a snack. And I won't let him sleep in my bedroom quite yet."

She hovered on the threshold.

I kissed her cheek and pushed her into the hallway. "I'll be fine."

"Call me at any time, okay?"

I waited until her squeaky trainers exited the building and marvelled at the feelings bubbling up inside me. I should have been questioning my sanity and checking into a psychiatric hospital.

Instead, I sensed a base note of grief, a heart note of curiosity and a top note of excitement. For the first time in forever, my anxiety had melted away.

Despite the early hour, I cleaned the kitchen. Call it middle age, but there was no way I was going to bed with a sink full of dirty dishes. I kept an ear trained for any noises behind me while I worked in case the leopard suddenly approached. I washed up, straightened the furniture, binned the cheese remnants and found a bigger bowl for Echo's water. The dish I'd had for him as a Bengal cat now seemed like a thimble compared to his real needs.

I returned to find him dozing, his long limbs trailing off the sofa and onto the wooden floor. "Echo?"

"Hmm?"

"Have you always been known by that name?"

He raised his head. "My kind have names that honour our ancestors. I have my forefathers' names, names that tell the wonder of war and service. But after the witch cast the glamour, Rajika called me Echo, and the name fit as snugly as a wizard's cloak. London is a city that changes all who come here. Why should I be any different? And so I am Echo, just as I am also my ancestral name, and when I return to India, I will cast off the glamour and the name, and all will be as it was."

His voice had lost its ferocity, and his sleepy state gave me the courage to inch forward and curl my fingers into the soft fur behind his ear. He purred and nudged his head into my hand, encouraging the petting. I responded, taking care not to venture too close to his powerful jaw. If I closed my eyes, I could even convince myself this was my Bengal cat and nothing had changed. His fur had similar markings, but his leopard fur had a thickness and richness that eluded him as a domestic cat. *My* Echo had been an illusion all along.

"Echo, why did you disappear when Mum died?"

"Even the most powerful magic has limits, Alisha. The witch's binding spell, concocted with the four drops of blood, fractured with Rosalie's death. With the spell broken, you regained true sight. I wanted to give you time to adjust before revealing myself."

"I missed you."

The leopard nuzzled against me, his body hot, his limbs wound coils ready to spring. "I was never far."

"What I don't understand is how Marina could see you too."

"Her scientific training dampened her magic. That is why

she couldn't see me before. Science and magic coexist unhappily together. I have seen it many times before," said the leopard. "What is more puzzling is why now? What changed to allow Marina Ambrose to see me now? The Otherworld is a fragile place. My best guess is that her empathy for you in your grief, your sisterhood, helped break the shackles of her constrained magic." He growled, suddenly impatient. "Enough questions. The hour is late. You must sleep, and I must hunt. Since you have no salmon in the fridge and kibble is not the correct sustenance for a leopard, I will arrange my own food. I am an opportunistic hunter. And you have been remiss in obtaining my preferred meals of wild boar, deer or fowl."

I raised an eyebrow in question.

"You cannot get these things from Lidl?"

I shook my head.

"How about Waitrose?"

"No, sorry."

He grunted in disgust. "Then I must make do with London street food, such as rats, pigeons, foxes and perhaps the odd stray Golden Retriever. They are juicy, but their hair sticks between my teeth in the most repugnant way. It is hard to be a king in this jungle."

"I'll leave the back window open for you. The sofa's yours tonight. Everything looks different in the light of day."

The leopard clambered up to all fours and leapt from the sofa. "I hope very much that you'll throw away the kibble by the time I return."

He stalked out towards the back bedroom.

I did what I was told. Then I crawled into bed and slept like a stone.

I ROSE WITH THE BIRDS, wondering if there would still be a leopard on my sofa or whether the previous night could be chalked up to a hallucinogenic episode after all.

The dozen missed calls from Marina suggested I hadn't lost my mind.

EvolveTech had left a voicemail asking where I wanted the courier to deliver my mother's belongings. I rang them to say I'd pick them up myself instead. I wanted to prolong my connection to her, and I was running out of ways in which to do it.

I dressed quickly, rolling over my grandmother's name in my head.

Rajika Verma.

Rajika Verma.

Dad rarely spoke of her, and Sahil and I had learned early on not to prod that painful segment of his past. Her name embedded itself into my consciousness as if it had a power all of its own.

I squeezed myself into my jeans, put on a T-shirt and looked for Echo. My breath caught in my throat as I saw him lying on the sofa, emitting a gentle snore. He must have hunted well because he didn't stir when I padded closer and snapped a couple of pictures of him. I tried to send the pictures to Marina with a reassuring text, but the images came up black like Mum's photographs.

Could it be that the defunct photographs weren't just about Mum? I sent Marina the words anyway and snuck out the door.

An hour later, I was at the EvolveTech reception.

The receptionist gave me a smile of recognition. "Alisha, how lovely to see you again."

"I'm here to pick up my mother's things."

"Of course. Please take a seat in the lobby. I won't keep you a minute."

I made my way to an empty sofa and sank into it.

A man opposite put down his newspaper. "Ms Verma."

"Sorry. Do we know each other?"

He had an easy smile and an angular face with a sprinkling of stubble. His slight paunch suggested he was in his late forties. "I'm Detective Jameson. We spoke on the telephone."

"Of course. I remember. Are you here on police business?"

"I have an appointment with the CEO to discuss your mother's case."

"You don't still think my mother's death was suspicious?"

"I take it you don't read the papers."

I pulled a face. "I tend to avoid the news. I've noticed it never puts me in a better mood."

"Well, your mother is not the only scientist to die of late. There have been two more accidental deaths this past week. They were killed using hospital equipment they had used hundreds of times before." He rubbed his hand over his buzz cut. Dark shadows sat underneath clear, brown eyes. "I haven't been assigned to the cases—budget cuts—but my instincts tell me they spell trouble. I'll get to the bottom of it." He rolled up the newspaper and swatted his palm, deep in thought. "You want to know what's really strange? The flower I mentioned growing from your mum's car, the Gallic rose—"

"That was Mum's favourite flower." My pulse sped up.

His eyes snapped to my face. "Now that's interesting. There were enough Gallic roses in there to fill a botanical garden. No shops within a thirty-mile radius stocked as many of that specimen, and your parents' bank accounts show no equivalent purchases. It's a conundrum." He searched my face. "I will find out if your mother had something to hide."

I held his gaze, worried he'd suss out our secrets like a human lie detector. I hadn't processed the fact I had swapped my husband for a talking leopard as a roomie, let alone the alien flowers. There was no way I'd be sharing anything until

I figured out what was going on. I wasn't a little girl in pigtails anymore. I had a bellyful of experience that told me that, without a solid explanation for the weird stuff in my life, I'd be laughed at, brushed aside or referred to the doctor for antidepressants.

A click of heels across the lobby floor saved me from having to answer.

The receptionist hurried over, a small cardboard box in her hands. "Here you go, Alisha. I've reinforced the bottom of the box with tape so it stays intact on your way home. Please do come and visit us when Rosalie's memorial bench has been placed."

"Thank you." I got to my feet and tucked the box under my arm, desperate to look inside, to find some remnant of my mother—a strand of hair, her scent, lipstick on her mug.

Detective Jameson pointed to the box. "It'd be very helpful if I could…may I?"

"Afraid not. Family first." I kept my voice breezy. "But I'll let you know if I find anything, shall I?"

6

I held my breath until the revolving door ejected me out on the pavement, half expecting Detective Jameson to grab my shoulder and insist on looking through Mum's belongings. Men didn't always listen when women said no.

When he didn't follow me, I skirted the building to access the EvolveTech gardens. Great oaks, Lombardy poplars and weeping willows dotted the green, interspersed with weathered wooden benches and triangular flowerbeds past their prime. The gardens had become public access some years previously as part of a goodwill gesture to the local community. It was a haven where Mum had spent many lunchtimes, shielded from the heavy traffic just yards away, and where commuters came for respite during the work day.

As I rounded the corner, I caught sight of Melissa, who had spoken at the memorial.

"Yoohoo," she called, setting down a copy of *Riders* and breaking into a warm smile.

"Hi, Melissa." I hadn't expected her to be a Jilly Cooper reader; turned out she was racier than I thought. I joined her on the bench and set the box at my feet.

"Just sneakily finishing a chapter before I get pulled into

the fray." She patted my knee. "How are you getting on? You picked up Rosalie's things?"

"Anything to keep busy. I'm fine, though."

"It's good to see you. You left the memorial so quickly."

"Sorry about that. I'm glad to bump into you. I've been meaning to ask: how did Mum seem to you in those last days?"

"Oh, you know her. Always busy, always working away at knotty problems." Melissa scanned my face. "She mentioned your fight. She said her words came out the wrong way, and she'd make it up to you."

I blinked back tears. "I wish I hadn't stormed off. She was okay at work, then, in those last days?"

The lines around her eyes deepened. "Now you mention it, she was uncommonly secretive about what she was working on. We usually shared our excitement and frustrations about projects, but this time she just gave me some spiel about needing to be ready. As far as I know, she wasn't up against any deadlines." She shook her head, brushing aside the thoughts like cobwebs. "In any case, what does it matter now?"

So Gaia had been right. Mum had been working on a personal project.

"I must get to work. It was so wonderful to see you, Alisha. Don't be a stranger." Melissa walked towards the front entrance, rummaging in her bag as she went.

She didn't see the man on the ladder working a few metres away. There was no danger sign and no high-vis jacket to alert her. He wasn't wearing a helmet or protective gloves. He didn't call out a warning.

Not even when the cable came loose and sparked above her.

Not even when it fell in her direction.

"Move out of the way!" I held up my hands, though I was too far to help.

Melissa spun around in my direction, a quizzical expression on her face.

I darted towards her, pointing.

A sudden gust of wind carried the sparking cable over her, missing her by a hair's breadth. It sliced Melissa's bag and landed at her feet just as a passer-by grabbed her by the wrist and jolted her out of harm's way.

Her bag dropped to the floor as she slammed against the passer-by's chest.

Fear swept across Melissa's face. She swooped down for her bag, chastising the man.

Only then did she notice parts of it had disintegrated. Her singed copy of *Riders* spilt onto the pavement, charred beyond use.

The sparking cable lay just beyond.

Melissa's eyes widened in shock as she absorbed what had happened. "Oh...oh my goodness. Did that cable just drop from the heavens? Did you pull me out of harm's way?"

"You must have the luck of the leprechauns on your side," the man drawled. He looked familiar. Grey eyes, square jaw. Where had I seen him before?

"This man saved your life." I looked around for the electrician. The idiot could have killed her.

His abandoned ladder wobbled in the breeze. He must have scarpered when he realised what had happened. Accidents happen, but he could have at least made it safe for the public. What a tool.

Melissa scooped up her things with jittery fingers.

"Don't touch the cable." I ushered her away from it with gentle hands. "It's probably still live. I'll wait here to make sure no one touches it. Could you tell reception what's happened? They'll have to cordon off this area and get onto the electricity company. Make sure you get a cup of tea and load up on the sugar. That was quite a shock."

"Yes, yes, of course. Thank you." She cast one last look at her saviour and hurried into the building.

I turned to Melissa's rescuer at last. "I know you. You handed me my dropped keys a few nights ago. You seem to have a knack for turning up when the moment requires it. Thank God you whisked her out of the way."

"Don't mention it. I'm glad the lady is safe." His voice was deep and had a slight rasp.

Just perfect for pillow talk.

My stomach fluttered. It seemed like a lifetime since I'd been hyperaware of a man, but my body was definitely saying yes to this one. I hadn't looked at another man that way while I was with Alex, not even while we were dating. I took promises of fidelity seriously, and however relieved I was not to have to deal with Alex anymore, I'd been heartbroken to break my marriage vow.

Till death do us part.

But there were upsides to everything.

"I'm Alisha," I said, pulling my ponytail over my shoulder, a flirting tactic from my university days. What on earth was I doing?

He leaned against the side of the building and lit a cigarette. "I'm Ezra."

I tore my eyes away from his soft lips and the smattering of stubble across his chiselled jaw. He was over a foot taller than me, with a lithe body and broad shoulders. His long brown hair, greying at the temples, flopped into calm, clear eyes. It was tousled and a little grubby, like he'd just spent the day on a building site. He wore low-slung jeans with a thin sweatshirt and a silver chain with charms suspended from it. I read quiet confidence in his grey eyes. This wasn't a man who had to try hard to stand out. Judging from how he'd leapt in to save the day and the energy coiled into even his resting stance against the wall, this man was as capable as he was dangerous.

"Melissa would have been fried chicken without you here," I said, but my tongue tangled, and it came out as, "Melissa would heat fried chicken here."

He raised a puzzled eyebrow and blew out a ring of smoke just as Detective Jameson and EvolveTech staff hurried out to secure the electricity cable.

"Nice to meet you, Alisha," Ezra said. "I'll be seeing you."

I considered giving him my number but decided not to be a hussy until I'd written a list of pros and cons for inviting a man into my life again. He would say no anyway. No way that hot stuff was in my age bracket, let alone my league.

He ambled down the street, and I hurried to retrieve Mum's box from the gardens before I provoked a bomb scare.

I STOPPED off on Balham High Road on my way home. Balham might not have been central London, but it had everything I needed within a few square miles: leafy parks, the tube, supermarkets, pubs, independent shops, eclectic restaurants, supermarkets, a library and charity shops where I rummaged for pre-loved clothes.

First, I popped into the fishmonger's for salmon, then headed towards the butcher's for rare steaks since Echo had turned his nose up at kibble, and I didn't want dead dogs on my conscience. It was a win-win situation, despite the expense. I figured a well-fed big cat was less likely to turn on me.

The door jangled as I entered the shop and made for the counter. I wrinkled my nose at the overwhelming smell of meat. The butcher took my order and loaded the steaks on his chopping board before slicing them with a sharp blade and deft hands.

"Having a party?" he said.

I took out my wallet. "A party for one. Not for me, actually."

"Lucky fella."

"You could say that."

Back at the flat, I kept a few slabs of meat in the fridge and stuffed the rest into the freezer.

A thud behind me alerted me to Echo's presence. He followed his nose into the kitchen, purring in anticipation. "Where have you been all morning?"

"Just you wait." I avoided him as I put a few choice pieces in his dish, not quite ready to brush up against a leopard yet.

He sniffed the meat and dove right in, swallowing it as easily as a child eating ice cream. "Now I know why they call London a city of food connoisseurs. Never before have I tasted such finery."

I made myself a cup of tea and sat at the kitchen table with Mum's box in front of me. Knife in hand, I sliced the gaffer tap holding the box shut down the middle. Inside, I found Mum's leather-bound appointments diary, a photograph of me and Sahil, a fluffy pencil case with her favourite pens, a cardigan, a book, a chipped mug and a pair of sensible, black heels that she'd sometimes changed into for meetings.

I buried my nose in the cardigan. The scent of her Estée Lauder perfume—white lilies, rain and leaves—made my breath catch in my throat. I reached into the box again and found it empty.

I wanted more. More clues and more of her.

I leafed through Mum's calendar, looking for something to jump out at me that she could no longer tell me herself. Nothing but team meetings, project deadlines, lunch appointments with Melissa and the odd optometrist and doctor's check-ups, together with our family birthdays. I shouldn't have expected anything else. She hadn't been the sort to write her feelings down or to write poetry.

Echo padded over, too close for comfort, his breath hot on my neck.

"Keep your distance, will you?" I said. "I can't concentrate with you so close. This side of you takes a bit of getting used to."

"That's gratitude for you." He swung around, his rump close to my nose, then headed for the living room with his tail swaying in anger.

I was considering whether more steak would soothe Echo's hissy fit when the doorbell buzzed.

Marina's grainy image came up on the intercom. "Only me."

I buzzed her in, left the flat door open and returned to my seat.

She tumbled into the kitchen, still in her work scrubs. "Where's Echo?"

"Sulking in the living room."

Marina took in my face and Mum's belongings in front of me and gave me a hug. Then we caught up on our respective days. Having her as my best friend surpassed having a husband. Alex's concept of conversation had been waiting for his turn to speak. He'd forgotten how to listen within a year of marriage. I might as well have been having pillow talk with a lamp post.

"This knight in shining armour sounds like a worthy notch on your bedpost." For Marina, sex wasn't about relationships. She didn't overthink the act or where it might lead. Enjoyment came first as long as everyone had the same expectations. Anything else was a happy bonus.

"More like a knight in worn denim. I couldn't believe the electrician scarpered. Shame I couldn't put in a complaint at his company."

"Shame you didn't get Ezra's number." She reached for the book. "What's this?"

It was a hardback with the image of a plant on it, with

swirly black lettering that read *The Rose of Jericho.* "Oh, I don't know. You know what Mum was like with gardening. It was probably her latest craze."

Marina flicked through it and frowned at the stamp on the internal page. "Hmm. That's odd. It's from somewhere called the Celestial Library. Never heard of it, and I know all the libraries within a stone's throw of here. Let's run an internet search."

Marina spent so much time watching over animals post-surgery that she was a whale reader—she'd been known to tear through the catalogues of all the libraries in a thirty-mile radius of her surgery. She petitioned for new books enough that most local librarians knew her by name. There were fewer brick-and-mortar libraries in London these days, but it was still impressive.

She pulled out her phone and typed into the search box with chewed fingernails. "Now that's strange too. No hits on the ISBN either."

I peered across at her phone. "That's strange. No location or online catalogue? Not even a telephone number to ring?"

"Nope."

"Did you type it in wrong?"

Marina rolled her eyes and continued scrolling. "Hold on. There are a couple of obscure mentions on an online forum for spiritualists."

I grabbed her hand. "What if our reality isn't true? Talking animals. Disappearing photographs. A mysterious library. Do we really want to find out?"

"You mean, like *The Matrix*?"

"I guess. Wouldn't you rather this all goes away?"

"Hell, no." She grinned. "Especially if I can have a nibble of Keanu Reeves. I don't want to live a lie. The world's never been black or white. If we've uncovered something here, we have a duty to throw ourselves into it. What does *your* gut tell you?"

I bit my lip. "That there's more to Mum's death than meets the eye. That I owe it to her and myself to dig deeper. But I'm scared I'll find out things I don't want to know. We should have everything sussed by now. We're not teenagers anymore."

"Thank goodness for that. I couldn't deal with pimples as well as droopy boobs."

"I don't know if I can take a whole life-aligning event right now."

"Girl, after Alex, I think that's exactly what you need."

I stood up. "Echo?"

He didn't come.

"Echo?"

A growl and a thud, followed by his beautiful head appearing in the kitchen doorway. "You call me like a dog. Next time, I will pay as little heed to you as I would a skunk."

I stroked his neck. "My apologies."

Echo lifted his head proudly. "If you had included me sooner, I would have saved your meandering angst. I tell you, I am a leopard in service to your family line, and you are still treating me like a domestic companion. You will have to learn faster than this if you are to become a druid of any standing, Alisha Verma."

"You heard us?"

"My hearing is five times as good as yours, perhaps ten. I heard it all. I would also like a nibble of Keanu Reeves, Marina Ambrose. You must save me some delicious morsels."

Marina gawped.

"Echo, was my mother's death an accident?"

He growled, displaying his jagged teeth in all their glory. "Of that, I cannot be sure, but if Rosalie has a book from the Celestial Library, it's fair to say she was mixed up in peculiar matters."

"Can you tell me why I couldn't take a photograph of you

this morning and why Mum's photographs are disappearing?"

"Did your father teach you nothing? Did you never wonder why there are no photographs of your grandmother?"

I shook my head. I'd just figured that generation didn't have the means or technology to take endless photographs.

Echo sighed. "The vanishing photographs are the work of the Sorcerer's Senate, which governs this country's peculiars. The Founder's Law states that peculiars must hide the existence of the Otherworld from humdrums and re-establish secrecy upon accidental arousal of suspicion. A consequence of the Founder's Law is that photographs of peculiars involved in acts of magic in the humdrum sphere disappear if there is a risk of discovery. In cases of great magic, a whole lifetime of photographs can be destroyed. Call it magical programming. Or magical control. Either way, it's a way peculiars remain hidden from discovery."

A whole lifetime of photographs. I swallowed the lump in my throat. "How can I unravel this all? How can I get her justice?"

He inclined his head. "I may be more than a Bengal cat, but I am only a leopard."

My head spun. I needed to lock myself in my bedroom and unravel this all. "And where can we find this Celestial Library?"

"That, I do not know. The Celestial Library exists between the folds of reality, sometimes there and sometimes not. It houses the most powerful books and artefacts in the Otherworld, and only the Custodian always knows its location. Even those that find their way there cannot retrace their steps. I have been there only once, at your grandmother's command, and that, only because she was the Custodian."

"Well, I guess there's nothing for it but to pop into

Shanghai Moon tomorrow and ask Fei Yen and Faeza if they know anything about it. They're bound to know with all that tarot, voodoo stuff they're into."

Marina gave me a sweet smile. "Can you pick me up some Longjing green tea and oolong while you're there?"

7

I'd been avoiding seeing Dad, but I needed answers. The way to get them was to see him alone, face to face, so I could tell if he was lying. I knew where he'd be. He'd been there every morning since her death.

He'd think twice before telling a lie there.

I slipped on a hoodie and jeans, then hopped on a bus towards Streatham Cemetery. The bus lurched over potholes as it chugged along, narrowly missing heavy tree canopies lining its route. I leapt off at my destination and slipped in through the main gates. The cemetery was Victorian era, with two ornate chapels and rich grassland dotted with wildflowers. It was home to graves of fallen soldiers and a war memorial and would have been a sea of tranquillity had my heart not been beating clean out of my chest at the thought of confronting Dad. I used my yoga breath to calm my nerves. Ambushing Dad wouldn't get me anywhere. He'd just clam up.

I followed the path past daffodils that had sprung up in the spring sunshine. On my right, I passed graves buried in ivy and shadowed by six-foot winged angels.

Tears welled in my eyes at the sight of Dad hunched over

Mum's fresh grave; a watering can at his side. He held a spade and cuttings I recognised from their garden, a mix of pink roses and orange chrysanthemums. He dug into the topsoil and pushed the cuttings deep before refilling the earth.

I laid a hand on his shoulder and breathed in the scent of him, musky apricot soap and the sharp tang of acrylic paint, and my anger faded a notch. "Dad."

Dishevelled white hair and a twirly, white moustache over still, dark eyes. He turned and smiled. "Hi, Alisha. Perfect timing. Water these, will you?" He handed me the watering can.

I watered the plants as he compressed the soil, then joined him kneeling at the graveside.

His fingers, usually stained with paint, carried no colour. I hoped Mum's death hadn't blocked him—he'd die without his art—but it seemed too cruel to question him now. Instead, we worked together as the sunrays warmed our backs.

We'd chosen a simple, oval headstone in green slate upon a stone base. The inscription read:

In loving memory of
Rosalie Verma
1952-2021
Wife, mother, scientist
She rests where no shadows fall.

I squeezed Dad's arm. "It's beautiful."
"I wanted to give her the world."
"You did."
"She was my world."
"I know," I said. "I picked up some of her things from EvolveTech yesterday."
"You did?"
"I wanted to save you the trouble."

"Did she leave anything for us? A letter, maybe?" The hope in his voice was almost my undoing.

"No, I'm sorry."

His face clouded in disappointment. "We didn't have a goodbye."

I hesitated. "I need to ask you something. About Echo."

He searched my face and stood, trying to edge away.

I grabbed his arm. "No, we do this here. You won't lie here. Not in front of Mum."

"Don't ask me to unlock this Pandora's Box, Alisha. I won't do it. I won't make that decision without your mother."

I shook my head. "How can that be fair? She's gone. And you're saying you'll withhold *our* heritage. Well, it doesn't just belong to you. It belongs to me too, and I want to know. Is what Echo said true?"

"Damn that cat. He had no right. Stubborn creature. He detests this isle. He should have returned to his beloved India."

I exhaled. He wouldn't talk about a domestic cat like that. My pulse thrummed like a hummingbird's wings. "So it's true? You lied all this time. You even lied about the vanishing photographs. How is that okay? You must have known what that meant. What if all the pictures of Mum disappear? What if we can't look at her again?"

Tears rolled down his face. "We can't change the past. We can only try to live with it. Why do you think I did what I did? As long as I had the three of you and my painting, I could live with everything else. Rosalie and I wanted you and Sahil to live a normal life. To have simple joys. We thought when your mother chose science that you would be safe. We filled the house with scientific texts and cut the Otherworld from our lives. It's tricky for magic and science to coexist. They vie for dominance and suppress each other. We thought it'd be enough, but that midsummer's eve when you were four…" He shuddered.

I needed to hear it. "What did you do, Dad?"

"I didn't have a choice."

"Tell me what you did."

"I arranged for someone to bind your magic. Except I can feel the magic returning to our lives now that Rosalie is dead, and I'm terrified. I'm terrified for us all. I can't lose you."

"Dad, you'll never lose me. I'll always be here for you, but I'm angry right now. I can't help it. I want to understand this part of myself. Will you help me?"

His eyes filled with sorrow. "You don't know what you're asking. This isn't just about you. You know nothing about the Otherworld. You don't know the rules or the factions. You don't know the sacrifices or the demands. And you don't know how to survive. Magic has this habit of spilling over boundaries. Your choices impact us all."

"Then teach me. Please, Dad."

"How can you ask this of me? Magic took your grandmother. It made our choices more difficult. I don't know if I can help you. I don't know if I can."

"Will you think about it at least?"

He nodded, then turned back to Mum's grave.

I left him there, picking stones out of the soil, trying his darnedest to make her resting place beautiful.

A few rows farther, I turned back to check on him, a painful tightness in my throat. I hated hurting him, but I needed the truth. I was my mother's daughter, after all. Secrets set me off like a bloodhound, and facts were too important to bury. They needed to be examined and prodded in the cold light of day. Lives built on lies couldn't ever be rewarding.

"Tough losing someone," said a male voice behind me.

I turned to find an elderly gravedigger leaning on a shovel, skin like worn leather and beads of sweat lining his brow.

"It certainly is."

He rubbed the back of his neck. "Been a fair lot of that recently."

I took in the dozens of graves he'd dug that morning, and the hair on my arms stood on edge. It was definitely time for a wax. "I'm sorry to hear it."

Something skirted the periphery of my vision, a dog or a fox or something.

My imagination went into overdrive, pooling together all the Hans Christian Anderson tales of beasts with claws and teeth and nefarious intentions. While cemeteries were full of stories, they were also creepy.

Watery blue eyes rested on my face. "There's been so many scientists killed this past week. Graves piling up all over London, not just in this neck of the woods, and who knows who's been cremated?"

I gulped and backed away. Maybe I'd be giving Detective Jameson a call after all. Things were looking decidedly too serious for me to handle alone.

Echo and I spent hours scouring the internet and found multiple reports of scientist deaths. I fell off my chair when I discovered he could read, and he ticked me off *again* for not acknowledging his nobility. Later that night, I headed to my local police station. I could have called, but I wanted to look Detective Jameson in the eyes when I asked him whether the deaths were connected to Mum's.

Echo insisted on accompanying me as far as the entrance, although I wasn't in the mood to test his glamour theory. Sure enough, no one batted an eye when a leopard padded through the streets of London beside me. Turned out all they saw was a Bengal after all. I just hoped no one would try to stroke him.

I couldn't get my head around how the physics of it

worked. Echo the leopard was ten times larger than Echo the cat. And Echo the leopard was much less reliable. One false move and this kitty cat would release his inner hunter.

"Stay here," I hissed, shoving his rump into a nearby hedge.

He grunted but did as he was told.

My boots clipped against the dull concrete floor as I walked to the front desk. The policeman there didn't seem very bright or very gentlemanly. He looked me up and down at a leisurely pace, taking in the curves underneath my sweater.

I held his gaze and raised an eyebrow, my fists itching to punch him in the nose.

That wasn't the sort of thing you did at a police station without getting arrested, even if the bloke was a douche. Besides, I'd already hit one police officer that week.

"I'd like to talk to Detective Robert Jameson, please."

He scratched his nose and then scrolled through a database, squinting at his computer screen. A plop of brown sauce marred the front of his jumper like he'd missed his mouth during lunch. "Jameson, you say? Detective Robert Jameson? J-A-M-E-S-O-N."

"He's assigned to my mother's case: Rosalie Verma."

"Well, who do you want me to look up? Jameson or Verma?"

I took a deep breath to stop myself from swatting him. "Jameson, please."

"What's his badge number?"

"How am I supposed to know?"

"No need to get agitated, miss. A little politeness never cost anyone a thing. I'll just locate him on our system." He peered over the top of his computer. "No one by the name of Detective Robert Jameson here. Are you sure that was his name?"

I swallowed the urge to throw something at him and

smiled sweetly. "Are you sure you spelt it correctly? Maybe I should type it?"

"Don't be ridiculous. A non-police officer can't use police equipment. That's against the rules." He sighed. "I'm afraid there's no one by the name of Robert Jameson in the Metropolitan Police Force. Why don't you tell me how I can help?"

My annoyance fizzed. "You can help by telling me who's been investigating my mother's death and masquerading as a police officer."

He shrugged as if he didn't have a care in the world. "Impersonating a police officer is a serious offence. I highly doubt that happened. But who knows? It could have been someone having a laugh. Kids these days. I tell you what. You see him again, you call the non-emergency number and file a report."

Then he turned back to the keyboard, humming in a low key while using his forefingers to type.

I made for the exit. "Thanks for nothing."

On the ramp outside the station, I closed my eyes under the night sky and wondered whether to hang around for another officer with more than wool between his ears.

A low whistle sounded by my ear. "You've gone and done it now."

I remembered that voice and swallowed the glee that bubbled in my throat. "Hi, Ezra. Small world."

He raked his hand through dark hair interspersed with copper. "You shouldn't have done that. They're going to be furious. You want the whole of the Metropolitan Police on your arse? Come with me."

My hackles rose. Bloody men, telling me what to do. "Er, no."

"Suit yourself." He rolled his shoulders, and the muscles across his chest rippled under his T-shirt. His strong arms reminded me of a gymnast's. Dammit, he was handsome. "Don't say I didn't warn you."

"I've had enough of warnings. I'll make my own mind up, thank you very much."

The street lamps flickered. Echo emerged from the hedge, his gait slow and exact like he was stalking prey.

"Whoa, tiger," said Ezra, bowing. "Pleased to make your acquaintance."

"Now you've done it," I muttered. "Wait. You see him too?"

"You know full well I'm a leopard," Echo growled. "Ignore this dog, Alisha. He can never be your friend."

Ezra held out his hand to me. "Isn't it time you stop dancing around the truth, Alisha? You've been looking for it, I know, and for someone who has lived forty years as a humdrum, you've impressed me. You have natural talents."

"She knows she's a druid," said Echo. "And she doesn't need you because she has me."

"Not just any druid." Ezra's hand hovered in the air. "The last of an ancient magical druid lineage."

I laughed out loud, but I was intrigued. I couldn't help it. It still sounded so ridiculous, but I could listen to Ezra's voice all day.

Echo bared his teeth. "I know my history, dog."

Ezra ignored him, which was pretty impressive, given a leopard is hard to ignore.

"Just think what you are capable of. You thought I saved that woman yesterday, Alisha, but it was you who used your magic to propel the cable away. I saw it with my own eyes. Trust me." His eyes sparkled with warmth.

I looked from one to the other, ignoring the flickering street lamps and the heartbeat that thudded clean out of my chest.

Didn't I owe it to Mum to take this step? The Otherworld was involved in her death. Hadn't Echo said as much? I wanted to find out how. The only detective on the case wasn't even on the books, so what the hell was going on? I was tired of going in circles. This way, I didn't have to wait for Dad to decide. If I trusted a talking cat, why shouldn't I trust this mysterious man?

Besides, I wanted to believe there was more to life than a messy divorce and a nosediving career. I wanted to believe the secrets in my life could be unravelled.

Echo padded closer. "You're not going to follow this dog to the Otherworld, are you? You aren't ready."

"Ezra, have you heard of the Celestial Library?" I asked.

His eyes lit up. "Of course."

This couldn't be an elaborate hoax. This was real.

I put my hand in his. "Where are you taking me?"

He smiled down at me. His warm fingers folded around it. "To Crystal Palace Park, of course."

I nodded. I'd been there plenty of times in my childhood. It was just another South London park. This wasn't crazy at all.

Shivers of excitement shot up my spine.

It was time for an adventure. To draw a line under the past and find a new me.

"Stop," growled Echo.

"Take a deep breath," said Ezra's deep voice.

"Tell Marina where I am," I said as the ground disappeared from under my feet. "And Echo? There's steak in the fridge."

8

The world spun until it blurred around me in swirls of black and technicolour and patterns that threatened to break my mind. When I could take no more, I closed my eyes and focussed on the sensation of Ezra gripping my hand, holding on for dear life. Then suddenly, it was over, and we were spat out in another corner of South London, on the grassy bank that enclosed Crystal Palace pond.

Ezra released my hand, and I fell onto my hands and knees into the strands of grass while the world stopped spinning.

"You'll be okay," said Ezra, his hand on my back. "Teleporting is hard the first time."

I coughed up phlegm and then wiped my mouth with the back of my hand. That was attractive. "How did you do that?"

He sat down in the grass next to me while I caught my breath. "Long story."

"What are you waiting for?"

"You first," he said. "When did you find out your cat was actually a leopard?"

"A few nights ago."

Midlife Dawn

"That must have been hard."

Leaning against that chest of his would have taken the edge off it. "Tell me about it. Your turn. Can you teleport to other planets or realms? Like Mars or Middle-earth or Asgard?"

He laughed. "You do know that Middle-earth is fictional and Asgard was destroyed, right? And the answer is no. I can teleport across London easily. I could teleport to Manchester pretty easily. But further afield is tougher. Teleporting to Canada, for example, would wipe me out for a few days."

"Shame."

"Tell me about it."

"Are you going to tell me who you are? Because normal dudes can't teleport. At least, not that I know of."

"You're going to find out soon enough, so I might as well tell it straight," said Ezra. "It'll be like peeling off a plaster. I'll do it quick and let it sink in. Just do me a favour."

"What?"

"Don't scream."

Dammit. I was starting to regret leaving the safety of the police station and coming to a park at night with a strange man without my leopard protection. At least the ground had stopped swaying. I shifted my bum to put a few more inches between us and give myself more reaction space if I had to defend myself. My hand found the keys in my left pocket. If in doubt, I'd shove the Yale into his eye. A makeshift weapon was better than no weapon at all.

"I'm half werewolf, half wizard."

My mouth fell open. "Excuse me?"

He pointed to his chest as if I couldn't keep up. Like Tarzan explaining something to Jane. "Me. Half werewolf. Half wizard. Well, a full werewolf, as it were, and a pretty pathetic wizard, but my charms help."

He jingled his chain to underline his point, just in case I was dim.

I shut my mouth in case any night critters crept inside and then opened it again. "Okay."

"Okay? Okay, you get it, and it doesn't surprise you? Or okay, werewolves and wizards are up there with the Tooth Fairy, Easter Bunny and Santa."

"My man, Santa is real. Do not get me started."

Was I flirting again? I pinched myself hard on the leg, just to make sure I wasn't dreaming.

Nope. All present and awake.

I squinted at his charms in the dark: a moon, a thistle and what looked like a 0-1 hung from the chain, all silver in colour and smaller than the pad of my thumb. "So you're telling me you're a werewolf, and the charms on your necklace allowed us to teleport across South London?"

"Not quite. My ancestors, werewolves in my paternal line, are responsible for my portal magic, not the charms."

"Oh, that's much more sensible." I rolled my eyes. "And what do the charms do?"

"I don't share those secrets unless I must, and much as I like you, I don't know you, Alisha Verma."

"You know my full name. It's more than I know about you."

His laugh reverberated in my ear. "Touché. Ezra Neuhoff, at your service. One more question. Then we have to go. The night is never as innocent as it looks, especially under a full moon."

I looked up and froze in fear at the sight of the full moon in the clear sky. If werewolves were real, didn't they change under a full moon? I gripped the keys in my hand even tighter, weighing how fast a wolf could run and how quickly it could change. My eyes struggled in the dark to assess if the man in front of me was actually a beast of nightmarish proportions.

Ezra glanced at me. "I can smell your fear, but you have nothing to worry about. A werewolf as old as me changes on command. The full moon has no power apart from heightening the call of the pack and the need to run on four legs. You are safer with me than in your own bed, Alisha."

I released my pent-up breath. How old could he be with a body like that? "You said I could ask one more question."

He sighed. "I did."

"How did you find me tonight? It wasn't an accident running into you outside the police station, was it?"

The smile in his voice sent shivers up my spine. "Clever, beautiful and brave. This is turning into a very interesting assignment indeed."

"Assignment?"

"I'm a seeker, Alisha. I seek out new peculiars for the Sorcerer's Senate. I track them, log them, and if the conditions are right, I introduce them to the Otherworld. My wolf form gives me a great tracking advantage. I've been following you since your mother's death. It's been decades since I've tracked a new peculiar who discovered their powers at such an advanced age."

"Charming."

"Are you ready to meet the senate, Alisha?"

I gulped.

He stood up and dusted off his jeans. "Because they are ready to meet you."

"Now?"

He nodded and held out a hand to hoist me up. When he pulled me to my feet, the warmth from his grip transferred to my hand. "This way."

I should have known better than to follow a strange man into a park at night, but I did it anyway. I didn't understand why I felt safe with Ezra or why my curiosity counted for more than my safety at that moment.

Only, I'd always recognised the chasm in myself. Yes, I wanted to find out what had happened to Mum. But it was more than that. Perhaps this was the missing puzzle piece.

Perhaps this was how I could be happy. Not by throwing myself into a marriage that showed cracks as soon as Alex slid the ring onto my finger. Not by wondering if I should try to have a child before it was too late. Not by making everything about my students or my dad or my damn leopard cat. Although he was rock-star cool.

Maybe, just maybe, this was me claiming my future.

Maybe forty wasn't old. Maybe it was the beginning—the prime of my life.

If I ignored the first sprinkling of greys, the deeper lines and my need to wee more often.

We walked into the park I knew well from my childhood days, frolicking amongst the dinosaur models with my brother. The night wrapped its thick curtain around us as we passed the maze, the concert bowl, the Italian terraces and the sphinx statues. Just when I thought we might hit the farthest boundary of the park and it had all been a hoax, the scent of mulch and bark and damp lawn deepened, and a vast forest opened up in front of us.

I stopped mid-stride, staring at the ancient trees. "Why have I never seen this before?"

Ezra smiled like sunshine painted onto a blank canvas. "You have true sight now. You'll have to take it easy. Try not to overthink it. It's rare, but sometimes when a peculiar comes late to their gift, their brain can't cope with the realignment of reality."

"Are you telling me this might melt my brain?" I spluttered in disbelief, which turned into a coughing fit.

Ezra thudded my back so hard I feared for my ribcage. "No need to worry about brain-melting if you play it right," he said once I'd caught my breath. "You'll need to approach it like swimming in a fast current. Keep your head above water, but try not to fight it. Trust you will find your rhythm."

We continued in silence until he located a yew tree with a

strange symbol carved into its gnarled bark. He placed his hand on the symbol and stepped back.

An eerie glow preceded a vibration in the ground like the rub of tectonic plates.

I grabbed Ezra's forearm to steady myself.

He grinned, and I kicked myself for not choosing a tree to lean on instead.

I blinked rapidly. Instead of an expanse of moonlit sky, a group of buildings stood before us as if they had always been there. "Wow," I said. "That is some reveal. Can you do it again?"

"I never tire of that," said Ezra, his voice as smooth as whiskey. "Welcome to Wildwoods. Come on. They won't wait forever." He put his hand in the small of my back and gave me a firm push in the direction of the buildings.

"Hold on." How was I going to find out what happened to Mum without following her clue? "I thought you were taking me to the Celestial Library."

He shook his head. "I only said I knew of it. Not that I could take you there. No one who wants to live can go to the Celestial Library without the support of the senate. Certainly not an unregistered peculiar. How can you not know that? Wasn't your grandmother a Custodian?"

Why did everyone keep calling my grandmother a Custodian? What did she have in her custody? The skulls of braindead men?

I parked that for another day and pushed back against his attempt to lug me to the strange building. I should have listened to Echo after all. Or at least brought him with me. My self-defence skills were pretty great, but I didn't have the claws and teeth Echo did. I was certain he was stronger and speedier too.

"You're not really suggesting my life might be in danger?" I asked.

"Listen, sweetheart. Magic isn't just for party tricks, not in my world. It's blood and sweat, and sometimes it's dead bodies and running away in the night. It's not too late to turn around. I can arrange another binding spell, and we'll put you right back into your blissful state of ignorance. It's what your dad wants. And that cat of yours would be a lap kitty again. Just say the word." Ezra folded his arms over his chest, giving me a close-up view of his biceps.

Yep, still hot.

I lifted my chin. It was hard staring down a six-foot-something man. I had to make my five-foot-five inches count.

"I'm not your sweetheart. Don't you dare pull the wool over my eyes again. Just stop blindsiding me. I'm a druid of an ancient magical lineage, apparently, and I was born ready." I put up my fists to show I meant it.

He laughed, and I resisted the urge to leap on his back and dunk his face into the puddle. "Fair enough. Come on, hellfire. I'll give you the grand tour."

"Better than sweetheart," I muttered, trailing after him. My ex-husband called me an array of pet names, which I hated, but they were saccharine-sweet. Hellfire, I could just about stomach.

Wildwoods was made up of a series of interconnected treehouses and bridges, built in an ancient woodland I'd mistaken for a dilapidated corner of the park. A gentle light flickered from the buildings, even at this late hour. The only way in or out seemed to be a set of ten cable cars that rose from ground level on a pulley system.

"Wildwoods is many things. It is a school where peculiars learn their art. It's a safe haven for peculiars in need, and it's the seat of the Sorcerer's Senate. Only registered peculiars who have made the blood bond are able to activate the rune on the yew tree. You're with me, though, so you get a free pass."

My stomach fluttered.

"Central to Wildwoods philosophy and, by extension, the

Otherworld, is obeying the Magical Constitution. To disobey the constitution is to be an outcast at Wildwoods and to bring the wrath of the senate on your head. I wouldn't advise it." He opened the door to the first cable car, an earthy green that blended in with its environment. "They might feel rickety, but they do the job. Wildwoods has been like this for hundreds of years. The senate likes to keep technology to a minimum here to safeguard the pupils and stop magic from going awry." Ezra winked and pushed his hair out of his eyes. "A pulley system is more reliable than an elevator in an environment like this. After you."

We stepped in, and the cable car shuddered skywards, as if on autopilot, towards a network of buildings nestled in the trees. The air as we rose higher was cleaner than any London air had the right to be, as if the trees formed a barrier to the city smog. I drew in great lungfuls of air filtered by the ancient trees, and calm descended over me. The central oak must have been thousands of years old. It was taller and wider than any tree I'd ever seen.

Ezra pointed to an enormous vaulted cabin with stained-glass windows and a moss-covered roof suspended at the heart of the oak. "That's the seat of the Sorcerer's Senate and doubles as a space for whole school assemblies."

Smaller cabins fanned out around the large vaulted one, connected by rope bridges that swayed in the breeze. Some rested on the boughs of the large oak. Others nestled in their own adjacent trees.

"The pupils learn their magical arts in these stone cabins," said Ezra. "When I was a child here, I didn't have to attend humdrum school, but it's different now. Most peculiars have regular jobs, so most peculiars attend humdrum school and come here in the evenings. The Sorcerer's Senate only gives exceptionally gifted peculiars dispensation to study solely here. Those peculiars are destined for magical jobs."

"Like a seeker? Isn't that what you said you are?"

"Yes, like a seeker. I attended Wildwoods as a child. I never needed a humdrum education. I love it here. The way the outlying cabins sometimes change positions. The way new cabins emerge from the forest for strange purposes. The way the cabins transform with the seasons. We'd come back after the holidays, and they'd be something else entirely—a dungeon, a polar landscape, a summer meadow with scented wildflowers. It never got old. Wildwoods is not just a building. It is a living, breathing organism."

"What's that?" I nodded at a clearing east of the cabins, where an arena reminded me of an old gladiatorial ring, like in history books.

"It's where the pupils train. There are certain skills that can be practised indoors, but for most of them, the safest way to practice is out in the open, testing their skills against each other. Under strict supervision, of course."

I shuddered. "It's magnificent. But you don't expect me to come back to school, do you? I left that behind a long time ago, and to be honest, mean girls and soggy lunches don't really appeal."

He chuckled. "No, afraid there's a different system for late bloomers."

The cable car thudded to a halt, and he shoved it open with his thigh.

"Come," he said, "we're expected at the senate in a few minutes, but I'll show you the library if you like. Where else would I take Rajika Verma's granddaughter?"

My heart skipped a beat. What was it about this man that got under my skin?

I followed him across a rickety rope bridge, thankful for my sensible shoes. Turns out there were endless perks to consigning heels to the back of my wardrobe once I hit my thirties. Keeping up with werewolf wizards was one of them.

The cabin looked ordinary enough from the outside: an arched doorway painted in cobalt blue gave way to a

109   9781915151018   **109**

WH: Aisle 14   Row: Bay 2
Bay: Shelf 6

ZBM.90Y1

Title:	Midlife Dawn: A Paranormal Women's Fiction Novel (Druid Heir Book 1)
Cond:	Very Good
User:	bc_ravneetk
Station:	Lister 03
Date:	2025-03-18 18:56:46 (UTC)
Account:	Zoom Books Company
Orig Loc:	Aisle 14 Bay 2 Shelf 6
mSKU:	ZBM.90Y1
vSKU:	ZBV.1915151015.VG
Seq#:	109
unit_id:	2730646
width:	0.73 in
rank:	2,996,519

ZBV.1915151015.VG

delist unit# 2730646

xxxxx

| 109 | | 109 |

WH: Aisle 1-1　　　　Row: Bay 2
Bay: Shelf 6

TYPE MFM

Title   Bulletin Specialty Organization
            Memorial Hospital Medical Group
            HOSP-03-541
Zone   WH Zone-C
Size   31 x 23 x 6 in
Shipper   1.000 lb
Date   07/05/02 16 16:56:46 (UTC)
Account   Azura Books Company
Don Loc   Aisle 1-1 Bay Shelf 6
PICKUP   MFM-071
PSKU   VW-DH-DH-H0785VC
Seq#   1-1
um ch   212 oz lb
width   17 in
ank   KWE-510

WH-F-041-01-05-96

PK-ipk-2175058

deceptively large internal space packed with cherry-wood shelves that housed endless rows of books. I drank in their scent. Boughs entwined through the walls of the stone structure, and vines wound through the ceiling, forming a skeleton for the room. Desiccated leaves crunched underfoot in hues of deep green and burnt orange.

"I could stay here forever," I said.

His grey eyes lit up. "A girl who reads. I thought they disappeared with the advent of mobile phones."

I wrinkled my nose. "You know all the wrong girls."

A smile played around his lips. "You think?"

Heat pulsed between us. I'd been stuck so long in my loveless marriage that I didn't know this dance anymore. I was pretty sure Marina would have lunged for his lips. All I could think was that suddenly the space seemed too small.

My tongue ran away with itself. "Let's go meet these big, bad sorcerers, shall we? Or senators? I mean, are they wand-wavers or paper-pushers? Do they look like Gandalf? Or Aragorn? Or are they more like Bilbo?"

"Want me to go and fetch you a copy of *Lord of the Rings* you can climb into?" Ezra arched a brow.

"Why would you do that when I've just found out that reality is just as exciting? Don't worry. I know the way. I'm a fast learner. Do try to keep up." I darted past him, ignoring the smile tugging the corners of his mouth, hoping I'd not bitten off more than I could chew.

9

The door to the vaulted cabin—shaped like a railway arch and as heavy as a tombstone—creaked open of its own accord as we approached. Soaring ceilings and limited furnishings gave the room an austere feel. Only the stained-glass windows softened the impact, together with a thousand burning pillar candles. They piled onto window sills and in clusters in the corners of the room, on china plates and candelabras. A ball of light hovered above two semi-circular stone tables, split apart like a pizza missing a slice.

There sat people of varying bearings and fashion choices.

Nine faces turned to inspect us as the doors clunked shut, and I stifled a scream in my throat. It wasn't the Rocky Horror Picture Show, but it was close. I was almost certain I spotted pointy ears, deathly pale skin and fangs. One woman wore a plant twisted around her as an adornment, and a tiny man had a grotesque, overgrown wart on his cheek with a hair poking out of it. It was going to take all my powers of restraint not to take my tweezers to his face.

Ezra tugged me towards him, and his deep raspy tones melted into my ear. "Speak only when you are spoken to.

Don't volunteer information. Try to relax. You want to give the impression of being a predator, not prey."

Well, this was going to be easy. This lot looked so creepy I doubted I'd be making it home tonight. That meant more Golden Retrievers on my conscience once Echo worked his way through the meat in my freezer. Unless I could turn this place into a massive fireball using the surplus candles and then dropkick my way through a stained-glass window. My life was worth more than the guilt I'd feel smashing something pretty.

The senate stood. I counted six men and three women, although it was difficult to tell with one glance.

I considered jumping into Ezra's arms and telling him to teleport us the hell out of here. He seemed to be leading me to an imaginary spot closer to the weirdos. I wasn't walking into the gap between the tables and having it squeeze me shut in a pincer movement. No way. I stopped short a few metres away.

Ezra frowned and backtracked to my side.

"It has been a long time since we had a Verma in these hallowed walls," said a tall, bearded man with midnight skin. "I thank you, Ezra Neuhoff, and I bid you welcome, granddaughter of Rajika Verma. Welcome to Wildwoods School of the Wondrous."

I bowed my head and put my hands together in a namaste mudra like in yoga class. The occasion seemed to warrant it. "It's Alisha, thank you. I only figured out Rajika was a big deal a few days ago, and I don't have much of a connection with her yet."

Ezra kicked me. So much for not volunteering information. Oops.

"I'm Phinnaeous Shine, Prime Sorcerer of the Senate." His silver-streaked cloud of hair complemented his robes and gave him the look of someone who had long figured out who he was and didn't need to pretend anymore. "Your grandmother was a great friend of mine."

"I am Orpheus Might, Minister for History and the Today. I, too, welcome you to Wildwoods," said the man with the ghostly white skin and a too-still demeanour. "However, I'd rather you didn't destroy Wildwoods property. I rather like those stained-glass windows."

"Vampires can read minds," Ezra mumbled. "I should have warned you."

I scowled at him.

Phinnaeous sat, and the others followed his lead. "You will learn our names and ways soon enough, granddaughter of Rajika. We are nine, but we each represent many more: shapeshifters, elves, angels, werewolves, vampires, fairies, witches, leprechauns and druids, of course."

"Fuck me." I laughed nervously. My gaze darted across their faces, trying to discern whether this was some elaborate hoax after all and they were making a fool of me with special effects or drugs or something.

Phinnaeous sighed. "Language, please, lest those with tender ears are offended. In the Otherworld, words are more than tools of a sharp tongue or noisy mind. More even than tools of diplomacy and beauty or forgiveness and solace. Here, they are a force of creation and destruction by the spells that leave our mouths."

I bit my lip. I wasn't an English teacher for nothing. I loved the power of them on my tongue and their echo in my head. I knew how their impact lingered and how the right words said at the right time could change the world. I also knew that swearing was a good stress reliever, and hell, I'd just learned that fairy tales were real, so I think he could cut me some slack.

Orpheus, the vampire, was a hunk if you liked your men brooding—longish black hair, a Roman nose, stern lips and heavy brows to match his goatee. He sighed heavily and rolled his hand in the universal sign known to mean the Prime Sorcerer should just get on with it.

"As I was saying," said Phinnaeous, "some of us have held these seats for centuries. Others have taken the place of fallen comrades. All of us remember what it was like to learn our arts for the first time. Let Wildwoods be the safe space for you that it was for us. Let the Otherworld find a faithful servant in you."

Meh. I wasn't sure about the servant stuff. That sounded suspiciously like unpaid work, and I'd done plenty of that as a wife. I was more interested in which of these peculiars could help me figure out what had happened to Mum and whether the short guy with the big nose and boil on his face was a leprechaun. If I had the luck of the leprechauns, I would have magicked that bad boy away or, at the very least, nuked the hair that grew out of it.

Orpheus, the vampire, rolled his eyes in my direction.

Ezra kicked my heel again.

"Stop that," I hissed at him.

"Control your thoughts."

"It is unusual for a peculiar to come into their art at such a late age," continued Phinnaeous. "You have much to learn. For one, it was ill-advised of you to attend a humdrum police station tonight. From now on, you will bring your problems to your assigned mentor and, thereafter, to the senate. Peculiar business cannot be allowed to drift into the humdrum sphere so thoughtlessly. We feel it would be in your best interests to give up your humdrum job while you learn our ways."

I tensed. I might have felt stuck without prospects in my job, but as a newly divorced woman, there was no way I'd give up my independence. How was I supposed to pay my rent or afford Echo's steaks or my kickboxing classes? And there was that expensive skin cream I had my eye on too. And maybe those Kardashian control pants.

Orpheus the vampire spluttered, but I ignored him. He could bloody well stay out of my mind if he didn't like what he found there. I mean, Minister for History and the Today? What was that anyway?

I fixed my eyes on Phinnaeous since he seemed to be the spokesperson here, being Prime Sorcerer and all. "That's not going to happen. I need the income, and I'd miss my students. I refuse to leave them in the lurch. If you want me to learn about all of this…" I waved my hands at the thousand flickering candles and the freakish line-up ahead of me and noticed an older woman in luminous exercise gear from the 1980s. Next to her, a lightly built fellow with translucent skin had a reptile on his shoulder. He didn't even blink when it scuttled into his hair. Urgh. "Then don't get all heavy-handed about my other commitments."

Phinnaeous stroked his beard and exchanged glances with the rest of the senate, then turned back to me. "Highly unusual. Perhaps you might consider reducing your hours at least? As a gesture of goodwill for the resources we are about to invest in you."

I fiddled with my waistband, wishing I was home in my PJs. "Well, I suppose I could ask for compassionate leave. Just for a few weeks." I paused. "Speaking of Mum, I think there might have been some funky business going on with Mum's death. Like, magical funky business. I thought maybe you could help me get to the bottom of that."

Ezra groaned beside me.

Phinnaeous Shine leaned forward, his forehead knotted. "That is impossible. Our Magical Constitution forbids peculiars from harming humdrums. You will soon become familiar with it. What your mother suffered was an unfortunate humdrum accident."

"I'm pretty sure you're wrong."

Orpheus the vampire's eyebrows flew up so fast they almost disappeared into his hairline. "You would do well to learn not to speak to the Prime Sorcerer in that manner. Many have met a messy end for far less."

"Never mind, Orpheus. We, too, were once unrestrained," said the Prime Sorcerer. "Tell me, Ms Verma, did your mother leave you anything else of worth?"

I frowned. My mother's will was none of his business, but I had nothing to hide. "She left enough to cover her funeral costs. Our family home is their only asset, and it belongs to my father, just as it should."

"Your forty years have given you a good sense of what to value in life, granddaughter of Rajika Verma. If only goblins and the majority of humans would learn that lesson as well." He paused and turned to his left with a swish of his robes. "Perhaps now is a good time for you to meet Rayna Willowsun, our Minister for Magical Education. Rayna is Headmistress of Wildwoods and will oversee your progress in mastering your inherent talents."

The woman with the snaking plant adornment smiled and stood up. Long, grey hair flowed over her shoulders, interspersed with plaited strands. To my surprise, she wore a hip belt packed with clanking potions and a dagger. She'd not be wearing that down Streatham High Road without the blues and twos being called out. Knife crime in London was bad enough without old ladies openly carrying weapons.

Phinnaeous pushed back his chair, and the rest of the senate rose with him. "I'm afraid the senate has other matters to attend to tonight, but you are in good hands with Minister Willowsun and, of course, Mr Neuhoff."

Beside me, Ezra inclined his head.

"There is one last thing." Phinnaeous flicked his hand, and a flash of white emerged as if from an air pocket: a paper bird or butterfly or a winged creature of some sort. The beat of strong wings filled the air. "Learn it, granddaughter of Rajika Verma. Obey it."

The creature spun through the air towards me and fluttered at eye level in front of me.

"Oh. My. God." I eyed it in terror.

Ezra reached up and grabbed it, clasping hands together like in prayer, trapping it inside. For a horrifying moment, I thought he'd killed it.

"Ready?" he said, a gleam in his eye.

My heartbeat was like a wild drummer in my chest. I held out my cupped palms and nodded, not wanting to show myself up as a fool while the spotlight was on me.

He tipped it into my hands.

I winced as it pricked me. "Ouch!"

A pearl-sized drop of blood bloomed in the centre of my left palm. It stung like hell. Only then did the creature settle, warm to the touch, as if it had been alive.

"Happens every time," said Ezra, still and serious at my side. "That's the blood bond taken care of. Unfold it."

My fingers quivered as I unpeeled it. Now inanimate, the parchment was as robust as a rhino's skin. I read it once, then again, my body tingling.

-

Magical Constitution
by order of the Sorcerer's Senate
The Pragmatist's Law:
Never meddle in the affairs of the gods.
The Administrator's Law:
All peculiars and magical artefacts must register
with the Sorcerer's Senate within three lunar cycles.
The Protector's Law:
A sentient peculiar who uses magic to harm a humdrum
will have their magic drained ad infinitum.
The Founder's Law:
Peculiars must hide the existence of the Otherworld from humdrums

and re-establish secrecy upon accidental arousal of suspicion.

The Jailor's Law:
It is forbidden to interfere with the compos mentis of another peculiar.

The Judge's Law:
The delicate power balance between coexisting peculiar communities must be protected.

The Educator's Law:
New users of magic must be supervised until they pass the trial.

The Monk's Law:
Black magic and necromancy are forbidden.

-

Who were the gods? Did it mean people with god-like powers? Because that paper bird trick had blown my mind. Fair enough if magicians with that amount of skill wanted to be left alone. I wouldn't mess with them. Did vampires drain the magic of disobedient peculiars the same way they sucked out blood in *Dracula*? What trial did I have to overcome before I could fly to Brazil for a beach holiday and see the Christ the Redeemer statue in Rio?

Orpheus, the vampire, turned with a pinched expression to his fellow senate members. "Mark my words; this one is going to be trouble."

"You are one of us now, granddaughter of Rajika Verma." Phinnaeous threw me a satisfied glance and walked away, followed by all but Rayna.

"Gah. It's Alisha." I gritted my teeth.

The candles dimmed in Phinnaeous's wake, leaving the orb floating above the table as the brightest source of light. It illuminated Rayna as if she were the virgin in a classical painting. She must have been pushing sixty, but her skin was wrinkle-free, and her long dress clung to curves a much younger woman would have been proud of. The lucky cow had obviously won the genetic lottery.

She whispered something under her breath that sounded distinctly like a spell. A soft L, a frothy M and an S rolled on a clicking tongue, and the orb darted in front of her and glided away.

"Come." She followed it at an easy pace. "The night has been long, and I need my sleep before Wildwoods is filled with young minds tomorrow. But there is time yet for a short nightcap in my office while we plan for your schooling."

"God help me." I passed through the tombstone door between Rayna and Ezra as if I were a sandwich filling.

The orb guided us into the night air, across two draw bridges and into Rayna's office, judging by the Headmistress plaque on the door. Her office possessed neither the grand flair of the hall nor the exquisite beauty of the library. It was an intimate space, with wooden furniture sanded smooth with love and silk drapes of muted, earthy colours. This was a woman who knew how to care for plants. Not one was shrivelled or dried up. Her collection included not just succulents but miniature orange trees and flowering fuchsia orchids. A mahogany desk with a green embossed inlay took centre stage, topped with an enormous bronze egg timer, potions in vessels of varying sizes and an inkwell and quill.

Rayna rounded the desk, settled into a high-backed chair and indicated to us to be seated. My ears pricked as she guided the orb to a stand on her desk with more whispered words.

I sat with a bump and felt, rather than heard, Ezra chuckle beside me. The chairs were lower at the visitor's side of the desk.

She pulled a piece of paper from her drawer, dipped her quill into the inkwell and turned her clear gaze to me. "Tell me, Alisha Verma, granddaughter of Rajika, what are you?"

"I am a druid." Unless Echo had been telling fibs. I

wouldn't put it past that wily cat. The word still felt strange on my tongue.

Rayna sighed and drew her hair across her shoulder, where it tangled with the weird vine adornment. "Of course, you're a druid. As am I. But what kind?"

I hoped she didn't think she'd be getting brownie points because we were both druids. She was giving me stern mum vibes, and I was no teenager. Besides, I knew nothing of my history. Wasn't Wildwoods supposed to be the fountain of knowledge for all things magical?

Still, I was nothing if not a trier. I decided to pick an answer and say it with great conviction. "I'm a druid of great magical lineage."

Next to me, Ezra barked with laughter.

I gave him a furious stare and tried not to notice his strong thighs straining against the denim of his jeans.

Rayna gave the patient smile of someone used to trying students. "Oh, dear. I see this might take a while. Let me try and explain in a more…humdrum way." She pursed her lips. "There are many types of cereal, yes? Healthy ones, chocolate ones, the one that goes soggy in the microwave."

"Weetabix?" I said helpfully. She wasn't the only one with the answers.

"Indeed," said Rayna. "And well, all druids aren't Weetabix. Some are healthy. Some are chocolate."

I frowned.

Ezra leaned forward. "I think what Minister Willowsun means is that druids have different talents. Some may excel at potions or spells. Others may have control of an element or take energy from natural or urban settings. A few, after decades of study, may be able to change into an animal form." He paused. "I have an inkling of who you may be, Alisha, but it is never wise to presume without clear evidence."

Rayna put down her quill. "Quite right, Mr Neuhoff. We are agreed then. You will become Ms Verma's mentor. You may attend Wildwoods around your other duties and use this safe space and the training arena to uncover and hone Ms Verma's talents. You will provide written reports to me every three days. As someone Ms Verma trusts, you are well suited to the task."

He nodded. "As you wish."

My hackles rose. It was rubbish, not to mention rude, for them to talk about my future like I wasn't even there. I kept my mouth shut, but I wasn't afraid to use it once I worked out what the hell was going on.

"Once Ms Verma's initial training is completed, we will see that she acquires knowledge in the traditional arts as befitting the Wildwoods standards: herbology, healing and ageing; weapons training; spells; magical history; and if she excels herself, wilding." She handed him a form on yellow parchment. "See to it that she is registered and that her knowledge meets the standard required to meet the trial unless, of course, she wishes to forfeit her peculiar nature at that point."

Ezra rubbed the back of his neck and accepted the form. "Time to go, hellfire. Goodnight, Minister."

My mind was like jelly. I needed sleep if I was to process this all. I scrambled after him. "Not sure if I'm up for a trial. I'm definitely up for my bed, though."

10

Ezra and I trudged across the rope bridges towards the cable cars to ground level.

"I tried teleporting out of Wildwoods once, but the rune on the yew tree doesn't care to be bypassed," he said. "Wildwoods catapulted me out of there quicker than lightning. I landed in the arms of a willow tree, which kindly shielded me from the worst of the fall. I couldn't sit for days. I now give it a healthy distance before I teleport, just in case."

I let his comment pass. There was only so much my brain could take. Besides, I was far too tired to unpick the Otherworld. The Prime Sorcerer's brush-off about Mum's death still bothered me, though.

"Ezra?" I asked.

Grey eyes turned to me as we glided along in the cable car. "Yeah?"

"Do you think Phinnaeous was right about my mum? That magic had nothing to do with her death?"

"Just because peculiars shouldn't interfere in humdrum lives doesn't mean they don't. They just haven't been caught. The senate's powers aren't all-encompassing, whatever Phinnaeous Shine would like to believe."

"Is it only new peculiars you seek out in your job?"

"No, I seek out criminals too. I seek out whoever the senate demands, and only work with their blessing. It is possible for peculiars to exist beyond the senate's reach, but it's not something I would wish for myself. Your father is a brave man."

We trudged out through the grounds towards the yew tree. The moon hid behind a bank of clouds.

"This should do it." He held out his hand to me. "I promised to take you home."

I shook my head, not keen on inviting back the sickening sensation. "Maybe I'll take the night bus."

"Sorry, hellfire. I can't risk you snoozing on the way home. Who knows who might be lurking." He pulled me towards him and teleported the second I hit his chest.

This time, when the ground disappeared from under my feet, and the swirls of black and technicolour enveloped me, I held on to him like a marooned sailor holds on to a rock at sea.

Only with sharper nails. And sniffing said rock.

He smelt of earth, roll-up cigarettes and mountain air.

"Easy with those nails," he said as we landed on solid ground.

I opened my eyes and found myself in my bedroom with a pile of clean underwear still on my duvet, waiting to be put away. That presumptuous dickhead. I pushed him away, despite the room still spinning around me.

"Whoa," he said. "You said you wanted bed."

"How on earth do you know where my bedroom is?" I shoved the underwear into a drawer.

"I told you I've been tracking you."

"To my bedroom? How does teleporting work anyway? Don't you have to imagine where you want to go?" No way he was playing me for a fool. I might not know all the rules, but I had an imagination.

He had the decency to look ashamed. "I've been in here

once to check you were still breathing when the leopard revealed itself, and you let it sleep here uncaged. But I didn't touch anything."

I raised an eyebrow.

Ezra grinned and held up his hands. "As beautiful as you are, a man who touches a woman without consent is lower than a pair of hairy balls."

Echo entered through the bedroom door, his paws padding on the carpet.

His roar made Ezra and I both leap, even though I'd seen him coming.

"Out, dog!" the leopard said, emerald eyes oh so still like he was ready to pounce. "You dare leave me behind when you take a Verma to the Otherworld? You presume you are better placed to protect her when I am hung better than you?"

Ezra shrugged and disappeared in a fizzle of light.

"What excellent timing, Echo. I'm sorry I left you behind." I scratched him behind his ear.

"He didn't take you to the Celestial Library, did he? Wolves are loyal only to their pack. As for you, a clueless druid is a dead druid," said Echo. "I hope you have learned your lesson."

I shoved his tush out of the door. He would have made a wonderful pillow if only I could trust him not to bite my head off. "Goodnight, Echo."

THE NEXT MORNING, I replied soothingly to a bunch of texts from my brother about his powers not manifesting and went for a run with Echo. I pulled on a fresh pair of leggings and a mismatched T-shirt and tied my hair up into a high ponytail to keep it off my neck, ignoring the curls that escaped to frame my face. Whereas once I would have planned my route to avoid dicey neighbourhoods and unkempt alleys, I could now run freely with my leopard protection in tow.

My body loosened, my legs stretched out, and the cobwebs in my head fell away as I ran through Balham past the cinema, the comedy pub and the charity shops where I rummaged for treasure. At the underpass at the corner of the park, small, knobbly, dull grey creatures holding brooms gave me a fright.

I sped up but not before catching the milky eyes of one. It raised a four-fingered hand in greeting.

"What were they?" I said.

"Dark elves cleaning the streets of magical residue, of course," said Echo. "You'll be noticing all sorts now. Best to prepare yourself."

My chest heaved with exertion. "But it's daytime."

"We're not all vampires, Alisha. I'd stay away from them if I were you. It was a dark elf that took your grandmother's life. That chapter might be over, but elves are still trouble."

I stopped short. "Oh, that's terrible."

"Many in the Otherworld struggle to forgive them. It is easy to be suspicious of them. They are small, quick-witted and nimble-fingered. The Sorcerer's Senate employs the majority of elves as clean-up crews, but they are just as likely to spray the buildings in their care with graffiti. When you get lost in London, it's inevitably because an elf has spun the street signs. Why do you think there are so many missing people in this city?"

My lungs were on fire. "The elves?"

"You do listen to what I say. They create dead ends with black holes, and some poor, unsuspecting person is always getting sucked in. If you listen closely enough, you can hear their screams at night."

"I thought that was mating foxes."

"They've even been known to move public telephone

boxes to disorientate city-dwellers. Personally, I think it is their mean streak. Who uses public telephone boxes—"

"Doctor Who?" How was he running so effortlessly when I had sweat running into my eyes?

"—unless they are in dire need? In any case, the succubi took up arms over the matter. They petitioned the senate to reprimand the elves for unfairly suppressing the prostitution trade."

"What are succubi?"

"How Rajika Verma could end up with a granddaughter like you, I'll never know," said the leopard. "But still, you're an improvement on the menfolk of this clan. The Y chromosome must be lacking in your kind."

Fifty minutes later, we looped back around to the flat, with me gasping for breath.

"Your fitness could do with some work." He was right, but he didn't need to know it.

My legs felt like jelly. "Huh. Well, it's not like I've had time for the gym recently. And I can run way faster with the right music playing. Although, I was tempted to stick my earphones in with all the moaning you did about the flyers. I only stuck a dozen up. How long could it have taken you?"

Echo grunted. "You try tearing down photos of yourself when humdrums are looking the other way. It was almost as stressful as fighting a leprechaun. Vile things. How the Prime Sorcerer stands for one on the senate is anyone's guess."

Well, that answered my question about the guy with the boil. "Phinnaeous sounded like he knew my grandmother."

"Rajika Verma made it her priority to know those who wielded power, and Phinnaeous Shine has been a man who commands respect for centuries."

"What is his power?" I wished there were an Encyclopaedia of Magical Persons so I didn't have to keep asking. Or a Wikipedia page, at the very least.

"Did the dog teach you nothing? Phinnaeous Shine is a

wizard with skin-walking powers, of course, singularly suited to the brief of Prime Sorcerer, which means he leads the senate but is responsible for infiltrating top levels of government, negotiations and planning missions. Most peculiars have humdrum jobs these days, but Phinnaeous Shine is a notable exception. His wealth is rumoured to rival the Queen of England's, and he has just as many charitable interests. Although, unlike the Queen, the Prime Sorcerer has a succubus housekeeper paying penance for her sins."

"Bloody hell." I pushed open the door to my building. "Is slavery still allowed in the Otherworld?"

Echo inclined his head and followed me into my flat. "Of course. Any number of situations wouldn't function without bondage. Peculiars are both hugely advanced and astonishingly retrograde. We are brutish and inspired, sometimes at the same time. It's a good thing you've called a family conference. Your father is right. Now you have stepped into the Otherworld, you will need allies, and you must expect to lose blood, whether it is yours or that of your loved ones." He paused. "Now go, or you will smell like old socks when your family arrives, and I will be too ashamed for you to hold my head up proudly."

"What about you? Surely it is beneath an Indian leopard to be stinky?"

"My tongue is more effective than any loofah."

I laughed and made for the shower.

A quarter of an hour later, I buzzed Dad, Sahil and Marina into the flat. She was family to me, the sister I loved more than my real-life sibling. I kissed them as they walked in, one after the other. Dad had already brought Sahil up to speed but, at my request, omitted to mention Echo's transformation. Call it sisterly love or sibling rivalry, but I wanted to be there when he jumped out of his skin.

"Got to tell you, Alisha, I'm going out of my mind," said Sahil. "I mean, one day you know you're more than ordinary.

The next day, you find out you're something else entirely. This is alien-level weird."

"You're telling me."

His eyes widened, lashes longer than mine. "I mean, I wish my talents would hurry up and manifest but just think. What if we can fly? What would I do with all my air miles?"

Marina stifled a laugh.

I ushered them into my living room without giving Sahil a warning about the enormous leopard lounging there. Partly to test whether he had true sight. Mostly for the glee of seeing him jump out of his skin.

He didn't disappoint.

"Holy shit," he said, almost leaping into Dad's arms, all hairy, five-foot-nine of him.

This time, Marina didn't hide her glee. She enjoyed seeing him squirm as much as me. He'd had a thing for her since our school days. I think he was miffed he'd never gotten in her pants.

Sahil gawped. "That can't be real."

Echo gurned like a living nightmare, all teeth and menacing big-cat energy. "Oh, I'm real. More real than the birthmark on the right side of your derrière."

"Nope. I refuse to believe it." Sahil paused. "How did you know about my birthmark?"

"Because I watched you grow up. And I've swatted you more often than I've feasted on Golden Retrievers, a sorry fact I must change."

"You can't be Echo." Sahil shook his head. "How are you so big? How can you talk? I need a beer."

"I'm not a maid, you simpleton," said Echo.

Dad's moustache twitched. Decades ago, it had been fashionable but now gave him a slightly ridiculous air. "I've not missed your sharp tongue, Echo, but your true form is a sight for sore eyes. If only I could convince you to sit for a portrait."

Echo nodded. "It appears we are on the same side again, Joshi Verma, son of Rajika. Perhaps in recognition of our new path together, I will let you paint me."

Sahil turned to Marina. "The cat is a leopard, and the leopard can talk."

She patted his arm as if comforting a toddler.

I raised a hand. "Sit, everyone, please. We aren't here to drink beer, trade insults or paint. I invited you here to tell you I've decided to recover my lost heritage and to ask for your support."

The three of them shared the largest sofa. Echo paced nearby in a deliberate attempt to lord his power over them.

I ignored him. "Yesterday, I went to Wildwoods School of the Wondrous and was allocated a mentor."

Dad's face flushed. "You're going too fast, Alisha. You know nothing of the Otherworld."

"I agree, Alisha," said Sahil. "You can't rush headlong into all of this. It's ridiculous."

"You're ridiculous," said Echo.

Marina raised her voice above the din. "Will you just hear her out?"

I sent her a look of silent thanks and ploughed on. "So you have made your choice, Dad? I don't expect you to make the same choice as me. We're not the musketeers. Even though I'm ready for an adventure, I have no intention of ruining your peace."

"I will stand by your side because I am true of heart," said Echo. "And I will teach and protect you until my dying breath."

"Was that cat always so dramatic?" said Sahil.

"Talk directly to me, you snivelling boy," said Echo.

Sahil ignored him, but the flicker in his eyes revealed his wariness. "Wildwoods, school of the what? You need to slow down, sis. This isn't like you. Is it grief because of Mum, because of your divorce?"

"Sahil's right," said Dad. "The Otherworld has tentacles further than you could ever dream of. Did you ever wonder what my talents were and what it cost me to give them up?"

I gulped. I'd been so caught up in my changes that I'd not given a thought to my dad's peculiar talents or even how genetics might influence my magic.

Dad continued. "Even as a young boy, they made me feel almost god-like. My mother had an inkling of what they could be. She put charcoal in my hands and colour pencils, even putty. It wasn't until I picked up a paintbrush that my talents were unlocked. I could draw a good likeness before I could read, and by the time I was nine, my artwork surpassed my tutors in India." He smiled. "They didn't know what my mother knew. Those very drawings were not merely oils on paper. I painted any creature my heart settled on—dragonflies, monkeys, cows and donkeys—and she could animate them. Those animals came to life before my very eyes. Behind closed doors, of course. This was no party trick to enthral the masses. It came with responsibility, but oh, the joy of creation."

No wonder he'd always seemed a little bitter about the past. To have those skills and to have to give them up must have been gut-wrenching.

"Heaven help us. Alisha and I aren't made from drawings, are we?" said Sahil.

Dad shook his head. "Don't be silly. I can't create humans. Not with my paints. What a ridiculous idea. You were made from a good old tumble between the sheets."

Sahil and I looked at each other in horror. Some things bonded even fractious siblings.

"You created animals?" Marina's mouth hung open. "Without mating and pregnancy and birth? You created real life animals?"

Dad nodded. "*We* did, my mother and I. Not willy-nilly. I

practised on insects, and as my talent deepened, the creatures grew larger and more complex."

"Wait, do you think I could do that too?" said Sahil.

I frowned. "What happened to the animals afterwards?"

"Once the animal serves its purpose, it is freed into the natural world," said Dad.

"Just think of all the species you could have saved from extinction this way," said Marina.

"Your partnership with Rajika was written in the stars, Joshi, but you betrayed her when she died," growled Echo. "She didn't devote her life to the Otherworld for you to turn your back on it."

"You don't think I mourned the loss of my mother and the magic she introduced me to?" said Dad. "I had to keep my family safe. We had already lost too much. And after she died, there was no one left to animate my paintings. I was useless, like—"

"A cricket bat without a ball," said Echo.

"A nightclub without the women," said Sahil.

I rolled my eyes.

Dad frowned. "Like a bow without the arrows. And the senate made it worse. The Celestial Library cut itself off from both warring sides. Lives were lost, and artefacts and manuscripts were out of reach. The senate was angry at my choice to cast ourselves adrift, and vengeful as they are, they punished me for it. They forbade me from displaying my art in public spaces in case another animator called forth the creatures. In case with my mother gone, someone else bonded to my gift, someone who didn't follow the Magical Constitution, someone who risked discovery by humdrums. I tried to rebel. Any submissions I made disappeared. If I enquired on the telephone, the line went dead. Eventually, I gave up and turned to greeting cards." He splayed his hands. "What else could I do? I had mouths to feed."

Tears filled my eyes. "Oh, Dad, I always thought you were

happy making your living from prints and cards. I thought you were too shy to show it in galleries. What a pity to have our attic stuffed full of your wonderful work because of senate orders. I'm so sorry."

Sahil nodded. "Sorry, old man."

Dad sighed. "What you need to know about the senate is that it didn't have to be that way. The witches' binding spell neutralised my magic. There was scarcely a chance of my original paintings causing trouble. But like all governing bodies, the senate can be as vindictive as it is benevolent, and their goals are often hidden from view."

I bit my lip. "You don't have to trust them, Dad. But can you trust me? I can't turn back now. I need my eyes to stay open."

Dad rocked back and forth like he sometimes did when he prayed. "Why, Alisha? Why is this so important to you?"

I locked my eyes on his. "You know why."

He swallowed hard. "Because of the flowers in her car. She was stolen from us, wasn't she?"

"Yes, I think she was." I turned to look at them all: the dad, who always put his family first; the brother, who had a softer side that only our mum could bring out; the best friend who'd always stood by me; the leopard, who said he'd die for me. "I won't let it go. Will you?"

"You're telling me I could be the next Iron Man or Doctor Strange," said Sahil. "Of course, I'm in."

"I'm in, too," said Marina. "I mean, talking leopards, sexy men and a senate that sounds like it was filled with all sorts of kink? Women with hip daggers and candlelit meetings? Sounds like my sort of scene. Bring it on."

A sad cloud passed over Dad's face like it did now when he was thinking of Mum.

"That's settled then." He pulled the three of us into a bear hug and left Echo out of the mix.

"No turning back," I said. "We owe her that much."

"Not unless we are ambushed by a pack of leprechauns in the dead of night." Echo's lip curled up to show an impressive incisor. "Then we scream like banshees and run. Or call the sneaky wolfman to teleport us out of there. Even dogs have their uses."

11

Dad chomped his biscuit. "There comes a time when a father realises he is too old to interfere in his daughter's decisions. I thought Alex might protect you, but instead, it seems you have a wolf and a leopard at your side."

It wasn't enough to be a kickboxing, mini-marathon running, husband-slaying woman. He still wanted a man to look after me.

Marina shot me a sympathetic glance.

Sahil had long since disappeared to his North London penthouse after a flurry of messages from his PA. It seemed the London property market stood still without him. He had left me with Dad in a melancholy mood that I hoped I could snap him out of. To add to the drama, Ezra had crept in through the back window. Lucky Echo had only grazed the leg that had come out of nowhere. We could have been dealing with an amputation.

The three of them sat in different corners of the living room.

"It's your own fault." I dabbed some antiseptic cream on Ezra. "You could have used the doorbell like a normal person."

"I was trying not to invade your space by teleporting in." He gently pushed away my fussing hands.

"Ignore him," said Echo. "I barely gave him a scratch, and wolves heal fast."

"Stop moping, boys. We have work to do." Marina's singsong voice couldn't possibly offend, especially when she used her winning smile. "Anyone would think you need nursemaids."

Echo purred. "You are right, of course, Marina Ambrose." Of all my family, he had thawed the quickest with Marina. He padded over to nestle next to her like he'd done in his Bengal cat form, and she almost didn't flinch. "What would you have us do, Alisha? Your wish is my command."

Ezra's thigh muscles bulged as he stood up. "We have to get on with your magical training. We have three days before I must submit the first written report to Minister Willowsun."

I shook my head. "First, we connect the dots about Mum's death. The training comes next."

"That's a mistake," said Ezra.

"You will regret—" said Echo.

Marina beamed. "So you two agree for once?"

"I'm not moving on this," I said. "I've seen enough CSI Miami to know how quickly the trail goes cold. I've been up all night, and I just can't find the common thread. Who is Detective Jameson?"

Dad shuffled forward, visibly shaky. "Your mother and I argued a few weeks before she died. I never told you kids because what happens in someone's marriage is for them alone. But now, I think my instincts were right. Something was off."

"What is it, Dad?" I said.

"Rosalie did something out of character, and wouldn't explain why. She got in trouble at work for releasing a load of mice and monkeys meant for trials. Dr Williamson docked her pay and gave her a warning, but they watched her closely after that. Rosalie seemed on edge."

I bit my cheek. "Detective Jameson mentioned that. I thought he had his wires crossed." I'd always hated the part of her job that meant she had to experiment on animals. So had Dad. "That's totally unlike her. Why would she do that?"

"I couldn't figure it out either, and she didn't want me poking my nose in it. We didn't have secrets. I couldn't understand why she wouldn't come clean even with me. But when you mentioned that old lady from the memorial…"

I scrunched up my face, thinking back. "Gaia?"

Dad froze. "Her name was Gaia?"

Ezra went from a slouch to a poker-straight back in two seconds flat. "Well, I'll be damned."

I looked from one to another. "What am I missing?"

"I pray I'm wrong. Because if I'm right, we're in deeper than I thought." Dad's words came out slow and ponderous. "I think Rosalie released those animals as an offering. I think Gaia is none other than *that* Gaia, Goddess of the Earth."

"And the Titans and the Cyclopes," said Ezra.

"Don't forget the giants," said Echo.

All air left the room, punctured only by Marina.

"As an atheist, this is a bit farfetched for me," she said.

"The gods are real, Marina," the leopard said. "I have seen them many times over the centuries, though they change their skins to blend in. They can be recognised by the havoc they leave in their wake. You can believe they exist without thinking they deserve power."

"*If* we choose to believe this, let's follow the line of logic," I said. "Why would Mum have made an offering to a god?"

"My gut tells me Rosalie went to the goddess for help," said Dad. "It makes sense, doesn't it? It explains why Gaia was at EvolveTech that day. It shows she's on our side."

"*None* of this makes sense," I said. "Why wouldn't Mum have shared any of this with us? What was she thinking, putting herself in danger like this, all by herself? How could she hide it even from you, Dad?"

Dad hung his head. "All I know is Rosalie was the cleverest, most devoted woman I know. She must have had her reasons. I have to believe that. And if we put our trust in her, we have to follow her lead. We have to speak to Gaia and find out what she knows."

Ezra raised his hands. "Hold on, hold on. You might be an outsider, Joshi, but I work for the senate and abide by the constitution. The first law, the Pragmatist's Law, states that we *never* meddle in the affairs of the gods. That is a non-negotiable. There can be no winning against the gods. Only deep pain comes from walking that road."

"Pah," said Dad. "Those rules never protected anyone from pain. The senate doesn't need to know. And how is it meddling to talk to Gaia when she approached Alisha first?"

"Technically, I'm still an unregistered peculiar until you hand in that form, right, Ezra?" I asked.

Grey eyes narrowed. "Yeah, but the blood bond was taken when you caught the constitution. It must be taken seriously."

"So must Mum's death. If the Prime Sorcerer wanted me to abide by his rules, he shouldn't have shut down my concerns. Echo, how do I summon a god?"

"With an offering that speaks to their interests, of course. Just like Rosalie did before you," said Echo.

Ezra folded his arms across his chest, straining against his sweatshirt. "This sounds like trouble, hellfire."

"Sorry, Ezra. I'm not going to change my mind." I laid a hand on his arm.

A growl from Echo. "You better hold your tongue, dog. Snitches get stitches."

"Alisha's under my care now." Power pulsed from Ezra, causing Echo to whine. "You best focus on the real enemy because, mark my words, they'll be coming for us now, and she's about as ready as a lamb."

WE MADE the offering at dusk, just in case Gaia made a scene. It was easier to hide from humdrums in twilight than under bright skies. I convinced Dad and Marina to let me, Ezra and Echo handle it. Dad couldn't protect me with his paintbrush, and Marina had no idea why she had true sight yet, so she was as useless as me. Echo waited for Ezra and me in a quiet corner of Wandsworth Common while we carried out our mission.

"I can't believe we're doing this," I said. "Will she look the same as she did at the memorial? Like a little old lady in a green sari?"

Ezra frowned. "It's not my area of expertise. The gods are beyond even the remit of the senate. I doubt the Prime Sorcerer himself could answer that question. But my guess is she'll look the same. Rumour has it they are weaker than at any other time in history. In the Otherworld, our talents come from our bloodlines. The power of the gods stems from something else entirely. Their strength gains or weakens in relation to how strongly their believers pray. And in this modern world, churches, mosques, temples and synagogues are not central to our way of life. They are merely a train station people pass through. Money is the real currency, the real god. My bet is that Gaia can't shed her skin as easily as in previous centuries because the lack of prayer will have diminished her."

"What if she doesn't respond? What if this isn't the kind of offering she wants?"

Ezra raised an eyebrow. "Then I'd breathe a sigh of relief. Centuries of toeing the party line, and I break the law within a week of meeting you. Trust me, hellfire, this is not how it usually goes."

I raised my eyes to meet his and then dropped my focus to his lips. I couldn't help it. "How does it usually go?"

"I do my job, tick my boxes and move on to the next job." He tucked a loose strand of hair behind my ear, and it made me feel twenty years old again. "But something about you tells me, even if I bailed out on you and reported you to the senate, you'd still carry on this path, and I'd be left wondering if you made it out in one piece."

My heart danced. I'd learned not to rely on Alex. Even if what I had with Ezra was a cheeky flirtation that never went anywhere, it was nice to feel protected. As long as he didn't get overbearing and didn't mind me calling the shots. There was no way I was ever playing second fiddle again. In this next stage of my life, I wanted to be the queen, not the maidservant.

We were outside a pet shop on Streatham Hill hours after closing time. Inside, beyond the window display full of dog beds, hamster wheels and bags of sawdust, an array of parrots watched from their cages. I'd taken a leaf out of Mum's book and decided that perhaps the Goddess of the Earth would be pleased by us freeing caged animals, and an internet search had brought us here to Dr Doolittle.

"Are you sure they won't have CCTV?" I said.

"Unlikely. The leopard scoped the place out, didn't he?" Ezra grinned. "But don't worry, no one's going to recognise you in that ridiculous getup anyway."

I smacked his arm. I'd worn four jumpers on top of each other to change my body size and borrowed one of the wigs Marina wore in her bedroom antics. It was a Tina Turner-style wig in a golden brown, miles apart from my own dark locks, and it obscured my features to boot. If, at forty, I was going to break into a pet shop, I was sure as hell going to take precautions against getting caught.

I eyed Ezra. "You could have borrowed a dress, you know. Paired with Marina's Little Mermaid wig, you would have been unrecognisable."

"I'll take my chances." He reached for my hand and pulled me closer. "Come on, hellfire."

He wrapped an arm around me and teleported inside.

My stomach roiled, and I opened my eyes to a couple of parakeets in one cage and a pair of African birds of some sort or another. The birds squawked, not in terror, but wide-eyed and yapping, in a kind of greeting.

"How many?" I said. "Will a cage each do?"

"That's fine. It's a gesture." He grabbed the larger cage. "Hold on tight to yours. We're not hanging about."

The gentlest touches on my hand, and we were away again, spinning through the swirls of green and grey. I didn't know what was bird, what was cage, and what was night. We landed more roughly than before, in a bump of bodies, metal and squeaks and whistles. This time, the birds sounded distressed. I opened my eyes to Ezra righting both cages.

"Sorry about that. My hands were too full for a calmer landing," he said. "We lost your wig on the way."

"Marina's going to kill me." I caught my breath and peeled off three layers of jumpers.

"I'll buy her a new one."

"What took you so long?" said Echo. "I hunted three squirrels in the time you've been away, and I turned my attention to a lost Jack Russell. You could have told me they are fearless fellows. His bark almost deafened me. But you are here now. Let us call the goddess and get this over with so I can snooze on the sofa."

I smoothed out my outfit and arranged the cages in an orderly fashion. We stood in a circle of oak trees, our mission lit now only by the stars and a sliver of moon.

"How do I call her, Echo?" I asked.

"By thinking of her, of course, and saying a silent prayer

using her name. That should do it, together with those birds. Although, if you don't mind, can I hide in that hedge over there and be your hidden man? I wouldn't like the goddess to think I was part of the offering. A creature of my stature should not be offered up like a piece of fruit. Neither would I like her to slit my throat."

I gaped at him. "Oh my goodness, she won't expect me to kill these parrots, will she?"

The birds squawked in alarm.

Ezra shrugged. His nonchalance at blood on our hands made me wonder about the killer in him and whether he hunted in his wolf form. "The gods are wily. Who knows what she'll expect? But from what I remember of Gaia from mythology, she is more of a creator than a destroyer. At least, I hope so."

"Nevertheless, I bid you adieu." Echo took a running leap into the hedge.

"Guess it's just us." I pulled out my phone.

"What are you doing?" said Ezra.

"Texting my dad and Marina, *I love you*, just in case we don't make it."

I sighed and raked my hair, which was dishevelled from the wig. I wished I'd plucked out the odd grey at my hairline that morning. It wasn't every day you met a goddess.

"Here goes nothing."

I closed my eyes, pictured the old woman in the green sari and said a silent prayer to Gaia.

The trees around us shuddered, and I almost peed my pants.

12

The oaks swayed and shed handfuls of leaves that rained down around us. This continued for a good three minutes until I lost my fear and wondered if anything would ever happen. I looked at Ezra with a questioning frown.

"Any second now, I can feel it." His hands were shoved in his pockets as if summoning a god was just run-of-the-mill Otherworld stuff when I knew for a fact it wasn't, but his eyes were alert for trouble, and a vein throbbed in his neck.

She materialised before us in light so momentarily blinding that we shielded our eyes. The trees seemed to bend in prayer towards her.

Echo emitted a low growl from the hedge.

Gaia turned with laser-sharp eyes to his exact location. "There is many a beast out tonight. Here, kitty, kitty."

Echo padded out, whiskers twitching, and lay at her feet with his belly exposed.

"Traitor," said Ezra.

Gaia bent over to tickle the leopard's tummy, then turned her attention to us. Her face and body were that of the old woman I remembered, but this time her sari was the colour of the deepest ocean and her blouse the silver of a distant planet.

She raised her hand to wave absentmindedly at the trees. "I'm sorry for all the drama. There was a time when I could appear without theatrics. Now it seems it's all foreplay and a little fizzle at the end." She paused. "But back to business. This is not the first time I have been summoned by a Verma. I wondered how long it would be before you came looking for me."

I'd thought of her as a harmless old woman, but now I wasn't so sure. This was no meandering, toothless senior citizen waiting for someone to paint her nails and comb her hair. In hindsight, she had been more than capable of dealing with the security guards.

She frowned. "Speak, child. What are you waiting for? And why have you brought the wolf abomination with you? Is he my offering? He's not the usual calibre, but as this is your first time—"

Ezra cursed next to me and took a step back.

"Gaia, Goddess of the Earth—" I started.

"No need to use my full title," she said generously.

"The wolf and the leopard are with me. We brought the parrots for you."

"Oh." Disappointment clouded her face. "Well, I suppose my love for the earth's creatures knows no bounds."

"They were rescued from a pet shop."

Gaia perked up. "You did well. A plague befall all pet shop owners."

I'd already committed one evil against poor Dr Doolittle. I hoped he didn't wake up in a bed of locusts. "Thank you again for your kind words about Mum when we met at the memorial. I wondered if you could be more specific about your dealings."

Gaia swung her thick, black plait over her shoulder and puffed out her rosy cheeks. "What can I tell you, granddaughter of Rajika? Tell you too much, and I jeopardise your growth. Tell you too little, and I jeopardise your path. What is the barest truth to push you towards what the fates predicted centuries ago?"

Echo whimpered at her feet.

"Sounds like a lot of pressure, hellfire," murmured Ezra in my ear.

"You have learned by now that things are not always as they seem," said Gaia.

I nodded.

"And that sometimes a pawn is a queen."

I had already lost her, but I decided to play along because it didn't seem right to ask a goddess to repeat herself. Reading mythology taught me that gods were big on respect. One look at Echo revealed that he was in a dreamlike state of bliss, but maybe Ezra would catch Gaia's drift if I kept her talking.

"You are an insect that has landed in a spider's web, but all is not lost. Centuries of cunning are on your side. My power is too diminished to stand against the dark, but if, with my help, you live up to the task, all will be well."

My stomach roiled. Dad had been right. It seemed Gaia was on our side, but if she was involved, this was more than a pauper's game. If a goddess was not powerful enough, how could I succeed?

"You see, granddaughter of Rajika, centuries of prayer nourished the heavens and the gods, but when belief dwindled amongst humans, the heavens crumbled." Her dark eyes grew wide with pain, and in them, I saw demons and fire and great cracks tearing through a plain of unbearable beauty. "The father of the gods could not survive. His remaining children flew to Earth on his last breath."

I broke out in a sweat. I had definitely bitten off more than I could chew.

Gaia continued. "The gods languish here in London, like

wretched relatives unable to live together or apart, bored of humans and life itself. Boredom corrupts, and an immortal being has no get-out clause. What is there to look forward to when you have seen the pyramids built, civilisations rise and fall, world wars play out, a man on the moon and Concorde fly? What is there when you have kidnapped Marilyn Monroe to sing and pout for you and to stand above an air vent in a barely-there dress? What do you do when all that is left is to watch the rainforests burn? Nothing compares to the scientific revolution, the Renaissance and the Industrial Revolution." She sighed. "Humanity is trifling to the rest of the gods. Especially now, humans are more likely to worship Silicon Valley products than they are the gods."

Right on cue, my iPhone beeped. I grimaced.

"See? Even the book of faces has taken over from the book of God."

"I think that was a text, actually. I'm old school like that."

Gaia nodded pensively. "Time and fate will decide if your innate values and strength are enough to tip the balance, druid."

"But what does this have to do with my mum?"

"The power of the gods is not what it once was, but we are still meddlesome by nature, especially without the Almighty to restrain us." Her eyes flashed fire. "Bored and vengeful gods do not make for good neighbours. How much they desire to be relevant, to be central to mankind again. For temples to rise and casinos and conglomerates to fall."

My heartbeat thundered like the pounding of hooves across a green. "I still don't understand."

"What is happening is a game of bored gods who long to be worshipped like in the olden days. It's inspired, really, targeting scientists. Where is humanity without science? Without healers, humanity would succumb to plagues, like in the dark days of Egypt. You are a race of boils and rats and distorting cells without scientific invention. Of flat-earthers and ape-like tendencies." Gaia was on a roll. "Where would you be without Albert Einstein, Marie Curie, Charles Darwin, Stephen Hawking and my personal favourite, David Attenborough? Kill the scientists, and cause suffering. An increase in suffering means an increase in prayer. It's a great shame about your mother, though. I liked her."

My blood ran cold. "Are you telling me Mum was killed by a god?"

"Yes, dear," said Gaia. "I thought I'd been speaking plain English. Do let me know if I accidentally slip into Hebrew or Aramaic. It has been known to happen. But yes, I believe your mother was on the brink of a discovery, and that's why she was targeted. You know, it's been centuries since a mortal made such an exquisite offering as hers."

So Dad's hunch was true. Mum releasing the lab animals might have been out of character, but she had a logical reason.

Well, logical if you accepted the need to satisfy the desires of a goddess.

"But what led her to summon you, Gaia?" I asked.

"There comes a time in the twilight of a woman's life when she wishes to find out more about her ancestors. Rosalie Verma made a surprising discovery that cast doubt on the decision to shield you and your brother from the Otherworld. A mother's intuition is strong. Like your father, she believed the Otherworld is full of perils, but she realised you would eventually take this path. So she asked for my help to keep you safe."

"Did you give it?"

Gaia raised a hand. "I have already told you enough. It is up to you what you do with this information. I displease the other gods at my peril. While they may not be able to drain my immortality, they can imprison and torture me or hurt the things I love as a proxy for slicing my flesh." She sank her hand into Echo's fur and trailed it along his back while he purred in ecstasy. "They see my nature as weakness, mock me for injecting my immortality into dying pieces of the earth. But I need not worry now. He will find you, and if you prevail, we will talk again."

"Why does this feel like I am David in the lion's den?"

"Because you are." Ezra set his lips in a grim line. He looked like he was fighting the urge to teleport me out of harm's way. "I told you nothing good comes of meddling with the gods."

The goddess toyed with her braid. "The wolfman is right. It will not be easy, but you will not be alone."

"If a god kills, does that even count as murder? Is it even possible to stop an immortal?" My heartbeat exploded in my chest. "And what do you mean he will find me?"

Gaia shrugged. "Gods have an inkling when we fill someone's thoughts. Once, we sensed small and fleeting thoughts. That is no longer the case. We lost that skill as our power dwindled. But if you turn your full attention on him, he will sense you. Just as I knew when you turned your attention on me, he will know, and he will come for you to destroy the threat."

The word *destroy* rang in my head like a bell, over and over again. What had I done?

I turned to Gaia, pressing my palms together in prayer, entreating her to help. "Please. There must be some way to appease him."

"But, child, the gods will always want more. How can you appease that? But do not fear. When you feel small, remember, they are neither the gods of the Bible, nor the Torah, nor the Qur'an, nor the *Bhagavad Gita*. They are not the gods of the *Iliad* or *Odyssey*, or even *Dante's Inferno*. They are small enough to take everyday jobs, and their power is diminished."

"I still feel like I'm bringing a pitchfork to a gunfight," I said.

Gaia's face shone with light. "If in doubt, child, believe. A little belief goes a long way."

"How about you—Gaia, Goddess of the Earth, mother of the Titans and Cyclopes and giants," said Ezra. "Do you have an everyday job too?"

"My landscaping company went out of business some time ago. I am an old lady in the neighbourhood. I look after strays and waifs and live on social welfare." She turned to Echo and sighed. "But now it's time for me to take my leave. It was good to meet you, Chanakya Gunbir Hredhaan of Maharashtra."

My eyebrows shot up.

"You didn't know the leopard's true name?" Gaia's mischievous eyes flashed, and she scratched behind his ear. "You may go, magnificent creature, to fulfil the promise made by your forefathers. But one day, I may call upon you, and you will come with joy in your heart."

Echo nuzzled his head against her hand and then made a deep bow before padding to my side. For the entirety of the summoning, my usually very opinionated, sometimes obnoxious leopard had not uttered a word.

Gaia came towards us in a rustle of silk to inspect the bird cages, prompting us to edge back.

"Goddess," I said. "I'm nothing. I'm not even a fully-fledged peculiar yet. Give me one reason you are trusting me with this."

Her eyes glinted in the moonlight. "Because you're vegetarian. Vegetarians are easy to trust. It's the cannibals I'm wary of."

Ezra sighed heavily. "Says the goddess who has encouraged blood sacrifices since the dawn of time."

"We live, and we learn," said Gaia.

"So you're not going to sacrifice the parrots?" I said.

"What do you think?" She opened the cages, and the birds

flew in celebratory loops and landed on her shoulders with a flourish.

"I expect they were already well trained," said Ezra in my ear.

Gaia whistled low and long. A scuttling sounded a few metres away, and the lost Jack Russell appeared from behind us. He pranced over to Gaia with his tail wagging, despite the proximity of Echo. She scooped him up in her arms and kissed his muzzle. Then, she closed her eyes and formed an O with her mouth, emitting a soft hum and sigh rolled into one.

With that, she was gone, leaving only her voice in the wind. "Farewell, druid, and good luck. It is my hope we meet again and that you do not meet an early death."

I released my pent-up breath in a whoosh and flicked Echo, who still seemed bathed in some sort of godly afterglow. "Fat lot of good you were. Now, what was your full name again?"

13

My encounter with Gaia felt like a dream. I sifted through the revelations, analysing each word, but the jigsaw still missed pieces. Ezra refused to let me rest on my laurels. For him, the meeting with Gaia had been evidence of a raised threat level. For me, it showed Mum had blessed this path. It might even help to ease Dad's reservations, knowing Mum's wishes. She might not have succeeded in her efforts to ensure my safety, but she had loved me enough to try, and that healed some of the broken parts of me.

"Two days, hellfire, until your progress report is due with Minister Willowsun. You've learned nothing about your druid nature. But within minutes of embracing your peculiar identity, you have broken the first law by summoning one god and attracting the wrath of another," said Ezra. "I don't know whether to shake you or protect you—"

"Or kiss her?" said Marina. "Has she reached that level of annoying when you just want to kiss her to shut her up?"

"He's my mentor, not my lover." I swung my hair forward so they wouldn't see me blushing. "And we've got bigger things to focus on."

Saying that it'd been an age since I'd been kissed properly, the thought of kissing Ezra was too delicious for words. Alex had been a wham bam thank you ma'am kind of lover. Ezra looked like the type of man who'd take his time, and the gruff wolf side of him would be fun to discover in bed. Plus, I was starting to like how the word hellfire rolled off his tongue.

I made an effort to get my head back in the game and thanked my lucky stars he didn't have vampire mindreading powers.

Ezra's eyes dropped to my lips. "Like I was saying, today, we make a start on your training. I cleared it with Minister Willowsun that you can tag along, Marina. The minister suggested Sahil come too, but I wanted to keep the numbers down. New magic is unpredictable."

"Who will mentor my brother?" I wanted us all to be ready.

If what Gaia had said was true, we'd all need to hone our strengths to stand a chance of survival. I still hadn't managed to get hold of Detective Jameson and had no idea if he could be trusted, what with his disappearing act. With or without his help, there was no way I was giving my mum's murderer a free pass.

Not even if he was a god.

"I suggested your dad would be the safest bet to mentor Sahil. Something tells me if your brother joined our training, it would be less harmonious." He tossed a look in Echo's direction. "As long as the cat plays ball, this should be a fun morning."

Echo descended from a nearby tree head first, his golden fur shimmering in the early morning light. He scowled at Ezra. "Your taunts do not harm me, dog. They merely add fuel to my conviction of your insignificance."

"There, there." Marina patted his head. "He is just jealous of your name, Chanakya Gu…"

"It is Chanakya Gunbir Hredhaan of Maharashtra. Thank

you for trying, Marina Ambrose. For the uneducated amongst you, it means 'Bright, Brave One with a Great Heart'."

I still worried the sight of Echo in the city would cause panic, but his glamour held. Indeed, the witch's glamour was so sophisticated it targeted speech as well as his appearance. His words to humdrums came across as a series of miaows. The young mums pushing their little darlings through the park or haring after scooters didn't bat an eyelid at his presence.

I quelled the sadness in my chest. As much as I was relieved at my freedom from Alex, I wondered what it would have been like to nurse a child, read stories and tuck them into bed at night. Still, my breasts were probably perkier than your average mother's, and I liked my lie-ins, especially now that I could roll over in bed with abandon without a great lump fighting me for space and the duvet.

Ezra hadn't been sure about teleporting the four of us to Wildwoods, given Echo's propensity to claw his eyes out. So instead, we'd driven over in Marina's vet van, with Echo complaining the whole way about the stench of inferior animals. I was pretty sure he meant Ezra rather than household pets, which didn't bode well for training.

We walked the stone terrace past a pair of terracotta sphinx statues. A rumble sounded as they turned their heads to look at us, stone lips curving into a grimace as Ezra nodded hello.

"All quiet today, boys?" he asked them.

"Yes, sir," they said in unison. "The arena is all ready and primed for action."

Marina clutched me. "I'm never going to get used to this."

"Tell me about it. Just wait until Wildwoods appears. No prior drug use can prepare you for what you are going to see."

"Not even that weird pipe we smoked in the Amazon?"

"Nope."

We arrived at the gnarled yew tree.

"There is one magical institution in every country, " said Ezra. "Places here are coveted. Today will be a mind-expanding experience, but remember, Wildwoods is a haven. You are safe and amongst allies here." Ezra placed his hand on the small of my back and pushed me ahead of everyone towards the yew tree. "Alisha, press the rune."

Heat sizzled up my spine. "Me?"

"You made the blood bond with the constitution. Only the Prime Sorcerer can revoke your rights to enter Wildwoods now. You must, however, register formally with the senate within three lunar cycles. This is to allow you enough time to understand our ways. Think of it as a probationary period on both sides."

I pressed my palm against the rune. Warmth shot up my arm, and the ground shuddered beneath us. This time, I turned away from the shifting trees and materialising school and faced Marina instead as realisation dawned and her reality warped. Deep in her irises, I discerned the outline of Wildwoods. Her eyes widened in wonder, and a beaming smile stretched across her pretty face.

"This is wild!" She ran towards it without waiting for us.

Echo bounded behind her in protection mode but soon shed his dutiful side and playfully leapt from ancient tree to tree, rolling in the grass, hiding behind the cable cars, chasing a butterfly that landed on the end of his nose and eventually heading for the arena, which had been prepared with a variety of objects.

"That leopard has more sides than a pentagon," said Ezra. "Centuries old and acting like a cub. Give it a few minutes, and he'll be sharpening his claws and turning murderous eyes on me."

I laughed. "Don't mind him. I just bring out the protective side in him, that's all."

He tugged a hand through his hair. The copper flecks in

his eyes mesmerised me. "Funny, you have that effect on me too."

"I do?"

"Isn't it obvious?"

I swallowed hard. "Come on. It's about time I learn what I'm made of."

"The students won't arrive until after humdrum school, so we have a clear morning to do our worst." He took off at a run towards the arena, his jeans riding too low for comfort. "Race you."

I'd dressed in a sports bra, T-shirt, yoga pants and trainers that morning. I was a hundred per cent ready for action but still reached the training arena a full minute after him, my chest heaving.

Ezra cleared his throat. "Wildwoods School of the Wondrous has been in existence since the earliest days of the Sorcerer's Senate. Our peculiar governance structures are the oldest in the world, established not long after the death of Merlin. We are the blueprint which is mirrored in peculiar societies globally. However, there can be no specific structure to a peculiar discovering their powers. It is, I'm afraid, rather hit and miss, even for those of us who found our essence in our youth." He pointed to a triangular structure. "Your first task, Alisha and Marina, is to climb to the top of the obelisk and jump off it."

"This should be good." Echo departed to the edge of the area, lay down and licked his paws without a care in the world.

I guffawed. "You can't be serious. That's got to be twenty metres high. Why would we do that?"

"To test flight, of course," said Ezra. "The height has been carefully calculated to allow enough depth for hidden wings to materialise."

"But what if we can't fly?" said Marina. "Will muscly men appear to scoop us up mid-air?"

"Not quite, but the arena adapts to its students." His eyes were on mine as if everyone else had disappeared. "Trust me. I wouldn't put you in danger."

"I don't know. I want to trust you, but we've only just met," I said. "Aren't there any safety videos we can watch first?"

Ezra grinned. "Technology-free zone, hellfire. I thought you had bigger balls than this."

I gritted my teeth and pulled Marina after me. The frame was cool steel against my sweaty palms, and I was conscious of how big my bottom looked from Ezra's vantage point. We climbed as fast as we could for middle-aged women who were a little wary of heights and a lot worried about falling to our deaths. The only solace I took was that, as the sworn protector of my bloodline, Echo would not allow us to endanger our lives. But he had previous experience of sleeping on the job. At the very least, he'd maul Ezra if we landed in a splat of bones and cells on the sawdust floor.

"You ready?" I took in Marina's terrified eyes.

"Hell, no. But I've done stupider things. One-two-three, jump!"

We jumped—no, plopped—off the side of the obelisk and plummeted to the ground, our hair pointing up like arrows, with no wings in sight. Marina, taller than me, was a pink whirr, a little closer to the ground.

I was going to watch my best friend die.

I opened my mouth to scream and instead found myself in Ezra's arms and then just as quickly deposited on the ground next to Marina, who was coughing up bile.

I held her hair back for her and then spun around and shoved Ezra hard against his chest. "What the hell? I thought you said the arena would catch us?"

"That was more fun." He was obviously enjoying himself. "I guess neither of you has wings. That rules out flight, instant armour and probably reactive adaption too. On to the next round. Leopard, you're up."

Echo sauntered over, a glint in his emerald eyes.

I tensed, sensing trouble, and pulled Marina to her feet. She shook like a leaf. She might have been brave in matters of the heart and would put an arm into a crocodile's throat without a second thought, but this was something else entirely. It had started to feel more like an onslaught than a game of equals, and we hadn't even decided on a safe word. If I called out *stop*, would Ezra and Echo even react?

Pine trees shot out of the sawdust, although they had no business growing there without soil and would never have grown so quickly within natural laws.

This is magic.

I tucked Marina in behind me, limbering up and raising my fists. Behind me, Marina's breaths came in jagged puffs as if she were close to hyperventilating. I didn't blame her. The trees had by now multiplied by the dozen and then again, making up a maze of pathways, blotting out the daylight.

I heard Echo behind me before I saw him. The hair on my nape stood on edge, and I knew he had turned into a malevolent foe by the roar on the wind. "Run!" I said.

We scrambled forward through the pine trees, disoriented, not knowing where we should run and who would help.

She clutched me. "Oh, my god. He's going to eat us."

I gulped, tempted to drag her with me behind the foliage. A chink of silver caught my eye. "Aim for the structure."

A sob caught in her throat. "I can't."

"You can." I grabbed Marina's hand and pulled her after me.

We ran down a passage, both hyperventilating, pine needles crunching underfoot, our access blocked and the trees' branches too slim to hold our body weight. Besides, hadn't I seen Echo climb just that morning?

Marina's ashen face crumpled. "We're going to die. I should have packed those bloody tranquillisers."

I nodded. "We'll be more prepared next time. Who did we think we were? Wonder Woman and Supergirl?"

"What next time? They're *never* going to find our bodies."

"Shh."

"I love you, Alisha," said Marina.

"Save it. We're too young to die."

A pounding of the earth. An eighty-kilo leopard bearing down on us. A roar at our backs.

I stopped and swung around, my movements jerky, pearls of sweat on my upper lip.

Echo snarled, ready to pounce. His emerald eyes shone with fierce intent.

I held up my hands and reached out for him. This was my cat. My beautiful Bengal. He wouldn't hurt me.

"I heard his stomach rumble," said Marina. "Don't, Alisha. Please."

I inched forward and relaxed my body, loosening my shoulders and jaw, trying to exude calm.

Echo roared and jumped, flexing his claws mid-air.

I winced, squeezed my eyes shut and sprang back towards Marina. Her eyes were wide open, and her fingers crossed in a desperate plea for good luck. At least we'd die in each other's arms. My ears zeroed in on a bump, followed by a sliding sound. I opened one eye.

A glass wall separated us from Echo. He lay in a heap on the ground, his limbs tangled, evidently out cold.

I extracted myself from Marina's embrace and knocked on the glass. Nada. My killer leopard was sleeping off his exertions. I had a right mind to send him back to India. Protector, my arse.

The ground hummed as the pine trees dropped into it, and the glass faded away.

"Oh hell," I whispered. "Time to move."

A deep voice behind us made us jump. "It's okay, hellfire. He won't harm you."

I inched closer to Ezra and pulled Marina with me. "He won't?"

"Nope, the training exercise is over."

I turned cold eyes on Ezra and thrust out my chest. "Why you…I have nothing to say to you. Nothing at all." I walked away and then spun back. "Actually, I do. Talk about throwing us in the lion's den. He's my cat, dammit. My leopard. And you turned him on us."

"It was Echo's idea and a pretty good one. We now know you are unlikely to have time manipulation or an unending supply of good luck. You don't have speed or invisibility and cannot tame wild or domesticate creatures. I was hoping that would be your talent, Marina. As a vet, it would have been really cool. Still, the universe doesn't always give us the most useful gifts. Pretty neat idea of yours to aim for the highest ground."

I glanced over my shoulder to make sure Echo hadn't moved. "We didn't make it, though, did we? For heaven's sake, man. There has to be an easier way to discover our talents than this."

Ezra frowned. "Although from the viewing and sound booth, it looked like you precisely identified Echo's motives, Marina."

"The viewing and sound booth?" Marina found her fury at last. "What is this, a production set? I thought you said this was a technology-free zone."

"All magically powered, of course."

"Of course." Marina shot him a dark look. "What do you mean by his motives? As in, he really wanted to eat us?"

Echo padded over to us, the venom gone from his eyes. He rolled his body into a lazy stretch. "I am a man-eating leopard, Marina Ambrose. I thought I had told you as much—"

"No, you hadn't. So much for your great heart. And you can eat the wolf man first, thank you very much," said Marina.

Echo gurned, disgusted by the thought. "I did indeed want to eat you, but only because I reverted to pure instincts for the purpose of that training exercise. I am now myself again."

"Well played, cat," Ezra said.

"Thank you, dog. I am pleased you didn't merely make me your administrative assistant in these matters."

"Hang on a minute, Ezra," I said, undecided whether I preferred the two of them at each other's throats or in cahoots. "I distinctly remember you saying in Minister Willowsun's office that you had an inkling of what my powers could be. And that I was the one who saved Melissa from that rogue electric cable."

"Easy, hellfire. There are no shortcuts to this process. We'll get there in our own sweet time."

I pointed a finger at his chest. "But there is no time. You said as much. What if the god attacks and we can't protect ourselves?"

Ezra folded his arms across his chest. His biceps rippled. The show-off. "Gaia didn't say anything about the threat being immediate."

I snorted. "Did you even listen? The goddess said a god would be dispatched to *destroy* me. What, you think a killer god is just going to play footsie with me?"

He gave Echo a sideways glance as if *they* were natural allies. "You have me. And the leopard."

"Have I? Hell," I retorted. "I feel like Little Red Riding Hood. Unprepared and at the mercy of you all. I don't want you to protect me. I want the tools to protect myself."

He came towards me, and the air thinned despite the vast expanse of arena around us. The scent of him filled my nose—

the musky scent of roll-up cigarettes and mountain air—but this time, it didn't turn me on.

I saw red. I held out my hands to ward him off, and my palms tingled. The gust sent him sprawling, his hands windmilling through the air, before he landed five metres away, an enigmatic expression on his handsome face.

"There it is, hellfire. I knew it! A druid with power over the wind. That was some move. Just wait until we really see what you can do." He got to his feet and dusted himself off. "One thing I don't understand. Rajika Verma was an animator. Your father is a painter. The question now is, can you do what they can do, and where the hell did your powers come from if not?"

I studied my hands in astonishment.

"What about me?" said Marina in a small voice.

Ezra lifted a single eyebrow. "You're a problem for another day."

14

Our four-hour training session in the Wildwoods arena left Marina and me battered, bruised and sweating like pigs. Ezra caught my sense of urgency at last, and I almost wished he hadn't. I preferred a relaxed mentor to a demented one.

"Will you stop chucking objects at me?" I gritted my teeth and sent a spiky projectile thudding to the floor. "Poor Marina is a sitting duck, and I could do with a break."

My hands had a mind of their own, as if my magic was instinctual rather than learned, but my confidence needed work. I didn't want to take a hit to my face, and I kept squealing and cursing even as I defended myself. Marina cowered behind me, running when I ran, entirely at the mercy of whatever Ezra and Echo could dream up next.

"Wildwoods won't let any undue harm come to you," said Ezra.

Marina poked her head around me and recoiled as some sort of cannon sounded to our left. "*Undue* harm? What does that even mean? Like you'd be okay if I sliced my knee, but you'd draw the line at losing an ear?"

Ezra lit a cigarette and took a drag. "The school has an

infirmary for the worst battle wounds, although I'm not sure the nurse is there at the moment. I could probably rummage in there for a healing potion, though. How else are you going to learn how to defend and attack? The fact you're a runner and a kickboxer means you're strong, Alisha, and have decent stamina, but in the Otherworld, that's not enough. The talents at your disposal are rudimentary right now. Druids of your kind should be able to manipulate the wind and cause hurricanes, tornadoes and thermal spirals."

"Not even Rajika could do that." Echo's eyes narrowed. "This is very unconventional. If I didn't like you, I would dip a stick in your blood and ask for heritage tests."

"Actually, DNA tests are done with a cotton swab and saliva," said Marina.

Echo inclined his head. "I bow to your knowledge of useless things, Marina Ambrose."

"Gee, thanks."

I scanned the arena to make sure Ezra hadn't lulled us into a false sense of security. My trust had taken a knock after our experience with the menacing Echo. Who knew what this half wizard, half werewolf was capable of or how much kindness and care remained if you were half beast?

Ezra chucked his fag away and ground it into the sawdust, where it glowed for a moment before disintegrating entirely. "Right, that's enough for the day. Next time we'll work on close combat, speed and knowing your enemy."

We retraced our steps out of Wildwoods. The yew tree shimmered as we passed it, and once it was behind us, the air grew thicker again, filled with London smog and the buses that hurtled past the park on the main road. We traipsed through Crystal Palace Park, past two humdrum teenagers flying rainbow kites with trailing ribbons, oblivious to the vast magical world only moments away. I raised my hand and sent their kites skywards, prompting shouts of delight until the kites took on a life of their own, jerking away from their owners, and heading directly for the sun.

"Oops," I said.

Ezra grabbed my hand and pulled me on. "Keep walking, hellfire. That rookie mistake is the sort of thing that could cost you. The fourth law, the Founder's Law, states—"

"Peculiars must hide the existence of the Otherworld from humdrums. Got it. Sorry." I paused, rubbing my shoulder, which had come up black and blue during a tumble in the arena. "What I don't get is why we had to go through the whole palaver this morning. It seems an unreasonable way to learn a skill. Why can't I look up techniques in a druid manual? The Wildwoods library must have something of use."

Echo lifted his head from the puddle he'd been lapping and caught up with us. "Druids are literate, but they are prevented by doctrine from recording their knowledge in written form. Besides, you can't learn everything from books. Somethings you just *do*."

We exited the park towards the side street where Marina had parked her van. She opened the rear doors. Echo sprang in, his hulking weight sinking the vehicle closer to the asphalt, and settled himself on blankets there. She eased the doors shut and then clambered into the front. Ezra and I rode up front with her. I plugged in my seatbelt, noticing Ezra didn't bother. Echo snored in the back, his bulky body causing havoc with the van's suspension as we sped over South London potholes.

"Maybe I could ask another druid to help me," I said, "like Minister Willowsun or my dad."

Ezra shifted in his seat, his thigh parallel to mine. The physical toll of learning magic had been high, and I longed to nestle into him. For comfort only. I still hadn't forgiven him for conspiring with Echo to scare the living daylights out of us. And I had no idea why he had asked Marina for a ride when he could have teleported to Australia and back in the time it took for a traffic light to change. I made a mental note to ask him to take me there if we ever became true friends. I had a thing for kangaroos and koalas.

"The minister is too busy to focus on one student. She has the whole of Wildwoods to oversee. Your father hasn't practised druidry for a long time. You could take your chances with him just like your brother. Druid skills are varied. You wouldn't ask a violinist to teach you how to play the cello just because they both play in an orchestra."

"There must be a common language, surely?"

"I've been doing this a long time, hellfire. It pays to have me in your corner." His deep voice reverberated in my ear, laced with a challenge. "Bottom line is, you muddle along, shooting breeze at unsuspecting strangers, you join a druid tribe—apart from the South London druids, there are some in France and maybe some in Asia—or you suck it up and put all your effort into mastering what I can teach you. What's it going to be?"

I held my tongue, weighing up the options, then shrugged.

"Awkward." Marina switched on the radio. Kings of Leon blasted out of her third-rate speakers, more feedback than crooning rockers.

Echo growled, and the hairs on my arm stood on edge. "When I wake, I will induct you in real music. Lata Mangeshkar, Mohamed Rafi and Jagjit Singh, for starters. For now, will you turn off that racket? Some of us are trying to sleep."

"Gigolo, who?" Marina turned the radio down to a background whisper.

I sighed, having seen enough of my friends' children and my infantile ex-husband to know the signs of hunger and tiredness. "I haven't a clue, but can you put your foot on it? He sounds grumpy."

A FEW HOURS LATER, I rocked up at the community centre to teach my night class. My body ached, and relief flooded me to leave magic behind. I'd left Echo in a steak-induced coma on the sofa, his drool pooling on the fabric. I had no idea whether Ezra lived in a house, a cave or a cottage in the woods, but he seemed keen to hang around my flat until I gave him a push to leave. I didn't want a minder or a protector. The Otherworld could be intense. After the morning I'd had, I just wanted some peace and quiet. Or even better, a drunken girls' night with Marina to wash away my troubles with the help of copious amounts of wine and some chaser shots. My newest favourite was Patrón XO Cafe, but I would settle for Tequila Gold.

With enforced compassionate leave from my teaching job prompted by the Prime Sorcerer, I might even have time for some naps. Joy bubbled up at the thought of starfish naps in my double bed that I didn't have to share with a man. There would be no stinky man smell to mask the scent of my spring daisies fabric softener. A little rest and relaxation before I got to grips with Mum's murderer and my druid heritage was just the ticket to make me feel like a new woman again.

First, I had to tell my night class they'd have a supply teacher for a few weeks. The news would go down like a lead balloon, given the supply teacher didn't offer kickboxing in her repertoire to supplement the language and grammar teaching. More fool him. I knew how to get the best out of my students.

I turned away from the whiteboard where I'd been writing a list of nouns to learn for this week's homework and tucked a lock of jet-black hair behind my ear.

"Nita! How many times have I told you not to play with matches?" I said.

I couldn't help but like Nita, despite repeatedly telling her off for conducting oddball experiments in class. There was no doubt biology was the right degree for her as soon as night class nudged her over the points needed to gain a place. So far this term, I had caught her teaching her students how to use deodorant as a fire canister, how to explode a Coke bottle and how to make invisible ink with baking soda. I'd confiscated ingredients for a hot ice and crystallisation experiment and been livid to discover a foam volcano she'd conducted under her desk to the delight of the rest of my students. I kept a pack of wet wipes in my work bag primarily because of Nita.

And to get rid of grime from riding the tube. London was a cesspool.

The thing is, I didn't mind Nita's messes. Other teachers might have mistaken her behaviour for disruptiveness or an inability to follow the rules. Not me. Here was an immigrant showing up week after week to my class, putting her hand up, doing her homework, making friends and showing she had a passion. That passion was something even adults struggled to find. It would set her in good stead her whole life. It didn't mean she wasn't a pain sometimes, but who said only children who coloured within the lines grew up to be upstanding citizens? I liked students who showed a bit of mettle. That's how I would have brought up my children had I been lucky enough to have them.

Caught red-handed, Nita bit her lip apologetically. "Sorry, miss."

She pursed her lips to blow out the match, but I lifted a hand, and a breeze got there first, blowing her hair over her shoulders at the same time. Well, technically, like she'd been blasted by a wind turbine.

Puzzled, she looked at the closed window and shrugged.

I hid a smile. I was pretty sure I wasn't allowed to practice magic without Ezra's supervision, but what he didn't know wouldn't hurt him. Besides, I was a grown woman. At forty, you'd think I'd be able to weigh up risk versus reward.

I slotted back into teacher mode. "Copy these nouns into your exercise books, look up definitions in your dictionaries, use the words in full sentences and bring them to our next lesson. No excuses."

Six grown men and four women groaned, united in their disgust of grammar homework.

"Can you show us that kick now?" said Nita. "You promised last time."

I nodded. "Of course. Up you all get. Find some space. Make sure you're not swinging your body parts at anyone."

Chair legs scraped on the floor as they stood up: nineteen-year-old Nita; the middle-aged Chinese women Fei Yen and Faeza, who owned the tea and occult shop; Marek, the Polish builder with the receding hairline and enormous biceps; Tomás and Santiago, the Portuguese couple, who wanted to be able to make friends at Pride; Farzad, the Iranian grandfather, whose goal was to have a conversation with other seniors at the bingo hall; Nagma, the Bangladeshi woman, who assumed I spoke Hindi because I was Indian; and Ethan and Hassan, two high school dropouts who came to my class as a way around a formal English grade at school.

A motley crew, reflective of the city and how it could be a microcosm of the whole world within a few square metres.

Add gods, vampires, werewolves, druids, wizards, fae and talking animals to that list, and my mind was truly blown.

"Before we start, I have something to tell you...I lost my mother recently. She died in an accident, and I need a bit of time to get my head straight. I'm taking a few weeks of compassionate leave. That means there'll be a replacement teacher to take my place."

Ten faces looked at me in sympathy and disappointment.

"We are sorry, Miss Verma." Farzad clasped his hands together. "We will pray for your mother."

"But no one can teach as good as you," said Nita.

"*Good* is an adjective, Nita. You mean the adverb *well*. A good teacher teaches well." I plastered a reassuring smile on my face and crossed my fingers that the killer god took mercy on me. "I'll be back before your exams, I promise."

"We saw Death and the Hanged Man in the cards," said Fei Yen and Faeza as one, giving me vibes of the twins in *The Shining*.

A shiver ran up my spine. Their innate weirdness sometimes marked them out as different, even amongst this group of oddballs, but there was no cure for that. All the best people appreciated weirdness anyway.

"Let's not dwell on it, eh?" I said.

They'd done readings for me in the past, but they really should have asked. I liked my tarot readings to be a bit of fun, not a true reflection of life. It's why I always avoided fortune tellers at fun fairs. Nothing good could come of knowing the future.

Fei Yen shook her head, tousling her silky black elfin cut. "You misunderstand. The card didn't speak of literal death or hanging. They spoke of sweeping transformation and doors opening."

Faeza nodded, her pink rosebud lips turning downwards. "And great pain."

"Well, aren't you two the life and soul of the party? Let's finish on a high note, shall we? Ready for that back kick, class? Check you have enough room behind you, at least two metres. That's it, Marek. You can push that desk back. Yes, you too, Nagma." I bounced up and down on the spot and stretched my limbs. "Copy me. Just a little warm-up so we don't sprain anything."

They wobbled and lunged in front of me, neither the fittest nor youngest group in the world, but mostly willing.

"Give it some welly, Ethan. You'll be back on the sofa soon enough. Nagma, it might be hard getting your leg up in that Punjabi suit. Just take it easy. We're just having a go. It's not going to be perfect, and some of you might not get your leg all the way up." I clapped. "Right, eyes on me. Turn on the spot. Lift your right knee to your chest. A bit higher, Santiago. Well done, Nita. Look over your right shoulder. Extend your leg backwards to your imaginary target, kick and swivel back to your starting position. Good. Excellent work, Farzad."

Ethan and Hassan sent a display flying at the back of the room, and Nagma got caught in the scarf around her neck.

I decided to call it a day before I got sued for negligence.

"That's it for today. Thank you, class." I made a mental note to myself to look at potential sportswear on eBay as a treat when they passed their exams. If Echo's steak money hadn't carved a hole in my finances by then.

They hovered around me to say their goodbyes when I lifted my eyes to find a stranger there.

"Excuse me." I frowned.

The estate had trouble a few months previously, and I had taken to locking the door from the inside while class was in flow to prevent any bother from the local riffraff. I wasn't sure how he'd gotten inside, but he didn't seem all there. Not that I was worried. I was pretty sure any of my students would have been pleased to try out the back kick.

"This is a closed session," I said, "but if you'd like to register for night class, I can give you the details."

"Druid," the stranger whispered.

Now I was hearing things.

I had no idea what was up with the heating or if I was having hot flushes, but my body was burning up.

The class stepped back, their expressions wary, giving me room to take charge.

His eyes were liquid amber, but their overall impact was cold. His short hair stood on end, and he wore a boiler suit in dull tones over a barrel-like flank. He was as strong as an ox, and my instincts told me to run, but that would have been stupid. He was just a man who'd wandered into the wrong hall. I'd probably left the door unlocked. Time off from work would do me a world of good.

"Have we met?" I stepped out from behind the desk, my skin crawling. I'd seen the suit before, albeit briefly, on the day Melissa narrowly avoided the faulty electricity cable outside EvolveTech.

Amber eyes glinted within a swarthy, leathery face. "There is no hiding from the sun. It stretches across streets and fields and icy plains. It reaches into buildings and creeps under the eyelids."

Farzad approached the man. "Strange man. You drunk. Go home."

He laid a hand on the man's shoulder to usher him out, then snatched it back and staggered away. It sizzled, his skin red and blistering where he had touched the stranger.

Nita screamed.

The stranger turned his unnatural eyes on her.

I put my body between Farzad and the man. I was impressed by Farzad's ability to put together a coherent English sentence on the spot, but he was more cut out for the bingo hall than playing security guard.

"Listen," I said to the man, unsure how he'd burned Farzad. Maybe he had some kind of battery pack under his boiler suit. He really needed to take the safety precautions of his profession seriously. "No need to intimidate me. I didn't dob you into the authorities for your dodgy work that day. You weren't wearing a badge. I'll get the first aid kit and patch up Farzad here, and you can just turn around and walk away. Although, you might need to get more training because I wouldn't want an electrician with your skills wiring a doll's house, let alone a public supply."

He gave a slight shake of his head like he had no idea

what I was on about. Maybe I'd pegged him wrongly, and he wasn't an electrician after all. Maybe he was just masquerading as one and had no affiliation whatsoever. Here he was, swanning around when he could have learned his trade—the cheek of it.

He leaned forward.

My students edged back, their faces beaded with perspiration.

"You can call me electrician. I have been many incarnations of myself." A ripple of amusement went through him. "You can call me all the names under the sun, but I will always be me."

"Are you on crack? There's an addiction group here on Wednesday nights. The sign-up info is in the hallway."

He frowned. "The game is underfoot, druid. And you'd do well to stay out of my way."

I froze.

There it was again. I hadn't misheard.

I'd barely stepped into the Otherworld, and here it was, following me to work in the guise of a threatening man. Let's face it; I'd dealt with dozens of threatening men before: outside building sites, inside nightclubs, on the tube and at sweaty gigs when I wanted to dance, not be groped.

But this one was creepier than the rest.

This was an opportune moment for my leopard protector to jump into the fray. I pinched shut my eyes and sent a silent message to Echo.

Come. I need you at the community centre.

We'd not talked about whether our minds could walkie-talkie each other, but I figured it wouldn't hurt.

"For now, I've decided to remind you that insignificant creatures would do well to stay out of the affairs of their superiors." He raised his voice and waved his hands grandly like a preacher at the pulpit. His thick, black nails made me gag. "Let this be a lesson to you all. If you had worshipped us in gratitude, we wouldn't have to cause you pain."

I took up a fight stance.

He didn't look like he was going to turn back meekly into the night. It was going to take some persuasion and maybe a kick to the face.

I stared him out and fought the primal urge to turn away. "Get out of our community centre."

"The guy's on acid," said Marek, like he'd seen it all before.

"Kick his behind, Miss Verma!" Nagma swung her scarf around like a whip, despite her advanced years.

Echo, where are you?

He'd made his point, whatever it was—that he didn't need an invitation, had bigger balls than us and had the right to be a shoddy electrician—but he was still here. I didn't have the faintest clue why.

The man walked towards us, unfazed, as if we were mere flies.

I hesitated and then unleashed a breeze that fanned his hair like he was on the beach.

Without batting an eyelid, he walked through it to Nita.

Nita spun, trying to execute a back kick, but he grabbed her shoe and flung it away. Her rubber sole seemed to melt.

"Get away from her." I went in for a crescent kick, followed by an elbow strike.

"Yes, miss!" shouted Ethan. He and Hassan seemed to be moving in from the side to help me.

"Stay back," I said.

The stranger squeezed Nita's shoulder, leaving her writhing to escape. The arm of her T-shirt disintegrated under the pressure of his fingers. Her eyes widened in horror, and a cry ripped from her throat. She was drenched with sweat.

"Nita, stay calm," I said. "You'll be okay."

"You did this," said the stranger to me. "In fifteen years,

she would have been at a Harrow laboratory on the brink of a discovery. I could have let her live. But what is a god without a little vengeance?"

My blood ran cold. It couldn't be.

He had come, just like the goddess had predicted—my mother's killer.

He hadn't come when I'd been on a run with Echo when my magical leopard could have protected me. Or on Wildwoods grounds when the school itself would have channelled its defences, or any number of peculiars could have helped.

This killer god had found me at my most vulnerable.

I kicked myself for being stupid enough to let it happen. I willed the universe to keep Nita safe.

Gaia. Echo. I need you.

A current pulsed between his fingers.

"No, no! Wait." I was defenceless against a god. Gaia had said he'd killed my mother. But how could I fight him with a few kicks and punches and a light breeze? If he wanted prayer, he could have it. I'd pray to him every dawn if that's what it took to keep my class safe.

I pressed my palms together in prayer.

The lights went out. Not switched off, but as if the light had been sucked into a void.

A spark flared, and then a scuffle ensued.

The swirls of black became limbs and tails and muzzles. I fought to decipher the darkness—slick fur and teeth.

A shape leapt at me, passing by a finger's breath away. Panting, an echo in my ears.

I was rooted to the spot, my heartbeat rattling until I couldn't distinguish between the sounds.

Then came a bloodcurdling cry.

15

The light returned to the classroom, though no one had hit the light switch. The god had fled, leaving upturned tables and huddled bodies. I swallowed hard, trying to keep my fear under control, though my instincts told me to get the hell out of there. I hadn't been able to make sense of the sounds in the dark.

My stomach roiled as I surveyed the room.

An enormous wolf lay next to Nita's crumpled body, his tail tucked in, nudging her with his paws. His thick, copper fur clung to his muscular frame, interspersed with silver-white.

When he turned his eyes on me, he howled as if in mourning.

My adrenalin had been racing for so long that I felt lightheaded. I took a deep breath, wiped the sweat from my forehead and risked a look at the class. "Are you all okay?"

Nine scared faces stared back at me. Farzad still nursed his hand.

"Fuck this, miss. I'm out of here," said Ethan, followed by a rush of feet.

Five remained, including Fei Yen and Faeza.

"Go," I said. "The wolf's not a threat. I'll deal with this."

They scurried out, eager to believe my lie.

I gulped. A fox in the classroom wasn't farfetched in a city overrun by them, but a wolf was the stuff of nightmares. They weren't scavengers; they were carnivores.

Nita looked asleep, most likely unconscious. Shock could really take the wind out of your sails. Her creamy skin was flushed, and her singed T-shirt made me wince. There wasn't a mark on her. That didn't mean it would stay that way.

Echo would have scared away or snacked on this wolf for sport, but he was nowhere to be seen, despite my telepathic S.O.S.

Sirens sounded in the distance.

One of the class had probably called the police. Good. I was ready for someone else to take responsibility.

I wasn't going to hang about, though. I needed to get the wolf away from Nita before it hurt her. What was it doing here in inner city London, away from its pack? I couldn't remember what you were supposed to do when confronted by a wolf. Marina would have known whether to back away, stare him out or make noise. Not that it had helped with Echo, but my preferred option—to run away—wasn't an option here. With no saucepans, blowhorn or vuvuzela in my pocket, I grabbed the nearest thing I could find—a stapler—and clicked it like our lives depended on it and added "go away" to the rhythm.

The wolf cocked its head like I had lost my marbles. If he were in a zoo enclosure, I would have called him beautiful. He yapped and pawed at Nita's chest, his claws retracted, and then dipped his head.

Outside, Marek and Hassan banged the window, trying to help out, and Ethan thudded some wheelie bin lids. Only Fei Yen and Faeza seemed morose and calm.

The wolf must have been deaf because the noise didn't faze him at all. I put down the stapler and edged closer, signalling my students to go away. I owed it to them not to add 'mauled teacher' to their list of traumas.

The sirens grew nearer.

Huge balls told me it was probably a male. "It's okay, boy. You can go now. Go on, shoo, before the police sling you in the dog pound."

He whimpered again.

For a moment, I thought he was trying to communicate. I must have been more under strain than I thought. I crouched down on the opposite side of Nita's body to the wolf, moving millimetre by millimetre.

All it would have to do was spring across her body to take me out.

I put my hands up and channelled my focus. My breeze had always worked for me in moments of terror. One false move and the wolf would think he was in a tumble dryer.

The wolf put his wet nose on my palm.

I almost emptied my bladder there and then. That would teach me to increase my water intake. His glossy fur smelt familiar, evoking a buried memory, but it was only when he turned his grey eyes on me that I noticed the silver necklace tight around its neck, threaded with charms: a moon, a thistle and binary code.

No bloody way.

"Ezra?" I breathed out in wonder.

He whimpered as cars skidded to a halt in the car park outside and blue lights flicked across the classroom.

Taking my courage in my hands, I reached for the soft fur on his neck and pushed him gently towards the door. "You need to get out of here before the police come. Find me later. Go, now."

I turned my full attention to Nita, although every cell told me to check Ezra made it out safely. "Hang in there, Nita. Help is on the way."

I put her into the recovery position, rolling her over onto

her side, rearranging her knee, tilting her head back a fraction and checking her airways. I stopped short. Her body was hot to the touch, feverish even, as if she'd spent the day baking on an exotic beach. London was a cool five degrees Celsius tonight.

My hands trembled as I checked her skin again. My own heartbeat became sluggish with dread as I checked for a pulse.

"Nita?"

I felt her neck, then her wrist, hoping my rusty first-aid skills were to blame for my panic. I stared at her chest, determined to see it rise and fall, and then listened for breath at her lightly parted mouth.

No. No. No. "Someone call an ambulance!"

I started compressions, worried about breaking her ribs but determined not to lose her.

Fei Yen approached from my peripheral vision and laid her hand on my shoulder.

I shrugged it off and continued the compressions. The seconds seemed like hours. What was taking the police so long?

Fei Yen squeezed my shoulder and then pulled me back. Her eyes filled with sorrow. "Why deny what you know to be true?"

"I have to help her."

"She's dead," said Fei Yen. "She has already crossed to the other side."

I knew she was right, even though Nita was unnaturally hot to the touch and not cold like dead bodies were supposed to be. I picked up Nita's slight body and rocked her.

Fei Yen waited a moment. Then she took Nita from my arms and laid her carefully on the floor, straightening her limbs and running a hand over her eyelids. Mascara crumbled from Nita's thick lashes.

"I did this," I said.

A heavy sigh. "No, you didn't. The god did."

A shiver ran up my spine. What did Fei Yen know about all of this?

There was nothing godly about murder. That so-called god had killed my mother. He had killed my student. He was responsible for the other deaths Detective Jameson and the gravedigger had talked of.

Weren't gods supposed to be benign and merciful? He had killed for no other reason than to create chaos for attention. So what if he wanted to be loved? I wanted to be loved. Everyone did. That didn't mean we went around killing people.

Rage unfurled inside me. Nita had been loved. She'd been loved by me, her fellow students and her family. She'd already been through so much leaving Turkey. It had been my job to protect her, and I'd failed. There would be no more mess in my classroom because of her. No more baking soda experiments or future glory. All her promise, all her passion and determination amounted to nothing now that her body lay lifeless on the classroom floor.

I needed air. I stumbled to my feet, and rushed outside into the black night.

Nagma made a beeline for me. "Miss Verma, is Nita okay? What happened to the wolf?"

Ethan's face loomed large. "Tomás and Santiago took Farzad to Accident and Emergency for his hand."

"Miss Verma, what's a druid?" Hassan asked.

Faeza gave me a sad smile, wrapped her arms around Hassan and ushered him away. "Did you hear druid? I heard druggie. Makes sense. That guy must have been on something."

I vomited onto the grass.

In the distance, under a crescent moon, a wolf howled.

It was close to midnight when two police officers gave me a ride home. I slumped in the back of the car and leaned my head against the window. Shadows lurked all around me, flitting in and out of my peripheral vision.

An officer leapt out to open my door. "Please get in touch if you remember any further details, Miss Verma. Don't worry; we'll catch the creep."

I nodded my thanks, although I doubted these humdrum police could catch the god, let alone hold him. They had even less information than me. They had no idea what he was, if he could change faces, who he'd target next or what Nita had died from. The police promises were as reassuring as a gerbil squaring up to a bear. They were completely outmatched and outgunned, just like me.

They did a U-turn while I walked to my building. I looked hard into the void of night, my heartbeat rattling. Nothing came for me, though I feared it would. The door opened before I put my key in the lock, and Marina tumbled out in a blur of pink.

"I'm glad you're here." I fell into her arms, ready for someone to look after me for a change. Whoever said grown women couldn't both be strong *and* need comfort obviously had no idea about women.

"I've been worried senseless since I got your text. I'm so sorry, Alisha." She pulled back to reassure herself I wasn't hurt. "Echo let me in through the back window."

One of my ex-husband's complaints was how often Marina came over. He was right. I should have given her a key

"Ezra's here too, even though Echo threatened to gnaw his leg. He said you told him to come by."

I raised a weak smile. "Something like that. Just let me have a quick wash and change into my PJs."

She gave me an encouraging nod. "I'll make you some tea and toast."

I ignored the voices in the living room, shut the door to

my bedroom and took a ragged breath before kicking off my shoes and peeling off my clothes. Then I headed for my en suite bathroom, turned on the shower and let hot soapy suds wash away the day's grime and soothe my soul.

Three faces floated in the nebulous pink of my closed eyelids: Nita, crumpled on the floor; the swarthy amber-eyed god; and Ezra in his copper-silver wolf form.

I sighed, washed my hair and stepped out of the shower before dressing in my PJs and yanking a comb through my hair in front of my steamy mirror. Not a scrap of makeup remained on my face, but I didn't care. I wanted my tea and toast. While makeup could make me feel ready to take on the world, sometimes I just wanted to be myself.

I padded barefoot to the living room, the remnants of coral nail polish on my toes and wet hair making my T-shirt stick to my back. The lamp lit the room, which suited my mood just fine. That was, apart from the slight whiff of a zoo, but a leopard and a wolf couldn't be expected to smell like a spa.

Echo purred in greeting. He dwarfed Marina on one sofa, taking up two-thirds of the space. A steaming mug of tea and a plate of thickly buttered toast waited for me on the coffee table a few inches from Ezra.

"Hey, hellfire." His gaze softened as it drifted over me.

"Thanks for tonight, Ezra. You put yourself in danger for my class."

"I did it for you."

My mouth felt dry. I must have been gagging for my tea.

He wore chequered boxers and a thin button-up shirt, only it wasn't done up to the top. There wasn't a goosebump on him. I figured wolves were warmer-blooded than humans and druids. The charm necklace that had been tight around his wolf neck now hung just above his pecks. A closer look told me he'd lost the top three shirt buttons. Had he ripped it off when he changed into his wolf form? The shirt sleeves were rolled up, and one arm had a nasty run of blisters.

"Don't let your tea get cold." Marina waggled her eyebrows.

Flushing, I gave her my best WTF look.

She grinned and gave me the peace sign.

I sat next to Ezra, averting my eyes from his bulging thighs. Then I reached for my tea, wishing belatedly that I'd put on a bra. Like most women, my breasts preferred to be wild and free, but hell, I wasn't twenty anymore.

My eyes flicked to the blisters. "What happened to your arm? Shall I get some antiseptic cream?"

"The dog heals more quickly than any of us," said Echo. "He has no need for humdrum lotions."

I missed the days when Echo would slink around my feet to show his affection. This Echo was tough as old boots.

"Echo's right. It's just a scratch." Grey eyes turned sombre. "Sorry I couldn't save the kid. That cuts deep."

Tears welled, but I pushed back my despair. There would be time for grief later. I wanted the killer god to pay.

"It could have been much worse, dog, if you hadn't been able to slip from the god's grasp," Echo said. "Who knows what the outcome would have been without your presence? I owe you my thanks for protecting Alisha when I was otherwise occupied. I admit the deer I caught in the royal park was the highlight of my year, but I would never have forgiven myself had Alisha been harmed."

I glared at him. "You were hunting when I sent my S.O.S., Echo? I could have done with your help."

Echo growled. "Did you use my full name? Usually, the magical post is more reliable, Alisha. I am sorry it failed you. I will have a word with the cloud master."

I blinked rapidly. "The cloud master?"

"Yes." He talked to me as if I were a distracted toddler. "You throw your message into clouds, where they are transformed into raindrops to be caught and held to the ear to decipher. Isn't that what you did? A system that works much better in London than in the Sahara, I might add."

"Er...no. I just asked you to come with my mind."

He threw up his magnificent head and emitted a strange honking noise I realised was laughing. "The granddaughter of Rajika Verma thinks I'm a *telepathic* leopard?" The honks continued. "Rajika's spirit is rolling her eyes; I just know it. You have a lot to learn."

"So everyone keeps telling me." I turned to look at Ezra because Echo liked being centre stage too much to stop the honking of his own accord. "How did you know to be there, Ezra? And what happened to the light? Did you hit the switch on the way in? Neat trick."

He rolled the moon charm between long, lean fingers. The silver threads amongst his chestnut brown hair made him more handsome. "See this? I told you my father was a werewolf. That's where my beast comes from."

"I remember." I took a bite of my toast and pulled my sopping hair over one shoulder. The wet patch spread too close to my chest for comfort. I grimaced. "I should have brought out a towel."

Ezra's eyes dropped to my chest. He looked away. "Shall I get you one?"

My stomach fluttered. It must have been my new single status. My hormones were obviously in overdrive. Hardly surprising, really. I had years of monogamy to make up for. I only had a decade or so before menopause and I wanted to enjoy myself before my libido took a hit. I pushed the thoughts out of my head. "Sorry, I interrupted."

"My wizard side is from the maternal line. My parents are dead, but when my mother died, her three sisters couldn't take me in. The pack wouldn't have it. They'd tolerated my mother, but to trust her witch sisters was a step too far. I was never going to be one of the great wizards. Pack law wouldn't tolerate it. It was more trouble than it was worth to go up against an alpha. My aunts knew that, but they loved my mother and wanted to give me a fighting chance. Werewolves tend to die young, especially werewolves with portal magic. We're rarer than an equinox. So my three aunts each gifted me a charm. I used the moon charm tonight. It allows me to suck away artificial light for a minute to allow escape. It gave me the edge of surprise." His eyes gleamed. "But if any of you betray this secret, I will kill you."

Marina smiled, showing even white teeth that had never needed braces—the lucky cow.

"What the hell, Marina? He just threatened to"—I pulled my finger across my neck—"and you *smiled*?"

"Easy tiger," said Marina. "I discovered something tonight."

"I'd prefer it if you didn't bring up other big cats in my presence, Marina Ambrose." Echo's head was too close to hers for comfort.

We all rolled our eyes at him.

He lifted his head in the haughty manner of a king who could not be lowered by mere subjects.

"What did you discover?" I said.

"You turfed Ezra out, and he teleported into my van just as I was doing a three-point turn. I got spooked, mounted the kerb and crashed into a post box. Long story short, I invited him back to mine to knock around some ideas about how to encourage you to embrace training more—you know, given you're in the shit with the gods more than I am—and something clicked in me. I just *knew* you were in trouble. I felt it. Like here." She patted her heart. "I shoved Ezra out of the door, trying to explain, completely forgetting he could teleport. Next thing I knew, his clothes were on my floor, and his naked butt had teleported out of there."

I quashed a pang of jealousy.

It's not like I had a claim to Ezra. If Marina wanted him, I wouldn't fight her for him. Sisters before misters. It's not even as if I really wanted him. It would be really bad juju to get into another entanglement without exorcising Alex from my head.

"Point is, I smiled because I *know* Ezra wouldn't hurt you. I feel it in my bones. Just as I felt in my bones that Echo wasn't himself in the arena."

"Turns out your best friend is an empath, hellfire," Ezra said. "She saved you tonight as much as I did. I wouldn't have known you were in distress without her."

I frowned, not liking the suggestion I was a damsel needing to be rescued. I had no idea how I'd manage it, but I was not putting myself in that vulnerable position again. I was not going to fail someone who needed my protection. Even if that meant I armed myself with kitchen knives and had to booby-trap my whole flat.

"So what does an empath do? Read thoughts and stuff?" I tried to keep my voice upbeat.

Echo groaned. "I don't know why I expect so much of you, granddaughter of Rajika Verma. I really must ask the Minister for History and the Today if I can look into your ancestral records to see if there are any unexpected blips there." He huffed. "Telepathy is reading thoughts. Empathy is sensing feelings. Even a troll would know that."

Marina squealed in glee. "I'm so excited to find out what I can do. And just think, if I know what you are feeling, I might be able to sense when animals are in pain too. Veterinary Awards, here I come!"

I was happy for her. She'd wanted so badly to find out what her peculiar nature would be and had cheered me on, despite her own pangs of disappointment. I'd even wondered whether it had all been a mistake and she was a humdrum after all. Logically, given she could see Echo's true form, I knew that couldn't be true, but the Otherworld was so new to us that we needed proof to believe each step. Marina would never have been a lesser person as a humdrum. She was extraordinary in every incarnation, but I was relieved to have her as my peculiar sister. I just wished I'd been there to find out first.

"It is not the done thing to profit from your magic, Marina Ambrose, but in this instance, I suspect only good will come of it," purred Echo.

Ezra shrugged. The skin on his arm had almost completely healed. "Technically, there's no rule against it, although the Sorcerer's Senate has discussed it according to the minutes of their meetings. It is *very* hard to profit from magic while obeying the other rules, so they didn't think an additional one was worth the effort."

A knock sounded at the door. At 1 a.m.. Who turned up at that hour?

Echo leapt off the sofa, energy rolling from his magnificent body, claws no longer retracted but ready to do damage.

"Holy shit, you think that's the god?" Marina was paler and stiffer than I'd ever seen her, as if she had soaked up all our fear.

"An *invited* guest would use the buzzer. Hit the lights," I said in a whisper. "That gave us an advantage last time."

Ezra shook his head. "My charm only lasts a minute or two. Best to just switch off the lamp the humdrum way."

Marina dove for the lamp in a poorly executed forward roll and yanked out the plug at the socket. I'm not sure it made covering the distance any faster, but I dug that she was getting into the spirit of things.

"Don't touch that!" I shouted, worried the electrician god would have sent a powerful current through the walls.

She stood up tentatively, right as rain.

A second knock on the door, this time more urgent.

I sucked in a shaky breath. "Maybe the electrician god is more polite than we thought."

"More likely he can't teleport like Gaia can or is saving his energy for bigger fights. Be great right now to be able to get guidance from the senate on his history. We're flying blind here," said Ezra.

"Stupid laws." I gritted my teeth and ventured into the dark corridor to open it. The rules of hospitality left me no choice. My house, my job.

Ezra followed on my heel.

"Get back here, granddaughter of Rajika Verma, or I will raise hell in this neighbourhood," roared Echo.

"You might need to," I said.

I nodded at Ezra, counted to three and unhooked the latch.

16

I opened the door a crack at a time, letting in a sliver of light from the hallway. Ezra's breath fanned the back of my neck. Echo and Marina stood alert and ready a few paces behind us. My fingers tingled, ready to unleash whatever I could at the murderous god—at least this time, I had back up.

A foot wedged the door open.

I saw red and used the door as a battering ram.

The squealing voice on the other side gave me pause, but I didn't care. I slammed the foot over and over again until I reckoned it was a pulpy mess.

For Mum. For Nita. For the scientists that could have done good in the world.

The god deserved everything that was coming to him.

"Yes, Alisha. Get him!" said Marina.

The foot stopped struggling.

The battle had been easier than I thought, so I opened the door a fraction more and frowned when the pool of light revealed a familiar trainer and sock. The ball of anxiety in my belly transformed into fury. I'd washed those stinky socks a million times before and bought those trainers for his last birthday before the divorce.

I wrenched open the door. "Alex? It's one in the morning. What the hell are you doing here?"

My ex-husband groaned, and happiness bloomed like a rose inside me.

Not only had we lucked out and avoided doing battle with the god, but I had dealt with Alex as easily as an exterminator deals with a rat. It felt good after all our angry emails and telephone calls to go to bat. He couldn't even blame me for thinking he was an intruder. I bent down to check on him.

I was an angry ex-wife, not an arsehole.

He gazed up at me like he was seeing stars. Blond hair and blue eyes with more wrinkles than in his prime, but we all had those. I'd still look twice at him if we didn't have our history.

"What did you do that for? I didn't even have a chance to tell you I love you." He reached for my cheek, and a cloud of beer breath hit me, possibly plus salt-and-vinegar crisps. "But I do."

Marina stormed over to us, flicked his hand away and stuck a pointy finger at his chest. "Don't you *dare* say that after everything you put her through."

Alex slid out from under her finger and staggered to his feet. "Still sticking your nose in where it doesn't belong, Marina? You girls been partying tonight?"

I cringed. When I started challenging him about his gambling, he took to using belittling nicknames for me: baby cakes, sweet cheeks, muffin, you name it. They made me want to hit him with a saucepan. "You reek of booze, Alex. It's late opening at The Rose and Crown tonight, isn't it?"

He held up his hands like I'd pointed a gun at him. "I only had a few."

He hadn't always been an idiot. There was a time when we could talk until the sun came up, laugh until our sides hurt, and we couldn't keep our hands off each other. Twelve years we'd stayed together, and not all of them had been bad, but there came a time when I gave up hoping that the old Alex would come back.

His eyes narrowed as he looked past me. "You've got another man in your bed already? That's low, pumpkin."

Ezra leaned against the door frame, completely at ease in his half-buttoned shirt. His muscular thighs burst out of the chequered boxers that rode dangerously low on his slim hips. His folded arms accentuated his toned body. He grinned, not bothering to correct Alex's assumption.

"You don't love me then, baby cakes?" Alex said.

"Afraid that ship has long sailed."

"Hallelujah," said Marina.

Alex curled a lip at her. "Then you won't lend me any money?"

"Jesus, Alex." I rolled my eyes. The man had become a worm.

His face turned green like he was going to vomit. Then he perked up. "Echo, my boy. Here, kitty, kitty."

Echo jostled Ezra aside and padded out. "Imbecile." He gave Alex a casual swipe. "Like I ever would have chosen to live with a gambling fool. You are worth less than the shit on a Verma's shoe."

Alex recoiled. "Why did he do that?"

"Blind as a bat and deaf as a doorpost, this one," purred Echo. "He wouldn't know the truth if it bit him on the rear end. Shall I?"

"No!" said Marina and I in unison.

"No, what?" said Alex.

"No, I won't lend you any money," I said.

He flushed. "Listen, sweet pea—"

"Go inside, the lot of you. I'll deal with this," I said. We'd probably woken the neighbours up already. I was bound to get an earful from Dotty, who lived a few doors down.

They turned to go inside when Ezra tensed.

"You catch that scent, Echo?" Ezra said.

Both leopard and barely dressed wolfman—with his perfect tush—stared down the length of the hallway. Echo growled and inched past me, his pupils dilating. His sense of smell was inferior to a wolf shifter's, but his eyesight was pretty darn good. Their sightline was obscured by Dotty's bicycle and boxes of recycling waiting to be taken out. The lobby lay around the corner. It always gave me the shivers when I went out, a perfect hiding place to get the jump on someone.

Echo roared, picking up speed.

My mouth went dry, and I considered using Alex as cannon fodder to slow down the god while we made a getaway. Maybe he'd do it to prove his love.

A man in a puffer jacket rounded the corner, his hands in the air.

"Call off the leopard," said the man as Echo bared his teeth. Ezra swooped in to twist the man's arm behind his back and pin him against the wall. "Call the wolf off too. I'm the police, you dimwits."

I squinted down the hallway. "Detective Jameson?"

"Duh," he said, in pretty spirited form, given his cheek was pressed against the grimy magnolia wall.

"Let him go." My heart raced. He'd recognised Echo's true form. And Ezra's. "I've been looking for you, Detective."

"I should rip this stranger's spinal cord out. That goes for your lowly ex-lover too." Echo backed off with a jaunty spring in his step, like he enjoyed hunting humans as much as he liked deer and Labradors.

"No need for that," said Detective Jameson. "I contemplated charging that one for drunk and disorderly behaviour. But seeing as he took the early heat of this encounter, perhaps we should give him a free pass and get on with our discussions. We have a lot to talk about, Ms Verma. It's about time we put our cards on the table, don't you think?

Given how I could just as easily charge you with perverting the course of justice."

The lights in neighbouring flats started to go on.

I gulped. My immediate future wasn't looking that rosy, but there could be fewer things worse than letting my shame play out in front of nosy neighbours.

"You'd better come in." I swung towards Alex, who was already being frog-marched towards the exit by Marina. "As for you, don't come back in a hurry." I wrinkled my nose. "And for heaven's sake, sober up."

We crammed back into my flat, and I switched on the lights before rounding on Detective Jameson.

"Can I see your badge, Detective?" I said.

He rummaged in his puffer jacket while I waggled my eyebrows like a demon-possessed at Marina and Ezra, hoping they'd get the hint. Detective Jameson might look human and act like a police officer, but given he hadn't appeared in the Metropolitan Police database, nothing was certain. We needed to be on high alert for fangs, hairy arms or worse.

"There you go." He shoved his badge under my nose.

I'd given it a cursory glance on the night we met, but this time I took care to memorise his warrant card number and check the photo. His hair had thinned since the photograph had been taken, but it was the same man. No obvious funny business stood out to me, but I still wasn't sold. The detective might think he had the upper hand, but this wasn't a one-way street. I had plenty of niggling questions of my own to ask.

I grabbed my dressing gown and pointed down the hallway. "After you. We can talk in the living room."

Detective Jameson edged towards the living room, his eyes trained on Echo. Judging by the nerve pulsing in his jaw, he not only had true sight but a healthy fear of Echo. I could use that to my advantage.

He wrinkled his nose. "What is that smell?"

"Just my leopard marking his territory." I'd noticed it

much more recently. Although Marina's nose seemed immune to putrid animal smells and Ezra was half animal, so he seemed to have a high threshold too. I murmured in Echo's ear. "Keep moving around the room. It will destabilise the detective until we know what he is."

Echo nodded. "With pleasure. This is a battle tactic your grandmother would have approved of."

My tiny living room couldn't accommodate us all easily, so I didn't invite Detective Jameson to sit. Instead, we stood in an uncomfortable face-off. Rainbow-haired Marina and barely dressed Ezra flanked me on one side of the room. Detective Jameson stood a few paces away. Echo prowled the outskirts, making everyone nervous except me.

My heartbeat had settled into a calmer rhythm than when I thought the electrician god had come for us, but I was still on alert. Even with the weirdness of the situation, never in a million years would I have swapped back to a life of sitting on the sofa with Alex while he watched reruns of *Top Gear*.

"A bit late to call around, isn't it, Detective?" I said.

"Some things can't wait." His face was all shadows and angles like he hadn't slept in a week.

Marina held out a hand. "I'm Marina Ambrose, Alisha's best friend. Your aura's really pretty."

"It is? Thanks." He shook her hand. "A pleasure to meet you. Although, it turns out you and your friends know far more than you let on. You've not been straight with me."

"This is between you and me. Don't bring Marina into it," I said. If he really was a copper, I didn't want to risk her landing in the slammer. This whole escapade had started with my family's secrets. Marina was guilty of nothing except being a great friend.

"Ah, but your friends are in as deeply as you, Ms Verma. They can't play the game and expect not to get burned."

Next to me, Ezra bristled like he was going to lose it.

I refocussed on Detective Jameson. "I went down to the

station a few nights ago. Turns out you're not on their books. Why is that *exactly?*"

Bleary brown eyes held my gaze. "I could have been more upfront with you. But then again, you're no ordinary woman, are you, Alisha? Ordinary women don't know about the Otherworld."

My heartbeat raced. Any minute now, he was going to transform into some hellish creature.

I didn't let him see my fear, though. "Ordinary men can't see magical leopards."

His eyes widened in surprise. "I thought he was a tiger."

"Dude, even five-year-olds can tell the difference," said Marina. "I'll give you a crash course if you like."

Detective Jameson nodded as if a tête-à-tête with my bestie was a real possibility.

"So go on, Detective. Who the hell are you, and what have you been hiding?" I said.

"I'll lay out my role in all this on the proviso you keep your mouths shut. You know how it is. If you spill, I'll have to kill you." No smile played on his lips. The man was deadly serious.

That expression told me he'd put us in a ditch and then go and buy doughnuts.

"Sounds a bit harsh." I looked at the others. Marina nodded, Ezra shrugged, and Echo looked distracted by a fly. "Okay, deal."

He drew in a deep breath. "I'm in the Shadow Squad. I apologise for the charade, but it's protocol. There's a reason why the Shadow Squad isn't on the Met database. All personnel files, in addition to past and ongoing investigations, are secret. There's a handful of us. We work alone."

Echo grunted. "This is a lie, granddaughter of Rajika Verma. Police officers do not work alone. Even I know the old joke—how many policemen does it take to screw in a lightbulb?"

I shook my head. "Not the time, Echo. Please continue, Detective."

My teaching career and gambling husband had given me plenty of experience sniffing out lies. The detective's story sounded dubious, but the boundaries of reality had shifted since becoming a druid. This week taught me anything was possible. My gut told me to hear him out.

"As I was saying, we are answerable straight to the Prime Minister. All interactions with the public are on a need-to-know basis."

I frowned. "What is the Shadow Squad responsible for?"

Shaky fingers pinched the bridge of his nose. "We investigate infractions committed by magical and otherworldly folk against humans."

"Well, smother me in cream and eat me up." Marina smiled at Detective Jameson as if he'd gone from run-of-the-mill copper to a light-sabre-wielding knight of the realm.

I knew that admiring, coquettish look well. It was the look she gave someone before she jumped their bones. I made a mental note to run an intervention when we were alone.

"I've never heard of a Shadow Squad," said Ezra. "And I wasn't born yesterday. If everything is hush-hush, how do we know you are telling the truth?"

"It's a conundrum, isn't it?" He paused. "Listen, mate, get some trousers and button up, will you? No need to flash your pecks in polite company. Some of us haven't had that body in twenty years. I've yet to meet a shifter who isn't an exhibitionist."

Ezra scowled. "That's how we roll, *mate*. Comes with the territory."

I pushed on, ignoring the prickles between them. If there was something I was good at, it was picking my battles. "Why did you come here tonight and not last week when it became clear Mum wasn't the only one who had been targeted?"

"What happened at the community centre tonight forced my hand. Things are hotting up. We know now beyond a shadow of a doubt the perpetrator is a serial killer. Not only that, he's enjoying the spectacle. That makes him even more dangerous than we thought."

"Who is *we*?" purred Echo. "Have you got any Labradors on your team? German Shepherds are too bristly, but how about Dobermans? I've never tried one of those."

The detective scratched his jaw. "Is he joking?"

I shook my head. "Afraid not. So what you are saying, Detective, is that you made me question my mother's competency at work and the foundations of my parents' marriage, *and* you didn't alert me to the known dangers of the situation. My student died tonight. She was a good kid. A great one. Now you're at a dead end, you come to civilians for help."

"But you're not civilians, are you, Ms Verma? At least, not in the powerless sense."

"Touché," I said. "But how do we know you're not something *other* too?"

"You'll have to take my word for it." Detective Jameson patted his slight beer belly. "To my great regret, I'm as normal as they come. Can you imagine investigating the Otherworld day in and day out and being utterly depressingly human? To make matters worse, I can't even tell my own father what I do for a living. He thinks I'm a traffic officer."

"Well, that sucks," I said. "Is there a magical x-ray machine we can use to be certain?"

Echo stopped mid-prowl and honked with laughter. "I must start to record these ridiculous things you say."

I gawped. "You can write, Echo? I didn't know that."

He held his magnificent head high. "That was a turn of phrase. Of course, I can't use a pen with *paws*. I'm not a primate. I don't have opposable thumbs. But if I could write, I would be the next Ursula K. Le Guin. Our paths crossed in Paris in 1953. Where else do you think all her ideas came from? As for an x-ray machine to scan for magical powers, there are no shortcuts in nature, granddaughter of Rajika Verma. This man will show his true colours, and we will be waiting to see if he has tried to pull the wool over our eyes."

Detective Jameson sensed Echo's implicit threat and swallowed hard.

I furrowed my brow. "How is it that you have true sight without being a peculiar, Detective? My understanding is that for humans, the veil is only lifted in the few moments before death."

"The Shadow Squad goes through training to both toughen and open up our minds. Hypnosis is part of the training. A hypnotist uses suggestions to achieve cognitive realignment. Not every mind survives exposure to the pierced veil. Some become trapped in a nightmarish twilight zone. But the success rate amongst recruits has improved over the years. Once you see the Otherworld, you can't unsee it. At least, not without magical intervention." He sighed. "The thing is, we're mostly an intelligence-only unit. We monitor. We clear up the debris. At most, my superiors reach out through diplomatic channels to have a word when the Otherworld gets out of hand. Our government doesn't have super soldiers knocking about. Captain America and Iron Man aren't waiting in the wings to suit up."

Ezra snorted. "It seems your Shadow Squad are toothless chihuahuas. It's best we work alone, Alisha."

"Maybe we should give Detective Jameson a chance." Marina sank into the sofa and tucked her bare feet up under her. She'd obviously missed my cues to stay alert at all costs. "His heart is in the right place. I can tell from his bright aura. Auras can't be faked, you know."

"Marina Ambrose," said Echo. "In Otherworld terms, you

are an infant. Less than an infant. You are an embryo. As much as your empathetic skills might seem en pointe to you, this muscle is as undeveloped as a sumo wrestler's waist. You should not act as a guarantor for strange men, especially if they flash badges to compensate for shortcomings in other areas." Green eyes dropped pointedly to the Detective's nether regions.

"Well, that was unnecessary," said Detective Jameson.

"The cat is right." Ezra cleared the detective's height by three inches. "We don't know yet that our goals align."

"I can't sit back and do nothing while people die," said Detective Jameson. "What use is information if I just sit on it?"

My stomach knotted. He really believed we could tip the odds in his favour. "Tell us what you know."

He hesitated, then spoke rapidly as if divulging the information went against his nature. "The preliminary post-mortem report for Nita Dogan shows she died from cardiac arrest as a result of electrocution. There have now been twenty-four other suspicious deaths across London, all of them scientists. All of them with oddities that show these aren't average murders. Your mother was the first. It was the roses growing from metal that first put her on the Shadow Squad's radar. She was assigned to me, but my efforts to close her case satisfactorily or predict the next target have come to nothing. Our government is impotent. Only the mounting bodies persuaded my bosses to engage with the Otherworld. When they reached out to their Otherworld counterpart, they met with a brick wall."

Ezra's grey eyes smouldered. "They spoke with the Prime Sorcerer?"

Detective Jameson gave a curt nod. "He didn't dispute the evidence we presented, but the senate refused to get involved. Their priority is not humans."

"Indeed," said Ezra. "They wouldn't want to bring the

wrath of the gods on the Otherworld. The Pragmatist's Law states—"

I groaned. "Never to meddle in the affairs of the gods."

Detective Jameson chewed the inside of his cheek. "The gods are closer to men these days than to all-powerful gods of mythology. The Shadow Squad doesn't have the resources or the reach of something like Interpol, but I was still able to piece together a sketchy history. Our unit was formed a little over a decade ago. Since then, the god we're after appears in our records sporadically. He's been a baker, a blacksmith and the owner of a tanning studio. Would you believe it? He's now a freelance electrician. He takes cash in hand and doesn't pay his taxes. He knows how to live off grid because he doesn't need the grid."

My heart raced. I put my fingers to my lips. "You know who he is. Don't say his name. He'll know. I'm his target. No need to give him another one." Hadn't Gaia said as much? I darted to the kitchen for a notepad and pencil. "Write it down."

Detective Jameson accepted the paper and knelt by the coffee table. He wrote two letters, then drew a symbol and handed me the paper. "If I were a betting man, I'd say this is our perpetrator. All roads lead here."

I looked down, suddenly lightheaded.

You can call me all the names under the sun, the electrician god had said.

Here, in smudged lead, was the detective's best guess. The electrician god was so confident he hadn't bothered to cover his tracks or hide his identity. His murderous image flashed before me: swarthy skin, amber eyes and black-singed fingernails. He had taken Mum, Nita and countless others. He had snuffed out lives like he was blowing out candles.

He was Ra, the sun god.

"Holy shit," said Marina. "I knew there was a reason why I wasn't religious."

Ezra read the word, only his stillness revealing his rage.

Echo came to rest by my side at last, and he, too, deciphered the page. "I do not believe it. If the sun god were here, he would have brought sunshine to this wretched rain-soaked isle."

I tried to keep my voice calm. "If the sun god is behind this, then why not kill us all? He can just decide to burn us all to a crisp or cover the world in darkness out of spite."

Marina's forehead knotted with worry. "Even if he went easy on us, a change in the light would be catastrophic. Crops wouldn't grow. There would be famines. Our bodies need vitamin D to function and melatonin to sleep. The sun even has an impact on testosterone levels."

"The power of the gods has been castrated. It took me a lot of legwork to piece it together. That's why he's an electrician. He might be less powerful than he was, but he's still lethal," said Detective Jameson. "His historic activities showed boredom and a disregard for human life but never such bloodlust. I'm still looking for a motive, but my instincts tell me his killing spree has only just begun."

Echo's emerald eyes glinted. "Did no one listen to the goddess? She told us his motive. The gods want us to offer more prayers."

"Fat chance," said Marina.

"Echo is right," I said. "He doesn't want to kill us all because there would be no one left to pray. He just wants to add to the weight of human suffering to make us pray."

"It's days like this I wonder whether I'd prefer being a community copper chasing down bike thieves." Detective Jameson sighed. "There's nothing for it, now. We need to neutralise him, and I'm going to need your help to do it. The ball's in your court. At some point, you have to decide whether to take a leap of faith. Can you trust me, Alisha?"

Ezra's breath fanned my ear. "He has given us more information than the senate would be willing to share. There's no turning back now the god has marked you out. You're under my protection. Seems to me we have no choice but to join forces."

Marina trusted the detective, Ezra had given his reluctant backing, and Echo could be swayed by the offer of a good meal, so his opinion was flighty at best. More allies could only be a good thing. This was the right call.

"You win, Detective," I said. "We can play on one team. Let's call it a time-limited partnership."

"I can get on with that." He pulled a business card from his jeans and handed it to me. "Here's my mobile number to save you from going down to the nick again."

I took the thick, cream card. There was no insignia, organisation, job title or email address, just his name and mobile phone number printed in block capitals.

"And one for you, Marina," he said.

Marina beamed and slipped the card into her bra.

I hoped Marina's instincts about him were right, but I had kept some wildcards in my pocket all the same. The detective knew nothing about Gaia, the Celestial Library or about my suspicions that Fei Yen and Faeza were peculiars.

Time would tell if he came through for us.

If not, Echo could chase him screaming into the night.

17

I should have heeded Echo's warnings about Ezra. It turned out he was like a dog with a bone. Barely six hours after he left my flat, he popped his head around my bedroom door, startling me awake.

"Rise and shine, hellfire," he said.

I groaned, emerged from the folds of my duvet and wiped the spittle from the corner of my mouth. The clock on my bedside table read 9.50 a.m. "Go away, Ezra."

He scanned my sleep-smudged face. "You can't rest on your laurels. Do the work. Get stronger, get quicker, and hone your skills. Or not only will this amber-eyed god hunt you down with the ease of a phoenix besting a pigeon, but the wrath of Minister Willowsun will rain down on me."

"Huh?" Complicated conversations before my morning cup of tea weren't a good idea. Ezra should have realised that already. We'd been spending more time together than I had with Alex in the heady heights of our marriage.

"Your progress report is due today. Minister Willowsun's office has already chased for it once. I am already known for my somewhat novel ways of fulfilling my missions. I could do without another black mark against my name, so will you *please* change into some active wear and come closer so we can be on our way? I've booked us some sparring time in the Wildwoods arena."

I ached, and my head was all over the place. "Sorry, no can do. Marina has to work, and judging by the snoring coming down the corridor, Echo needs his beauty sleep."

I did too. My wet hair had dried in loose waves that resembled a scarecrow more than a mermaid.

"An empath doesn't need to get into the thick of battles. The cat has plenty of experience using his teeth. You, on the other hand…"

I decided he was more bulldog than wolf, gave him my most unimpressed look and went to get changed.

Four hours later, I wiped the sweat from my forehead and put down the staff that Ezra had insisted I practice with. My kickboxing training meant I preferred to punch and kick during fights, but he wanted to push me out of my comfort zone. He armed us each with a bō, a Japanese staff. In Ezra's hands, the bō was a graceful, effective weapon he used to swing at and strike his opponent. In my hands, it was a crude instrument with which I slashed the air and attempted to poke his eye out.

Ezra's breathing was even, in contrast to mine. "No time in the ring is wasted. Every practice session results in quicker feet, better hand-eye coordination, and new sequences learned."

I panted like I'd just given birth. Or at least, how I imagined that would be from romcom movies. "Why do you even need to be combat-ready? As a wolf, you have teeth and claws. And as a wizard, you can teleport. Plus, you have the moon charm, so you can pull your light-switch trick."

He inched closer, and a slow grin spread across his face. "I can do much more than that, Alisha." Then he handed me my bō. "Let's go again."

I grew light-headed as the arena changed yet again

around us, an assault on my mind and senses. Objects emerged from the sawdust: not only trees but monoliths, great columns that belonged in Roman times and hideous statues of gargoyles. The air thickened around us or swarmed with bees. An eerie child's voice sang a nursery rhyme, and unfamiliar creatures chattered and squawked.

I tried not to overthink every moment, fearing my mind would melt. That I'd end up in some London crack den railing about my experiences, and no one would ever believe me.

Better to breathe, be present and take each moment at a time, one footstep at a time.

It was how Mum approached science and how Dad approached art. Hell, it was how I approached teaching languages. I just needed to hold on to the threads of my sanity and believe in myself.

"Wildwoods is in simulation mode. It tests your powers of concentration and your strategy skills. Use the arena to your advantage to block my advances or camouflage yourself. Your job is to overpower me. Let the arena become part of your toolkit rather than a distraction."

I ducked and dove around the structures. Ezra might have been faster, but I was lighter on my feet. I swung my bō in an arc and almost landed a blow, but he was too quick.

Monoliths fenced us in, and we went hand-to-hand, blow after blow. He was going easy on me; I could tell. He didn't teleport or put his entire weight behind his blows, but I didn't go easy on him.

I'd missed the gym and my punching bag. I let out all my anger on him—about Mum, Nita, and all the secrets that had been hidden from me.

I adapted my footwork from kickboxing to surprise him and landed the odd kick to his shins before following up with a strike with the bō and interspersing my moves with wind.

It felt good going on the attack.

The bō was mostly in both hands, so I could put as much force behind it as possible. The weapon suited me, so light and smooth it was almost an extension of my limbs. I released my left hand only to call the winds. The winds came more easily to me the more I practised, like breathing. My left hand was almost as consistent as my right, and I no longer knotted my brow in concentration.

My job was to come out as the winner and show him I was fearless. To prove I didn't need a protector and I could take him.

I closed in on him, ignoring the crackle of fire and the scent of smoke the arena had conjured. Ezra set his jaw and upped the ante. He didn't want to lose any more than I did.

I lunged towards him, got in close and jabbed his throat with my left fist. I landed my punch and didn't hold back. He'd said there was a nurse with a cabinet of healing potions in the main building.

Ezra swore and darted back. I swung the bō at his head.

He swivelled out of reach, stuck his bō in the ground and pole-vaulted over me like a gymnast.

Next thing I knew, I'd taken a kick to the small of my back and sprawled face-first in the sawdust.

My ego was more wounded than my body.

Strong hands grabbed me by the waist and lingered there a moment before setting me back on my feet.

Around us, the Wildwoods arena reverted to a blank canvas.

"You almost had me there." Ezra touched his throat, where a pink cauliflower bruise marred his skin.

"Sorry about that. That was some move you pulled at the end. What are you? Some kind of circus acrobat?"

"A wolf isn't a circus animal, hellfire. We aren't the performing type." He collected the staffs, and they vanished from his fingers like they'd been stored in a pocket of air. "Come on," he said, nodding towards the cable cars. "The school is alive with students today. It's a good day to show you around."

My knees were muddy from a swampland the arena had thrown at us. My ponytail of raven waves had so much sawdust in it that I could have been mistaken for a blonde. I smelt like a farmhand. Ezra, however, looked like he had stepped out of a Diet Coke commercial.

"I didn't bring a change of clothes," I said.

In this light, his eyes were molten steel. "We could skip the tour, and I could teleport you home."

I shook my head and made for the cable cars, determined to beat him there after the thrashing I'd taken in the arena. "No, just show me where the loos are. Five minutes in there, and I'll be sparkling new."

Ezra leaned against a wall outside the toilets. His eyes brightened when he saw me. "Looking good, hellfire. Are you ready to meet the big wigs?"

I tossed my still dirty hair and grimaced. "A little bit of spit and polish, and I'm good to go."

We'd ridden the cable cars up to the great oak, and I'd spent ten minutes in the less-than-sparkly pupil toilets, shaking the sawdust out of my hair, spot-cleaning my trousers, and blasting toilet roll around like confetti while I tried to dry the wet patches.

"We make our report about your progress. We keep things tight and necessary," said Ezra in my ear. "No spilling about Ra. Not yet. I don't want you falling foul of the senate just yet. First, you impress them. Later, we can talk to them about how you're digging your own grave, and maybe, just maybe, if they like you enough, someone will put themselves out for you."

"Sounds a bit like getting my mother-in-law on my side."

He grinned. "Did it work?"

"I guess. She wanted to feed me up like a prize pig. It would have been better if she'd hated me."

"Come on; they'll be on a tight schedule. It's a stand-out day in the Wildwoods calendar. With any luck, the Prime Sorcerer won't mind if you stay on and witness it."

"Phinnaeous Shine is here? Doesn't he have better things to do than hang around at a school?"

"The Prime Sorcerer always attends the ceremony. He has many duties, amongst them leading the senate and negotiating with humdrum agencies, but his office is here for a reason. Wildwoods is the centre of the Otherworld. Every now and then, he likes to teach a class. It's a good way of earning the admiration and loyalty of new students. His teaching is legendary at Wildwoods, as well as his habit of pop quizzes to catch out anyone who doesn't listen. On his best days, he could inspire the Mona Lisa to come to life."

"So he taught you?"

Ezra tugged at his charm necklace, visible tension in his neck and shoulders. "He's a shifter. Not my kind. Phinnaeous Shine isn't a mere wolf. He can shift into any two-legged form he touches. It gives him an affinity for those of us with similar talents. He knows what it means to shed one identity and inhabit another. What a toll it takes physically and psychologically. How you're never fully satisfied in either form, never whole."

"Sounds tough."

"Nothing's perfect."

I scuttled after him like a crab as he strode across the rope bridges, my legs still heavy from the training session. I could have sworn Minister Willowsun's office lay in the opposite direction. New cabins had sprouted up, literally by magic. We approached the cabin with the Headmistress plaque on the door. A curtainless window revealed two grey heads bowed together over files on the desk: the tall, reedy headmistress with long hair and a shorter woman with a full head of sassy, silver curls in luminous exercise gear.

"Who's the silver-haired lady in the exercise getup?" I asked. "I remember her from the senate."

"My aunt, Lavinia Drach."

"A witch?"

He lowered his voice to a gruff whisper. "Be careful around her. She might be family, but she's not always on my side. She heads up the coven, and her allegiance is to the witches, but she'll help me out if it suits her. You ready?"

Ezra gave a clipped knock on the door.

"Come in."

We stepped inside, leaving the bright light behind us and entering Minister Willowsun's boudoir of drapes, smooth wood and plants. The scent of vanilla and chocolate wafted over from a group of flowering orchids, in addition to the pong of hairspray holding Lavinia's curls in place, which smelled like it'd been concocted in chemistry class.

"Just like clockwork, Mr Neuhoff. How nice not to have to send a wraith to chase you," said Minister Willowsun.

Ezra gave a slight bow. "Ministers. I hope we're not intruding?"

Minister Willowsun shook her head. "Quite the contrary. We'd just finished. I'm looking forward to Ms Verma's progress."

Ezra's aunt approached and reached up to kiss him on both cheeks. "Let me feast my eyes on you. Why such a stranger? The coven misses you. That dirty old wolf Gunnolf must be keeping you busy."

"Actually, aunty, it's Alisha that's taking up most of my time these days. I'll be sure to pop into the gym when time allows."

Lavinia clapped in delight. "Oh yes, you could lead a weightlifting class for me. You know you're always a hit with our clients. Ravynne also quite likes a sweaty wolf. But how rude of me to get carried away with my nephew." Her sallow, lined face broke into a warm smile. "How lovely to see you again, Ms Verma."

"Please, call me Alisha." I curtsied and then felt stupid when Ezra chuckled.

His aunt swatted him. "Leave the poor woman alone. Alisha, you must call me Lavinia in private and save the minister malarkey for formal occasions only."

"Done."

"Come, let's go for a walk and leave these two to their boring business." She took my arm and grabbed her umbrella, a sturdy full-sized one with a dull brown canopy and shimmering brass handle.

"Oh, the weather is peachy. Not a cloud in the sky," I said. "No need for an umbrella."

"I'm going to have to turn you into an umbrella aficionado, dear. Don't you know, an umbrella is a shield against the sun and the rain. It's both a weapon and defence and much more besides. Queen Victoria herself had her parasols lined with chain mail after an assassination attempt. I always liked her—a lot of chutzpah for a queen. My umbrella is from the company used by the royal family. Their brollies keep royal hairstyles intact, even in the worst London downpour. Mine's been upgraded, of course. I'd be more likely to leave home without my dentures than without it."

What a strange old lady, waxing lyrical about an umbrella. "I'm more of a rain jacket girl, myself."

Lavinia winked. "Then you haven't lived."

Ezra gave me a wry smile over his shoulder as she ushered me out of the office and closed the door behind us. We walked the rope bridges in a circuit, surrounded by luscious tree canopies and twittering robins and blackbirds.

Lavinia hooked her arm in mine and swung her umbrella like a baton. "Tell me, are you interested in Zumba? We have a new class at the gym. If that's not your thing, maybe a spin class? My motto is eat and drink to your heart's delight. Just squeeze in some endurance, strength and flexibility training if you want to be swinging from the chandeliers in your old age."

I'd pretty much try anything if I could wear pink Lycra leggings in my sixties.

"You run a gym?" I said, a little overwhelmed by her friendliness. The woman could thaw an igloo with her presence.

She cackled, revealing a mouthful of pearlescent teeth that didn't look like dentures at all. "Yes, dear. Witches aren't all cauldron-loving, cave-dwelling hermits, you know. Or would you rather we were the Women's Institute? How quaint." She chuckled. "My coven aren't the sort for church bake sales and knitting needles. You must come by. We're in the heart of Wimbledon, next to an orthodontist's surgery." She let go of my arm and waved her hand in front of her face as if she could see the name in lights. "Baba Yaga's Gymnasium on Dundonald Road. White script on a green sign. You can't miss it. Plenty of tennis players for clients if you're into hot totty."

"But you serve on the Sorcerer's Senate too?"

"I'm Minister for Defence, dear. I keep my small witch army at full strength and train the reserves a few times a year. The last time we were at war was the day your grandmother died, but the threat never quite recedes, regardless of what the lily-livered think. My coven and I conduct security missions. We're always ready for escalation."

I had my doubts. A gym-loving granny wouldn't have been my first choice for Minister for Defence. Orpheus, the vampire, had been much more threatening. Even Rayna Willowsun, with her hip dagger, might have suited a defence role. Lavinia Drach's bubble-gum pink, effervescent cloud of hairspray vibe didn't scream danger.

But then, a chihuahua had bitten my ankle once. It had clung on for so long that I thought it had lockjaw. I'd needed stitches and antibiotics. So I wasn't one to knock the deadly impact of small packages.

"My humdrum gym is a lot of fun. We have a giggle and keep fit, so when the time comes, we can break bones. Of course, there is no point in breaking bones without having a sideline in healing and protection spells. It's very lucrative generating both supply and demand."

We'd come to the end of a bridge. She ducked underneath a rope and stepped neatly into a snug seat for two that had been carved into the bark of a tree.

"Come along, dear. Any longer, and I'll be on my deathbed." She patted the space beside her. "I discovered this nook many moons ago. To think, it's still here providing solace and joy. You know, I'm very glad to have run into you."

I gritted my teeth and took the leap over to the nook, finding it too snug a fit for two grown women's bottoms. From this close, I could almost taste her hairspray.

Her hazel eyes gleamed. "My nephew seems to have taken a shine to you. It's been a long time since I've seen him protect anyone other than the pack."

"You gave him the moon charm?"

"No, dear. The moon was my sister Chandra's gift. The thistle is from me." A sad smile tugged the corners of her pink-frosted lips. "As much as my nephew doubts my intentions towards him, he is the last living piece left of my eldest sister." She brightened. "Now, tell me. I'm an old woman now, and to be honest, I've not needed men for a long time. But I recognise attraction when I see it. Have you bedded Ezra yet?"

I spluttered with surprise. "Er...no."

She frowned. "Shame. But he has teleported with you?"

A frisson of wariness crawled up my spine. "Yes."

"Silly boy. He won't give his dear aunty a little drop of blood, but he'll sweep a stranger off her feet."

"Hardly a boy."

"Forty-four is nothing these days, Alisha. And repdigits—11, 22, 33, 44, et cetera—give a year real pizazz. It's scientifically proven. Then there's the devil, of course. Another case in point. Best not to say his number, though."

I grinned. Ezra had been decidedly cagey about his age. About his life, really. But his aunt was like an encyclopaedia.

Lavinia sighed. "Teleporting is such a nifty trick."

"Rather vomit-inducing, I'm afraid."

She raised a pencil-thin eyebrow. "Really? Oh well, I suppose vomit can always be mopped up. A bit like sea sickness, I suppose. Not a deal breaker by any means. He has that from his father's side, you know. I've always envied it. The places that his father Levi took my sister Morena. To Paris in autumn, Jerusalem in spring, Tokyo in summer and New York in winter. Just think of the adventures. And no jet lag! Teleporting in Levi's arms must have been worth all the downsides of being a wife. Of course, Morena would have married him even without the teleporting bonus. She was sickeningly in love."

"What happened to them?"

"Ah, that's a long story, dear, and we have a ceremony to attend." She pointed to pupils making their way to the yew tree rune, so far in the distance they looked like an army of ants. "It's not a day to be missed. You are staying? It's all rather brutal but necessary, much like childbirth."

The old ache throbbed, the one that groaned into being when I imagined children of my own. "I don't have children. I wouldn't know."

"Oh? Well, never mind, dear. A vagina has multiple uses, you know." She rolled her eyes. "All these mother duck types who go *on* and *on* and *on*, like a womb is the answer to their life's calling, are rather tedious, aren't they? The brain's a far sexier organ. Especially at my age when all the moisture's gone."

My toes curled. "Jesus."

"More like the Virgin Mary. You shouldn't take the Lord's name in vain, you know. He was a good egg, or so I've heard."

I pasted on a smile that likely resembled that of a constipated child's. "Ezra must be wondering where I am."

"Ezra is wise to make allies. His pack won't be enough in the coming fight. He's always been a good boy. I just hope his loyalty isn't his undoing. The senate has been preoccupied with pressing business these past few days. Darker times are coming."

My heart skipped a beat. Lavinia had to be talking about Ra. What else could she be referring to?

Maybe Phinnaeous Shine cared more about humdrums than Detective Jameson thought. He'd need a lot of firepower and cunning, but perhaps he planned to break the Founder's Law to protect them after all.

Relief flooded me. I preferred to be left out of the fight, being a new druid and all. The Prime Sorcerer was much more capable of taking on this fight than a virgin peculiar.

"The Prime Sorcerer is usually more philosopher than warrior," she said, "but this time, he's in a tizzy."

I wanted to trust Lavinia and tell her my secrets, but Ezra had warned me not to give anything away. "If you don't mind me saying, the Prime Sorcerer's household set-up seems rather combative. I don't know many who keep a succubus slave as a housekeeper."

Lavinia's laugh tinkled in my ear. "Oh, well, you've been missing out, Alisha. Having other people scrub your floors and fold your knickers is freeing."

"You're not wrong there."

"My intuition tells me there is a lot riding on the ceremony today. As you know, a witch's intuition is not to be taken lightly. Phinnaeous is hellbent on finding the eternal girl. Without her, we don't stand a chance."

I gave her a blank look. "The eternal girl?"

"Why, yes, dear. Your parents must have told you a version of the Chameleon Tale when you were a child as a bedtime story perhaps, or on special days as a treat."

"My parents read me Mr Men stories."

"How humdrum. Well, dear, it's all up to me then. The Chameleon Tale speaks of an eternal girl who blends in even though her talents are brighter than the sun. When Death opens the door, only the eternal girl may stop the coming Dusk, together with a disintegrating tome lost to the world."

"Sounds heavy," I said. "I prefer Mr Tickles."

"You have no idea." Lavinia glanced at her watch with a gasp. She picked up her umbrella. "That's enough nattering for today. My nephew will never forgive me for filling your head with my nonsense. I'm due at a senate meeting, but I hope to see you soon."

She pushed off the nook and dropped like a stone in a well.

I stifled a scream as Ezra's aunt descended to her death and summoned wind to cushion her fall. My attempt failed, and my fumbling hands managed only a slight flurry of leaves. I peeked over the ledge, anxious to find her splatted in the arena, being magically cleaned up like she was some gunk simulation.

Lavinia twisted in the air. She flung a Lycra-clad leg over her umbrella, then straightened her posture like she was on horseback. The umbrella jolted like it had come alive and carried her up towards me.

She hooted with laughter at my expression. "I told you it was handy! Oh, how marvellous. I've not surprised someone like that in decades. Toodle-oo!"

Off she went, gliding like a swallow to the other side of

Wildwoods, where she disembarked with the finesse of a gymnast.

Giddy excitement bubbled up in my belly at what I had seen. I couldn't imagine how anyone would choose to live like a humdrum when they could experience sights like this. When Lavinia faded from view, I dug out my phone and searched the internet for Baba Yaga's Gymnasium. They certainly knew how to keep old ladies fit.

18

Ezra and I stood mercifully alone in the vaulted cabin where I had first encountered the Sorcerer's Senate. Without the candles and soft furnishings, the cabin had an austere feel. Instead of the split stone table, a newly erected stage with nine high-backed wooden chairs commanded attention. Rows of trestle tables and benches in cherry wood filled the bulk of the room, arranged around a central clearing. The afternoon sun streamed through the stained-glass windows.

"The senate meeting might run over a few minutes," said Ezra. "We've been asked to keep an eye on the children until more responsible adults arrive."

"You could have warned me about your aunt. She's like a firework in a small room. You never know who's going to be hit."

He picked a twig out of my hair with careful fingers, despite it being greasy enough to fry an egg in. "I *did* warn you, but she's the kind of woman words can't explain. You have to meet her in the flesh. I was hedging my bets you could take care of yourself."

"Wait until Marina hears about her flying umbrella."

"If you let my aunt surprise her, you'll earn extra brownie points. Especially when the coven take to the skies en masse. It's better than the Red Arrows."

"How effective is she as Minister for Defence?

"She's the best one ever to hold the post. Her skills are legendary. They say you can judge how effective she is by the wars that *haven't* happened on her watch. Lavinia might look like Barbie Senior, but she's as sharp as a tack. The sort of foe that would stab you between the shoulder blades for the greater good. My parents wouldn't have died if she'd been there the night they died."

"I'm sorry."

"So am I."

"How good are her protection spells?"

"Good enough for the coven to make a killing out of their protection racket. Expensive though. And Lavinia doesn't take mere money as payment. She only takes what interests and amuses her."

I brushed aside his hair and checked his neck. "Not like you need her protection, though. Being a werewolf has obvious perks. The bruise I gave you has already disappeared."

His grey eyes sparked with copper at my feather-light touch.

I rambled on to distract myself from the electricity between us. "She seemed very taken with your teleporting powers."

He stiffened. "That'd be right."

"I liked her. She's more Dolly Parton than Machiavelli. She's sunny, clever and in cracking shape."

"I've been landed with an incurable optimist." He shook his head.

"How did it go with Rayna?"

"Fine, I think. She was underwhelmed by your talents. I

think she expected more from the granddaughter of Rajika Verma."

"Charming."

"Like a sparrow trying to live up to the legacy of a phoenix."

"You're not helping."

"You're too easy to wind up. It's one of the things I like most about you."

In came three girls and a boy carrying instrument cases. They wore slim, grey trousers with a crisp, white shirt that was more Burberry than Asda multipack. Instead of a jumper, the uniforms were topped with short, hooded robes in navy velvet.

Ezra nodded hello. "Don't mind us. We're just here to make sure you don't get into mischief."

The pupils gathered to the left of the stage, pulled out and set out four chairs in a circle and then tuned their instruments. A few moments later, they launched into a Bach piece, entirely in sync despite the absence of a conductor.

The quartet mesmerised me.

"They're incredible," I said. "I'm pretty sure they don't need supervision. If my new skills are anything like that, I'll be a happy bunny."

He laughed. "It's not the geeks I'm worried about. Today marks a special day in the Wildwoods calendar. It's a good day to experience the heartbeat of the school. We'll just lurk here at the back of the room so you can get a sense of the place and its culture."

I turned my attention to the stained-glass windows decorated with scenes from Grimm's fairy tales. I spotted Hansel and Gretel pushing the witch into the oven, the Pied Piper leading away children with his tune and Rumpelstiltskin tearing himself in two.

"The vaulted cabin is the biggest indoor space at

Wildwoods," said Ezra. "Pupils take courses in the smaller cabins according to specialised schedules and hone their skills in the arena. There's no boarding here. It's strictly a part-time offer. They'll be home before their parents finish work. The vaulted cabin is for senate meetings, school meals and assemblies."

"Impressive, but aren't the stained-glass windows a bit gruesome for this age group?"

"Are you kidding me? Teens in this day and age play gory computer games far worse than anything depicted up there. What's the point in wrapping them up in cotton wool when the world has teeth?"

"If you say so." I'd long decided any future children of mine would be raised on a diet of Mr Rogers and Sesame Street, supplemented by Peter Rabbit and Winnie the Pooh books.

Wildwoods had an old-world feel. This wasn't your bog standard comprehensive with sticky lunch trays, the clank of lockers, the squeak of trainers and stinky toilets.

The string quartet launched into Brahms, filling the room to the rafters with their sound. In came a column of children, aged from about eleven to seventeen years old, in their grey trousers, shirts and hooded, knee-length, navy robes. Each robe bore the school crest—a golden W—crowned with posies of plants. The children took their seats on the trestle tables. Some girls clutched each other, their eyes trained on the clearing.

London was a melting pot of cultures, but Wildwoods took difference to a whole new level. I absorbed every detail: pointy ears, diaphanous wings, teeth of varying sizes that no braces would ever help, far more hair than a pubescent teen should have and great big feet.

I smiled at a passing girl I pegged as a druid—she wore her uniform with matted locks and goth boots—and received a stony stare in response.

"Just your average day in South London," I muttered. "Where are the gorgons and goblins, the centaurs and trolls?"

"As much as Wildwoods likes to see itself as a bastion of equality, some peculiars would rather gnaw their own foot than come here. Representation on the Sorcerer's Senate is a big clue as to the movers and shakers in the Otherworld and who must skulk in the shadows. Nine groups represented on the senate and nine house colours."

A wolf boy at the table just ahead set his sights on a luminescent girl fluttering past with auburn hair that fell in ringlets about her shoulders. She wore a long, white gown underneath a navy robe that rippled behind her like the sea. The wolf boy launched a projectile at her, his aim strong and true. As the music crescendoed, the ball arced through the air and plummeted towards the girl.

I held up my hand, shifting the path of the ball slightly. Instead of hitting her square in the forehead, it ricocheted off her arm.

She jerked to a halt and identified the culprit by his raucous laughter. She blinked hard, her face a storm, muttering under her breath all the while. Wolf boy's trousers crept higher, over his belly button and higher still. He wriggled in horror, reddening with pain as they gave him an almighty wedgie. The material thinned, threatening to tear.

I poked Ezra. "Do something. The Prime Sorcerer told us to keep watch."

He moved closer, then stepped back. "She doesn't need any help."

"Are you serious? Men don't let women get away with that."

The girl blinked again, freeing the wolf boy. Wolf boy and his four friends stood as one, twice her size in both height and girth. They closed in, eyes flashing with malice. Within seconds, she was cornered, skittish like a deer, attempting to fly beyond their grasp as they pulled her down by her gown and bounced her between them as if she were a ping-pong ball.

"No magic without supervision, Mirabel," said the wolf boy who'd suffered the wedgie and started it all.

"Told you so," I said over my shoulder as I waded into the thick of it and shoved the bullies aside to stand back to back with Mirabel. I lifted my hands and skewered the ringleader with a fiery glare. "Back off."

He smiled with malice. "Make me, girlie."

It might have been my height, maybe the greasy workout hair or the hazy afternoon sun, but he seemed to think I was close to his age. Unlucky for him, I was old enough to have learned how to deal with bullies. I took a deep breath, narrowed my gaze in focus and flicked my wrists, sending all five bullies onto their bums.

Then I took Mirabel's hand and pulled her with me over their sprawled bodies.

"I thought I could handle it," she said. "Thank you."

Behind us, the wolves gathered again, but Ezra, his lips twitching with mirth, strode towards them. He laid a hand on the wolf boy, power rolling lazily off him in waves like he'd flicked a switch.

His gravelly voice brooked no argument. "That's enough. You had it coming. Go take a seat before bigger beasts decide to make an example of you."

The wolves whimpered and did as they were told, skittish and wary as they passed us to return to their seats.

I sent Mirabel on her way and leaned into Ezra when he returned to my side. "I could have done with that kind of authority when I taught at an inner London comprehensive school."

He laughed, low and easy. "You were pretty impressive yourself. I counted five foes."

"Of school age."

His voice was warm as honey around the edges. "Maybe. But you're a virgin druid, aren't you?"

I blushed. "I learn quickly."

"That you do. It's easy to subdue wolves of a lower rank. It would've been different if I'd tried that with a group of vampires. As a seeker, I have no authority with Wildwoods pupils. I'm not a member of staff. More like an uncle supervising naughty kids."

"High school life is hard enough without adding fangs and claws into the mix. Although Mirabel has guts. It must be therapeutic to thump a bully. Will they get in trouble?"

"I won't tell if you don't. Pupils are still learning to control their impulses at this age. Unsupervised children tend to get away with what they can. Bullying is rife for the more unsightly and unusual creatures and even worse for the mixed breeds. I love Wildwoods, but let's just say that Minister Willowsun has more of an affinity for potions and academic progress than pastoral care. It's not a deliberate oversight. She merely notices the emotions of plants more than that of the children."

By now, the trestle tables had filled with pupils, and a palpable sense of anxiety filled the room amongst the girls in particular, judging by the darting eyes and heads cowed together.

I gripped Ezra's arm. "What's going on?"

Ezra sighed. "A tradition as old as time. Cruel to boot. Whatever happens, try not to draw attention to yourself and keep your cards close to your chest. You'll soon find out—at Wildwoods, the walls have ears. Here we go. Wait for it."

The string quartet shuddered to a halt, and two hundred odd heads turned to face the stage, like a hall full of demented dolls programmed to exterminate. Nine ministers filed onto the stage, an oddball crew of imposing, misshapen and luminous figures.

Unlearning my humdrum ways wasn't an overnight

exercise. My pulse quickened. My eyes drank in every detail, and my mind worked hard to accept them.

Phinnaeous Shine took the central chair, flanked by Rayna Willowsun and Orpheus the vampire, whose heavy brows shot up when he looked in our direction. Lavinia, farther down the line, gave us a cheery wave. Ezra nodded to Gunnolf, the werewolf minister.

The Prime Sorcerer raised his hands like a preacher. "Welcome, all of you, to this remarkable day. There is a story, repeated so many times over the centuries, that it transforms every time it is spoken aloud. You have heard it many times from the lips of your parents, your friends and your teachers. You have heard it around campfires and whispered in the shadows. You've heard it when a girl-child is born into the Otherworld. The Chameleon Tale tells of our destruction and our salvation. Never has our need for the eternal girl been so great."

The room darkened, even though the sun had not faded from the sky and no curtains covered the windows, as if the vaulted cabin had a weather system all of its own. Lavinia appeared to be muttering a spell.

"Today is a chance to find the eternal girl. Only she may stop the coming Dusk. Only she may find the book," said the Prime Sorcerer. "The ceremony marks a rite of passage that all peculiar girls endure. Today, the youngest girls amongst you will stand in hope against the dark. Today, you will shine brightly, lighting the way for the eternal girl, even if you are not her."

He swirled each of his hands in the pattern of an eternity sign.

There was a collective intake of breath as freshwater crashed through the vaulted cabin, streaming from the stage down the aisles between awestruck and trembling students. The water pooled in the clearing, the droplets and rivulets clumping together, leaving the body of water suspended in a cube.

I squinted at the water as dark particles writhed at its centre. An enormous, bulbous head with large, intelligent eyes and eight limbs swam in the water. Hundreds of suckers protruded from its arms, trailing blue ink.

The air in my lungs constricted.

Five girls lined up, Mirabel amongst them, their faces painted with terror. They couldn't have been more than twelve. They cast their robes aside, exposing long, white gowns like Victorian nightdresses but without frills. The girls clutched hands, knuckles white.

"Is that an octopus?" I ask.

"Not just any octopus," said Ezra. "Kraglek is the most important creature in the Wildwoods bestiary. Centuries ago, he was touched by Ganga, the goddess of the Ganges. It made him immortal and gave him the ability to sense the eternal girl. At the beginning of her first term, every Wildwoods girl must spend a minute in the tank with him and will be rendered unconscious by his venom unless she is the girl in the prophecy."

"Are you insane? This is a school, not the London Dungeons, dammit." My stomach churned. Even the creature's name made me want to run a mile. "How can their parents allow that?"

"Think of it as a bar mitzvah or christening. This is integral to the Otherworld way of life. I've seen this year's list. The auburn-haired girl is Mirabel, a fairy. We met her earlier. The plump elf is Gaylia. Poor thing looks like she's going to pass out. The girl with the plaits is Maura, a witch. She has already made a name for herself in the first term for potion making. Then there's Nessa, a vampire girl, newly turned. She's still ravenous with hunger, and that will stand her in good stead to recover from Kraglek. If I were a betting man, I'd say of this year's cohort she has the best chance of being the eternal girl. The blue-eyed doe there is a druid. Soleis, I think her name is. Druids take the longest to regain consciousness, possibly because they are inherently pacifist by nature."

I thumped him. "Well, I'm not a pacifist. You think this is okay? I don't see you jumping into the tank with that thing."

"No, hellfire, I don't think it's okay, but I don't make the rules."

"Aren't they carnivores?"

"Yes, but Helio Woodwink, the Minister for the Bestiary, won't let that happen. Kraglek will have been well fed before the ceremony, and Helio has not once across the decades allowed a girl to be permanently dismembered. He'll be on standby for extraction." Ezra winced. "Although, there was an issue with the minister in the post before him."

I broke out in a sweat as the girls approached Kraglek, holding hands as if they were a chain of fragile daisies.

They took a deep breath and stepped into the wall of water.

"Do something." My voice was low and urgent.

Grey eyes full of sorrow. "I can't. We don't play by the same rules as humdrums here."

Kraglek shrank his gigantic form, compressing his arms as the girls entered his space, but his clever eyes were wide open, waiting to strike. The cube of water measured roughly six metres squared, and he lurked near the top surface. The girls trod the water towards the bottom of the cube, holding their breath. Their cheeks were puffed out, silken tresses floating underwater, dresses swaying in the current. They held fast to each other, moon eyes jerking and wide as they tracked the creature above them.

The Prime Sorcerer looked on with interest as if watching a horse race. A small man, who I assumed to be Helio, the bestiary minister, had left his chair on the stage and hovered next to the body of water, bright eyes following the beast's every move.

Inky fluid shot out from Kraglek, darkening the water further still and blackening the girls' dresses. They shrank from him in terror as his lumpy purplish arms stretched out, reaching for them in the confined space. There was a movement as quick as the strike of a cobra, water gushing as the octopus surged downwards, all nodules and prehistoric brain, even more terrifying in his squelchy bonelessness.

A scream built in my throat.

Kraglek reached for the elf Gaylia and the druid Soleis first, dragging them up and breaking the daisy chain.

I closed my eyes and buried my head in Ezra's side.

When I opened them, the two girls were limp, discarded by the octopus. Kraglek's purple tones had become the colour of the inky water, so I barely discerned him. Seconds became hours. The three remaining girls cowered, with only Nessa, the vampire girl, defiant in her gaze.

I held my breath, and those in the vaulted cabin breathed as one as Kraglek revealed his pink innards. A sharp, parrot-like beak emerged from his centre, where his arms converged. Kraglek dropped on them from above, his mouth open, venomous saliva at the ready.

The girls lost consciousness.

I couldn't hold back. I rushed at the cube of water, my mind a blur, my footsteps ringing across the floor.

Somewhere behind me, Ezra shouted, but I didn't break my run. I lifted my hands and sent a whirlwind through the cube. It spun diagonally, wrenching the cube of water apart and splitting it in two.

In one segment, Kraglek swam, enraged by my interference. His eyes bulged, his tentacles thrashed, and the disgusting beak-like centre snapped in vain.

In the lower segments, the girls floated, mercifully free of the beast but unconscious.

Ezra grabbed my shoulder as a rush of feet entered the clearing. "What have you done now?"

Helio, the bestiary minister, frowned at me and shocked the creature into submission with some kind of Taser.

Five small men hauled out the girls, leaving only limp Kraglek in the water.

A smattering of applause broke out from the students. They might have clapped for the girls or the spectacle, but all eyes were on me.

Not that I cared what they thought. Traditions like that belonged in the dustbin of history.

On the stage, the Prime Sorcerer sent me an icy look, flanked by Orpheus, whose eyebrows had disappeared into his hairline. The string quartet picked up their instruments and sprang into a rendition of Mozart's "Eine Kleine Nachtmusik."

Ezra leaned down to whisper in my ear. "It's my fault. I should have prepared you better for that. You've ruffled some feathers today, but at least the ceremony has concluded."

"That's what you're worried about?" I hissed.

"Alisha, it's okay. The girls are safe now. The leprechauns have them. A bit of luck, a night in the infirmary, and they'll be right as rain. In the morning, the girls will be heroes. Even the wolves will congratulate Mirabel. And hopefully, the senate will forgive you."

I breathed through the thickness in my throat.

My maternal instincts blazed. It didn't matter that I wasn't a mother. If the Sorcerer's Senate were willing to put small girls through this ordeal with a monstrous octopus, their constitutional laws could go to hell.

19

Baba Yaga's Gymnasium in Wimbledon didn't smell, look or feel like other gyms I'd trained at. Instead of masculine decor in monochrome shades, Baba Yaga's had a Barbie's Dreamhouse vibe, a sort of bubble-gum pop scheme that matched Marina's hair. A faint aroma of jasmine masked the stench of sweat. Judging by the turnout on a Friday morning, the gym had more female than male members, and all abided by an unspoken jazzy dress code. There were no black sweats and baggy T-shirts in sight. Here, sculpted bodies shimmered in Lycra and baby oil.

I shuddered, feeling like a rhino in a room full of gazelles.

Marina, of course, felt right at home.

I'd roped her into signing up for an aerobics class with me for moral support and her empath antennae. I needed to know if Lavinia could be trusted. The head of the London coven looked like butter wouldn't melt in her mouth. She was all smiles leading the class in a series of step touches, grapevines and bicep curls.

"Lucky I chose my best sports bra. This is wild." Marina whooped as "Love Shack" drifted seamlessly into "Video

Killed the Radio Star." She took a swig of her water bottle and then picked up the beat again.

I clenched my teeth. The music made me want to run for the hills, let alone the moves. All this prancing about was a far cry from the kickboxing training I was used to. I'd take a punchbag over shaking my booty any day. Lavinia had put us in a triangular formation opposite a floor-to-ceiling mirror.

Judging by our reflection, she had moves, but the rest of us most certainly didn't.

"And once more through the routine. That's right. Keep pushing. One...and two...and twist...that's it. Lunge left, lunge right, box step, and big finish—shimmy!" Lavinia beamed. "That's enough for today. Well done, everyone, especially you, Marina. What a natural. Good effort, Alisha. It gets easier. See you all next week."

I plastered on a smile and wished for the ground to open and swallow me up.

Marina mopped her brow. "I'm going to need another shower."

"I thought it would never end. Good thing you drove us. Otherwise, we'd be a sweaty mess on the tube."

She grinned. "Your aura is a muddy green. Shake off that insecurity. It doesn't matter if I wipe the floor with you at aerobics."

"Shut up. You're giving me flashbacks to you overtaking during athletics at school with that arsehole P.E. teacher."

"Miss Andrews?"

"That's the one. Enough to scar a girl for life."

Lavinia bustled over. Her hair hadn't moved an inch, and her skin glowed with a ladylike sheen of perspiration. "My dears, how lovely to see you. And in much better circumstances than last time when you embarrassed yourself at the Kraglek ceremony, Alisha. Still, I suppose in my youth I got up to worse. Like the time I commandeered a woolly mammoth from the bestiary to impress a lover. The yew tree still bears the scars from its tusks." She hooted with laughter. "How did you enjoy the class?"

"We had a blast," said Marina. "Didn't we, Alisha?"

I nodded.

Lavinia beamed. "How lovely, dear. The first one's free, you know."

"I would happily have paid, Minister Drach," said Marina. "And what a playlist. I especially enjoyed 'Wake Me Up Before You Go Go.'"

"Oh yes, wasn't George marvellous? We were great friends, you know. I advised him on the dance moves for 'Outside.' We had such a hoot." A shadow passed over her face. "But you mustn't use Otherworld terms here. Lavinia is just fine. Now come along. I have just about enough time for a smoothie break."

"If you're sure it won't put you out?" I said.

"Not at all. You must meet the other girls." She led the way out of the bright studio, nodding to clients as she went. "It can't have been easy witnessing the ceremony the other day, Alisha. I trust my nephew held your hand throughout—metaphorically, of course. These traditions we have can be quite disembowelling."

I raised an eyebrow at her choice of adjective. Lavinia had a bleak vocabulary, despite her bubble-gum facade. Perhaps she was more suited to the role of Minister for Defence than I first thought.

"We have a reception, the main gym floor, three studios, unisex changing rooms, state-of-the-art massage jet showers and a chill-out lounge with drinks and healthy snacks. Upstairs are living quarters for the team. Men are allowed by invitation only." She cackled. "We send naughty ones to the rats in the basement."

"You have a problem with rats?" I said.

"No, dear, our rats are more beloved than most men." She checked the coast was clear of humdrums. "We each have a rat as our familiar. What else would we choose in London? They are clever little things, easy to sneak into a pocket and make the best spies. Not to mention their ability to land a ferocious bite and to capitalise on the fear reaction they provoke. And do you know what the best thing is?"

We shook our heads.

Lavinia preened like a peacock. "Our rat familiars train secondary rats to run on power-generating wheels in the basement. That means we are utterly self-reliant. It was my idea to migrate to a more ecological model in the late seventies when I started worrying about the ozone layer. I've always been well ahead of my time."

"You're kidding," said Marina, slack-jawed.

Lavinia chuckled. "Would you like to see them?"

Aerobics followed by a basement of rats? What fresh hell was this? I shook my head. "Maybe next time."

"Just say the word, dear. They really are quite marvellous." She darted up the carpeted steps to the first floor like a woman half her age, not stopping for us to keep up. A palm against the handleless door at the top of the stairs, and it swung open. Lavinia disappeared inside.

"Into the lion's den," whispered Marina behind me. "Lavinia's a riddle. I like her, but there's something bubbling just beneath the surface."

"Stay close."

"Aye, aye, captain."

Curls of smoke from pungent incense sticks drifted through the inner sanctum of the London coven. Sumptuous wallpaper in ornate motifs lined the walls and begged to be touched. Here, pinks and reds bloomed alongside purples and blues. These were women who weren't afraid to make their mark on the world.

"Hurry along," called Lavinia's voice from farther along the warren of rooms.

We scampered after her voice, taking in tasselled lamps

and scurrying rats, spell books and golden chandeliers dripping in jewels that couldn't have been real. In every corner, umbrellas lurked: travel ones and golf ones, frilly ones and plain ones.

"So many umbrellas," said Marina.

I nodded. "Wait until you see their party trick."

"Fingers crossed they don't open those indoors. Think of all the bad luck they'd have in one fell swoop."

We continued in the direction of Lavinia's disappearing back. A woman with long, raven hair emerged from a steamy bathroom in a barely-there towel and smiled a hello, beckoning us to follow her.

In the kitchen, a tray of green smoothies and a plate of oatmeal biscuits waited on a marble island. The raven-haired woman pressed two smoothies into our hands and took her place in a circle of women sitting cross-legged on a rug.

"Come sit." Lavinia patted the industrial-style concrete floor. "We bury bodies here, don't you know."

We joined them in the circle, nursing smoothies that smelled of the sea and had the thickness of oil.

"Sisters, please wish a warm welcome to the druid, Alisha, who has captured our dear Ezra's attention, and her empath friend, Marina. Alisha, Marina, please meet my biological sisters, Isadora and Chandra. No less loved are my chosen sisters, Ravynne, Morgan, Elvira and Agatha."

A chorus of murmurs welcomed us.

All three Drach sisters had hazel eyes flecked with the same copper that Ezra, too, possessed, a trait handed down the maternal line. Whereas Lavinia had a head full of silver curls, her equally petite sister Isadora had a short red elfin cut. Chandra, the tallest of the three, had blond locks and a gentle manner.

"It's an honour to meet you all," I said.

"Drink up, and it'll give you the strength of a horse," said Ravynne, who had handed us the smoothies.

Marina raised her glass and tipped back her head, but I put a hand on her wrist.

"Please, you first." I smiled at the circle.

"The druid does not trust us, sisters." Isadora tilted her head like a bird.

Lavinia smiled. "A woman can be formed in many ways. Through adventure or misadventure, through battle in the home or workplace, through childbirth or a call to arms. This world offers so much wisdom but so much pain. I'd be more worried if forty-year-old women had the innocence of newborn babes. That would be toe-curling."

Marina raised her hand. "Actually, I'm not yet forty."

"Bottoms up, ladies!" said Lavinia.

I expected them to go into downward dog, but they downed their smoothies instead and slammed the glasses down in the centre of the circle.

I murmured to Marina. "Can we trust them?"

She turned her palms skywards like a set of scales, subtlety entirely lost on her. "I am getting a curious mix of readings. Their auras are aligned to each other, and there's a dark current running through I can't put my finger on."

"Fat lot of good, that is. We're going to have to hedge our bets." I held my nose and gulped down the ghastly concoction. Marina followed suit.

"That's it," said Lavinia. "Drink it all up."

The room swam. The glass fell from my hands.

"Oh shit." Marina clawed at my arm before collapsing onto my lap.

The witches' faces blurred before me. I lifted a hand and heard glass shatter.

"She's strong, that one," said a familiar male voice.

I cradled my best friend before I, too, lost consciousness.

A GENTLE HAND stroked my hair back from my face. A sofa beneath me. The hum of unfamiliar voices.

I struggled to remember where I was. When it flooded back to me, icicles of fear gripped me. I froze, playing dead lest the witches try to finish me off.

The hand at my forehead paused. "She is rousing."

"Let it be so," said Lavinia.

A glass at my lips. I clamped my lips shut and opened my eyes. I wasn't restrained.

"Shh," said a member of the coven. "It's water."

"You can trust her, Alisha," said a man's voice from the other side of the room.

I sat bolt upright, discarding all pretence and ignored the gentle witch that tended to me. "You! You're in cahoots with the witches? You bloody swine! Where's Marina?"

"Easy," said Detective Jameson. "You don't know all the plays on the board."

I whirled around, ignoring the coven and the traitor in their midst. If I had to turn the coven's headquarters into a whirlwind, so be it. I'd do it if they'd hurt Marina. I'd do it with a smile on my face if one rainbow hair of hers had been harmed. I'd send umbrellas and treadmills and yoga mats flying out over Wimbledon's Lawn Tennis Club if that's what it took, and I'd have no regrets.

"Tell me where my friend is," I said.

"I'm here, Alisha. I needed the loo when I came round. That smoothie really didn't agree with me."

I ran to hug her on unsteady feet.

"I'm okay. I'm okay," she said.

I turned my fire on them all. My breath came in short bursts, and my tongue was sandpaper. "What did you do to us?"

"Calm down, dear. It's just a truth tonic," said Lavinia. "No harmful effects, apart from the need to empty your bladder. Just honesty on tap."

"You haven't told them anything, have you?" I said to Marina.

She shook her head.

"We're not telling you anything. I will go to my grave with my secrets."

"No need to be dramatic, dear," said Lavinia. "We have everything we need. Ravynne, here, is a dab hand at extracting thoughts. We temper the truth tonic to allow her access. Not an easy thing to do in public, given she has to be washed and naked, but here in our own home, it's a synch—centuries of practice, you know. You shouldn't be disheartened. You really are quite young in Otherworld terms but show tremendous promise. We really are very glad you came by."

Ravynne, she of the long black hair and tiny towel, gave a friendly wave.

I bristled with anger. "Jameson, you double-crossing son of a—"

Marina gripped my hand. "I didn't get him wrong, I'm sure of it."

"Oh, the empath is quite right," said Lavinia. "Don't mind poor Robert here for coming to see me. He's a regular, after all."

"Your spin classes are something else," said Detective Jameson. "I wouldn't go anywhere else."

Lavinia giggled like a schoolgirl. "Oh, stop it, Robert. You're too much."

I scowled at Detective Jameson.

"I'm a police officer," he said. "We're not married, for goodness sake. I told you I am a member of the Shadow Squad. You think you were my only Otherworld contact?"

"Of course not. But you could have told us about where your tentacles reached. You're as bad as that octopus Kraglek."

My needling made no impact.

He exuded calm and focus. "Says the woman who hid that she had dealings with the earth goddess."

Lavinia patted her helmet of silver curls. "Kraglek is a pussy cat, really. You just have to get to know him."

I felt a stress headache coming on.

"What did you expect me to do when I suspected you were holding back information? Haul you down to the station and use a lie detector? I told you. The Shadow Squad doesn't work like that. We use our wits and our contacts. It's good old-fashioned policing, except the chips are against us because we can't rely on peculiar talents."

I turned to Lavinia. "Why did you drug us, Minister?"

She shrugged her bony shoulders. "I'm responsible for the defence of the Otherworld. I needed to know if you were a friend or foe. When Robert came to me because he suspected you were hiding information, we decided to act."

My heartbeat was a hummingbird in my throat. "What did you find?"

She stared me out while I tried not to flinch. I realised Lavinia's bubbly persona hid a steel core, just as Ezra had suggested.

But she didn't realise I could give as good as I got. I met her stare and added a curled lip.

"Tell her," said the dumpy, soft-spoken witch who had stroked my hair so gently.

Lavinia shook her head. "You know our code, Elvira. We only share the information we must."

"You mistake her for prey when she is a predator," said Elvira, her brown eyes wide like a doe's. "If we mean to act against the gods, we need to act as one."

"Very well. We found that the empath and you have a bond worthy of your own coven. She is governed by her loyal heart and has a peculiar love of unicorns, although this is a childhood fantasy and not worthy of a grown woman. We found that you are governed by logic and are attached to

Bengal cats." She frowned. "This is not optimal, given cats eat rats. However, more interesting still was that you met with Gaia and have therefore cavorted with the gods behind the senate's back. That in itself is a reason to expel you from the Otherworld."

Fear snaked through me. "Lavinia—"

She held up a hand. "But I am a practical woman and a protector of secrets. You see, this coven has seen plenty of humdrums and peculiars die in our time. We've been the cause of it. But we only condone killing when there is no other choice. Phinnaeous Shine might be prepared to turn a blind eye to humdrum deaths, but I am not." She smiled. "Of course, I have a price."

Detective Jameson regarded us with sombre eyes. "If you want to stop your mother's killer, you'll hear her out."

20

"I know how we're going to do it," I said to Marina on the telephone. "I know how we're going to defeat the electrician."

We were reluctant to say his name out loud, in case it had the effect of summoning him when we weren't ready, like some sort of Candyman.

"Of course, you know how to defeat him," said Marina. "I wouldn't expect anything less. Are we going to send him to one of Her Majesty's prisons or maybe resurrect the purpose of the Tower of London?"

"Er, no."

Excitement bubbled down the telephone line. "Ooh, ooh. Don't tell me. Let me guess. We could put on a WWE match between him and Gaia. Maybe at the O2 Arena or the Millenium Stadium so they have enough room and can be contained. Or better yet, in the gardens of Buckingham Palace so the Queen can have the winner over for high tea."

"I think the Queen might worry about her prize roses being felled. You do know that wrestling is playacted, don't you?"

"Killjoy. I know, we could set Echo on him."

"Actually, that's not a bad idea," I said. "Now listen up."

If I had learned anything from my time as a wife, it was how to use my feminine cunning and wiles for short-term gain. Sure, my marriage had combusted like a dump truck hit by a flame thrower, but there had been moments when things had gone my way, and those victories were sweet.

Chief among my tactics was throwing a party. I much preferred that to putting on doe eyes and batting my eyelashes or slipping into lingerie.

Who didn't like vol au vents served with chilled white wine and wiling away the evening under a starry sky with friends? How utterly perfect, too, that vol au vent was French for *windblown*. Light and airy puff pastry vessels whose name spoke to my druid talents and Mum's birthplace.

As if the gods were on my side tonight.

Except they clearly weren't.

Still, there were many benefits to this not being my first rodeo. Twenty-year-old me would have found it hard to think with a man like Ezra in spitting distance. Forty-year-old me could savour his handsomeness without seeing stars. That gave me a fighting chance of pulling tonight off.

To defeat Ra, I needed Ezra to trust me enough to give me his bodily fluids, and I had roped in my best wing-woman and cat to help.

I gave myself one last look in the mirror. The nude lipstick had a nice plumping effect, and the glossy black eyeliner brought out a sultry side. My hair tumbled around my shoulders.

I wasn't classically beautiful, but I was proud of my body. The lines and bumps and stray grey hairs I'd accumulated over the years were signs it had served me well. I hadn't hidden the circle of dots on my inner arm. My skin glowed, and my waist was trimmer from the training we'd been doing, especially with the added help of my control pants. For once, I'd picked a balcony bra instead of a comfortable one. My curves looked amazing in the little dress I had squeezed into—black was so forgiving—and I'd decided to swap my trainers for heels. My toes protested a little, but heels made me feel sexier as long as I didn't have to walk anywhere.

A smile tugged at my lips. I'd missed this feeling of being a woman who knew her own power. The divorce had taken the wind out of my sails, but that was behind me. I felt more like myself than ever before.

Still, I couldn't host the party at my flat, not if I wanted a good ambience. Since Echo had shed his Bengal form, there'd been an uptick in marking his territory, and my poor flat had suffered. He'd been spraying urine upwards in the corner of the living room to get his scent as high as possible, and I'd noticed it happening more since Ezra had been coming round.

Thankfully, he hadn't marked his territory with droppings yet. There was a limit to what I could stomach.

The resident's roof terrace was usually used for drying racks of my neighbour Dotty's enormous, greying underwear.

Tonight, I'd reserved it and decked it out with candlelit lanterns and cushions. An ice bucket with bottles of prosecco and sauvignon blanc waited for us, together with a bottle of tequila. I figured Ezra was more of a whiskey man, but that wasn't as fun as shots. At the last minute, I prepared a plate of cubed salmon for Echo. A glass dome I'd inherited from Mum covered vol au vents filled with garlic mushrooms and brie and cranberry. I wanted her to be a part of tonight. And to protect the vol au vents from London's wretched pigeons.

Echo slinked up behind me, his fur caressing my bare legs. "Va va voom." His emerald eyes shone. "You didn't dress up like this for the other one."

"I'm not a car, Echo."

"Not vroom vroom. Va va voom. From a Nicki Minaj song.

I decided if I have to live in this century, I should make an effort to learn the lingo."

"I'm impressed."

"You can count on me to elevate the conversation tonight," purred Echo. "I have learned lyrics from the Bee Gees and the Spice Girls. I thought 'Stayin' Alive' and 'Viva Forever' were particularly apt, given we've incurred a god's wrath. Although 'You Win Again' and 'Goodbye' could work equally well."

"Actually, Echo, you're here tonight in more of a bodyguard role."

A growl, far too loud to be overlooked by neighbours. There were only so many times I could use the noisy dishwasher excuse. "The granddaughter of Rajika Verma mistakes me for a bodyguard. A bodyguard is traditionally a corpulent male of human origin with gold teeth who hopes his fists will meet a jaw, only to fall asleep on the job, stinking of nicotine and body odour. That is most certainly not me."

I leaned my forehead against his head, mimicking the affectionate nuzzling he did when he was my Bengal cat. "I need you tonight, Echo. If the electrician shows his face, I need my family around me. We'll need to work as a team."

He relaxed, allowing himself to enjoy my caresses. "It is good to know that you view me as family. This part of you is akin to your grandmother. Your father, however, saw me as a mere appendage, like a wart on an otherwise pleasant face. Or a—" Echo raised his nose into the air. "I smell wolf. And the fresh citrus notes of Marina's favourite perfume."

The intercom buzzed.

"It is time, granddaughter of Rajika Verma, to put your plan into action. I wish you fruitful hunting."

We sat on the rooftop of my building under a medley of stars, picking out the constellations we recognised: The Plough, Orion's Belt, Castor and Pollux. I'd been filling Ezra's glass, but he showed no signs of intoxication.

Although the sun shone brightly over Balham during the day, the evening cooled quickly. Goosebumps chased up my bare limbs, and my teeth chattered. I could have fetched some blankets from downstairs, but as a true London stalwart, I decided instead to down alcohol to warm my cockles. Copious amounts of booze needed a solid base, ideally a burger or a kebab with a good dollop of garlic sauce. Vol au vents, with their airy, fragile nature, were about as much use as a set of dentures on a vampire. I ate them anyway, one after the other, matched mouthful for mouthful by Marina.

I'd missed our time together. She knew how to make me chuckle and when to call out my bullshit. So we drank. We drank with abandon and glee. With each clink of our glasses, Marina's habit of staring directly into my eyes to avoid seven years of bad sex became more and more comical. Before I knew it, we'd polished off two bottles of prosecco and most of the food between us.

"You know, this empath thing has been working out brilliantly," said Marina. "I've not had a migraine in weeks. I mean, can you imagine if I never have to deal with one again?"

"That's brilliant. I'm so happy for you." I thought about how I couldn't share this with Mum. How she would have kept Marina's secret but investigated the science behind it.

"*And* I've been able to make some uncanny diagnoses about the animals in my care. The colours of the auras are so pretty, and they're a guiding light, even without x-rays. I've saved my own skin a few times too. I got a flash of anger from a pet snake the other day and warded off a volatile hamster before it stuck its teeth in. The nurses just can't work out how I'm doing it."

Echo propped his paws on the guard rail to gaze longingly at a passing poodle.

"Come down from there, Echo," I said.

Ezra's T-shirt had ridden up to reveal the bronzed skin of his abs. He lounged against a pile of cushions and looked at me from under hooded eyes.

Like, *really* looked at me.

Marina waggled her eyebrows at me teasingly. She was about as subtle as a ten-tonne truck.

I flushed and offered him some vol au vents. "Have some more."

My control pants were starting to cut off my circulation.

"Mushrooms aren't my thing," said Ezra. "But the brie and cranberry were delicious."

"How about *mushrooms*?" Marina left no doubt about why she had been suspended twice from school.

Ezra grinned. "Also, not my thing."

"Shall I top you up?" I said.

"Sure. You know your wines. This one is excellent." He knocked back the rest of his glass. The stem looked fragile in his hands.

"My Mum was French. No one understands wine better than the French." I swallowed a burp, masked only by a Cafe del Mar playlist I had on in the background, and poured more wine into his glass.

"The Germans would beg to differ," said Ezra. "You should come by my place sometime and try a bottle of Riesling. I have one that is aged to perfection."

I blushed. It was probably the prosecco wreaking havoc with me because that definitely hadn't been a come-on.

Echo bounced off the guard rail, knocking over a trough of yellow crocuses. He stalked over to us, the rosettes on his golden coat breathtaking in the evening light. "Where do you live, dog? I have been unable to picture your kennel. With your teleporting skills, it occurred to me you could live anywhere. It must be nice not to be subjected to border controls like other humanoid creatures. Luckily, I, too, possess the wit and skill not to be subjected to a pet passport."

Ezra chuckled. "I live in a farmhouse near Windsor, as per pack law. Although our alpha Gunnolf turns a blind eye when I disappear for a while. He understands it's part of the nature of being a seeker. The farmhouse backs onto woods ideal for running when the moon calls. Those woods are more home to me than the house itself."

Marina tumbled into the ice bucket, sending the bottles crashing.

A whoosh and Ezra was at her side, righting the bucket and steadying her.

I frowned. Either werewolves had a higher tolerance to booze than us, or Ezra's tall, muscular frame meant he needed more to hit a high. My plan didn't work without him being happy-clappy drunk.

A frisson of anxiety spread in my belly.

Maybe he was a mean drunk or a hopeless one like Alex. Or one of those people who kept drinking until sunrise and then dropped out cold.

I needed him lucid. Pliable, not comatose.

"Tequila! We need tequila." Slurring my words wasn't intentional. I stumbled to my feet, resisted the urge to kick off my heels and swayed over to the booze, sensing Ezra's eyes on my arse. My control pants rolled down like they wanted to escape me.

He was at my side in a flash, his hand cupping my elbow. "Are you sure tequila is a good idea?"

"Hell yeah, cowboy." I poured out three shots.

"I live on a farm, not a ranch."

The world spun around me. "Why aren't you drunk?"

"Why do you want me drunk?"

I raised an eyebrow in challenge. "I like living dangerously."

His eyes smouldered. "I'd choose tedium over danger every time. Time for wild runs and skinny dipping. Time for deckchairs in the sun and rereading favourite books. Time for watching the changing expressions on a loved one's face. Time for sunsets and breakfasts in bed."

"All right, grandpa. Tonight, we live on the wild side. I propose a drinking game." I put the plate of cubed meat in front of Echo and handed out shot glasses to Marina and Ezra, together with a wedge of lime and the salt shaker. "Go ahead, load up. A shot to get us in the mood. Ready? 1-2-3, tequila!"

We took the shots, grimacing after sucking on the lime, and I refilled our glasses and put the plate of lime wedges and salt between us. "The game is called Fabled Creatures. It's a twist on a game we used to play as kids around the dinner table. Marina and I will call out names of mythological creatures. If we hit the jackpot with a creature that exists in the Otherworld, Ezra must drink. If we are wrong, Marina and I will drink. Got it?"

Echo huffed, his tail swishing. "This is what you people call fun?"

"Echo, you may eat a cube of salmon with each wrong or right answer," I said.

He purred with pleasure. "This is an honourable game, granddaughter of Rajika Verma."

"My turn first." Marina screwed her eyes up in concentration.

We'd been mythology geeks in high school. I knew she could reel off as many as me.

"Unicorn." She tossed her freshly dyed rainbow hair and pointed to the tattoo on her arm.

I shook my head in rue at her lousy guess.

"They don't exist," said Ezra.

We drank.

"Manticore," I said.

"Nope." He shook his head.

We drank.

"Centaur," said Marina.

"Nope," said Ezra.

"No centaurs? I don't believe you," I said. "Is he lying, Echo?"

Echo lifted his head from the plate, strings of fish hanging from his teeth. "The dog is correct."

"Why, thank you, cat," Ezra said. "It appears our protégées are basing their guesses on Narnia."

"The pleasure is mine, dog. C.S. Lewis had nothing on Ursula K. Le Guin," said Echo. "Drink, ladies."

We drank. The plan was well and truly off the rails now.

I crossed my fingers. "Dragons?"

"All dead."

I punched the air. Dad used to make up tales of dragons. Forty-year-old me was still attached to them. "Ha! So they lived once?"

He nodded.

"So we all drink."

He shrugged and knocked back a shot with us. "Continue."

Marina chewed her lip. "Lizard folk?"

"Nope."

"Whose side are you on, anyway?" I threw a cushion at her.

We drank, and I reconciled myself to having the most brutal hangover in the morning.

"My turn." I tried hard to stay upright. "Let's double the stakes."

"You sure you can handle that, ladies?" drawled Ezra.

"Bring. It. On." Marina went cross-eyed.

"I got this." I cast back my mind to the stories Dad read me as a child. "Basilisk."

He drank a double.

"Oh wow," breathed Marina.

"Satyr," I said.

Another double. He recoiled from the taste.

"Selkies."

"Of course. The Minister for Information is a selkie." He downed another two shots, shaking his head at the nearly empty bottle. "Enough, enough, or I will be useless."

Four storeys beneath us, a dog barked.

Echo lifted his head from his bowl and crooned the melody from 'Bohemian Rhapsody'.

"Did the leopard just hum Queen?" said Ezra.

"He has been swotting up on popular culture. Nicki Minaj, Taylor Swift and now Queen, apparently," I said.

"Blimey," said Marina.

"I have something to ask you, Ezra," I said.

He smiled. "Go ahead."

"We need to give Lavinia a drop of your blood in exchange for a protection spell against the electrician."

He frowned, processing my request. Then his face turned cold, like a trapdoor had closed, and we were on opposite sides. "No. Absolutely not."

I reached for him. "Just think about it for a second."

His whole body tensed. "There's nothing to think about. Is that what tonight was about, an elaborate ruse to manipulate me?"

"Alisha's not capable of that." Marina rode on a wave of tequila endorphins. "She would never harm you. She *adores* you."

"I would harm you," said Echo, eagerness brimming. "But I like you enough to do it quickly."

The dog at street level gave a plaintive yowl.

Echo hesitated, gave a guttural moan and then raced to the guard rail to take stock. "The poodle is taunting me. I will only eat a third of him. That will leave enough for his burial."

"Echo, don't you dare!" I said.

He leapt off the rooftop, landing cleanly in a nearby oak.

"It's nature. You can't stop him," Marina said with the detached passion of a wildlife commentator. "He'll get as close as he can, then dispatch it with a bite to the neck."

I rushed to the guard rail. He was no longer my pet but a beast driven by instinct. And his timing couldn't have been worse, judging by the storm on Ezra's face.

"Echo, get back here, right now!" I called.

"I will pull my kill into the tree. No humdrum will know what has happened here."

"There's a little old lady attached to the lead." I prayed she was deaf and couldn't hear my pleading.

Echo clambered down the tree headfirst. He stalked his prey, belly inches from the tarmac, keeping close to the shadows. I found my Dutch courage, kicked off my shoes and climbed up past the crocus boxes on the roof rail in my bare feet.

"What are you doing?" Ezra grabbed my wrist.

I twisted away from him and jumped, holding my hands out at my sides and channelling my power. The wind eased my descent, and I jerked downwards in spurts, my dress thankfully moulded enough to my body to stay in place. I landed just as Ezra materialised beside me.

His pinched expression said it all. This was duty, not friendship. "I was ready to rescue you."

"I don't need rescuing, but thanks for being by my side."

"What's the plan?"

I took a deep breath. "Distract the old lady. I'll deal with Echo. He's less likely to turn on me than you."

We ran, side by side, to the street corner where the old lady tried to tug her unwieldy poodle onward. Echo waited in a bush to pounce. His body simmered with tension, eyes on his target.

I crept up behind him and took my chance, grabbing his tail and holding on.

He swung around, growling. "You dare to come between a leopard and his prey?"

Betting that his duty to protect my family would outweigh his anger, I leapt onto his back like I was riding in a rodeo competition. He shook me off like a fly and refocused on the poodle. I thudded into a bush. Its prickles sank into my feet and scratched my limbs.

Next, I directed a blast of wind at him, but Echo's four legs and hunting posture low to the ground meant he barely noticed my efforts.

I risked a look at Ezra. He'd engaged the old lady in conversation. My foot squelched into pigeon poo as I ran over to them. To be fair, I'd stepped in worse in London. I did my best to ignore the gunk on my foot and prayed Echo hadn't decided all four of us were fair game.

I channelled calm, even though my heart hammered. "What a beautiful dog."

It was clearly a lie. A severe underbite meant it was no show dog. It needed a good dunk in the bath to loosen the filth in its coat. I ignored the yapping and scooped it up in my arms. It struggled for a second and then let me feel the full force of its dog breath.

Or periodontal disease.

Ezra unleashed a dazzling smile that didn't reach his eyes. "Darling, how many times have I told you to wear shoes when you are out walking? This is Julianne. She lives around the corner in the same house she moved into when she and her husband were young sweethearts. Milo here is a nuisance if he doesn't get his nightly walk. I was telling Julianne about the robbery the other night and offered to walk her home."

The man could charm a statue to life.

"Nice to meet you, Julianne," I said as dog slobber dripped onto my shoulder.

Julianne beamed, her snowy perm a halo in the street light. "What a lucky girl you are to have a man like this. A gentleman and a looker to boot. You would have had a fight on your hands had I been in my prime. There's no need for you to walk me home. I can see my flat from here. But next time I need some muscle to take out the bins or replace a lightbulb, I'll know where to come."

Ezra winked, his playful nature in stark contrast to his true dark mood with me.

I returned the poodle to Julianne, and she hobbled towards her flat.

"Thank you for your help," I said to Ezra when she had gone.

"I could hardly let you blast your way through a humdrum neighbourhood. You're under my supervision, remember?" He paused. "I thought we were friends, but I guess not. All this time, I've avoided giving the coven what they wanted. You know nothing about this life and what people will stoop to. How can you presume to do a deal behind my back?"

I balled up my fists. "I haven't promised Lavinia anything. I just wanted you in a good mood before I asked you. But in case you hadn't noticed, my mum was *killed*. Nita was *killed*. Countless others too. How can you just sit there and do nothing if we have a chance to stop it?"

"The first law—"

"The first law is obsolete. You heard Detective Jameson. The senate knows what's brewing, and still, they do nothing. But your aunt is willing to step up. She just wants a small drop of your blood. That's all."

Copper glinted in Ezra's eyes. "Have you listened to a word I said? You're like a newborn babe picking up a weapon. You have no idea what is at stake here. It's not our call."

"Then whose? *Nothing* happens in this world unless we stand up and fight."

Ezra gritted his teeth. "In the Otherworld, a drop of blood

is not just something to be mopped up. A drop of blood is needed for the most potent spells. It can be used to steal powers or harness them. It can be used to control, sacrifice or even kill. To boil a foe's blood, track their movements or corrupt their souls. Blood magic is something to run from, not towards. And my aunt can't be trusted. Who are you to decide otherwise?"

"Come back to the rooftop. Let's talk about this."

All gentleness had fled, leaving stony eyes in a chiselled face. "No, I don't think I will."

"I'm sorry."

In his voice, I heard the wolf. "Find another way."

My disappointment stung.

He vanished, leaving the night empty without him.

I could have asked Marina to bring a syringe from work and stolen his blood, but I couldn't bring myself to stoop that low. Ezra was my friend. I wouldn't go behind his back, even though every cell of my body screamed it was the right thing to do.

Without him, there was no deal with Lavinia's coven. Without him, we were just two girls in control pants plus a poodle-mad leopard trying to defeat a god.

I bit my lip and drew blood. I wanted to stop Ra so badly. I wanted him to pay for Mum's death. It hurt to give up, but I didn't have another choice.

Without Ezra and the witches, I didn't stand a chance.

21

It wasn't often that I regretted not owning a car in London. The city's Victorian streets were often gridlocked, and owning a car was expensive. Public transport made sense unless a magical leopard decided to accompany you.

Even in his Bengal cat form, Echo would have raised eyebrows hopping onto the bus with me. It was okay for a spaniel to follow its master onto a bus, but cats had no master. A free-range cat on the 219 would have prompted too much attention, so I dug out a cat carrier from the back of the wardrobe.

I had no idea how Echo's glamour worked metaphysically —it would be a nifty trick to squeeze my forty-year-old self into my twenty-year-old clothes—but there you go. He fitted into the cat carrier, and I carried him onto the bus, ignoring his plaintive miaowing.

"You are wise beyond your years, granddaughter of Rajika Verma, to trust your own instincts over the wolf," said Echo. "He should have agreed to your plan. It was a good one."

"You're just sore he stopped you from devouring the poodle," I said in a whisper, testing his excellent leopard hearing. The bus passengers could only hear miaows, but I had no such glamour and had to be careful.

"This may be true, but alas, my anger propelled me to seek thrills further afield. The royal deer herds of Richmond won't forget last night in a hurry."

I groaned. "I'm glad the poodle escaped, at least."

Echo grunted. "How the mighty fall. One day, I taste a deer's fleshy behind. The next, I, Chanakya Gunbir Hredhaan of Maharashtra, have been stuffed into a handbag."

"Well, you didn't have to come." We were heading towards Tooting Bec to see Dad.

"As much as I tolerate your minuscule flat, I have a fondness for the Verma family home. It was my first abode here with Rajika Verma, and I will not pass up the opportunity to relive my grander days on this measly isle."

"It's a cat carrier, not a handbag, by the way."

"It is beneath me. And it stinks of urine."

I sighed. He wasn't going to let me forget this. "Well, you shouldn't have released your bladder at your last vaccination appointment. It would need an industrial cleaner to get the stench out."

"A magical leopard doesn't need to be vaccinated against feline diseases. At least this year, I won't have to suffer the indignity."

"Actually, Echo, I signed up for a three-year vet plan, and I'd much rather we kept up appearances."

He emitted a roar that frightened the beautifully coiffed lady on the opposite aisle of the bus.

I gave her a sympathetic smile and made a show of poking Echo through the netting of the bag. "Be quiet, you silly thing."

He bit my index finger and drew blood.

"Ouch!" I sucked the puncture wound.

The beautifully coiffed lady threw us a disturbed look and changed seats.

I had a right mind to leave Echo on the bus. To teach him a lesson, I stood to ping the bell and let him sweat it out without me while the driver propelled the bus through the last mile towards Dad's house. When the doors opened, I grabbed the carrier at the last second and jumped off the bus.

"You are walking a dangerous line, granddaughter of Rajika Verma, by treating me like a housecat," hissed Echo from the carrier. The scar across his eye gave him a savage air, especially when his tail swished like a python in attack mode.

I turfed him out of the carrier onto the street before he decided to maul me. "You'll all be relieved I've dropped the thought of challenging a killer god. We'll be much safer if I just have you to deal with."

Echo prowled along next to me. "So you have reconciled yourself to being a lily-livered spectator, have you? Where is your oomph, druid?"

"What else can I do? Ezra barely trusts me. The deal is off with Lavinia, and Jameson seems not even to have a truncheon to take to this fight. I should stop trying to be more than I am and take small steps. Plus, Dad needs me. I need to concentrate on him."

It had been the series of texts last night that had given it away. For the first few weeks, he'd busied himself prettying Mum's grave. Gaia's revelations that Mum had been killed by Ra had hit him like a tonne of bricks. He'd distracted himself from grief by mentoring Sahil. It meant a great deal to him that the senate had entrusted him with the task, although he would never have admitted it to them. It had been a way to bridge the cracks with the Otherworld that had formed when he had abandoned it.

Only he and Sahil had come up against a brick wall.

They were no closer to discovering whether Sahil had any Otherworld talents. So Sahil had decided to clear out Dad's attic and ignore any further attempts at training. Dad consoled himself by eating Mum's freezer food.

Two grown men, not speaking to each other and acting like schoolchildren.

While Sahil grunted in the attic, hauling boxes back and forth, Dad had eaten every last morsel of the meals Mum had batch cooked for the days she'd worked late. The last taste of her lovingly made meals had sent him over the edge.

His texts had come into my phone like an S.O.S.

Your brother and I aren't talking.

I miss your mum like a hole at the centre of my life.

Her ratatouille tasted of love, and I've eaten the last bite.

Oh wait, I have found her Roquefort and caramelised onion tart in the freezer. I think I will be okay until morning.

Truth be told, I'd not given Dad the time he'd deserved since Mum had died. I'd been too caught up in my own wild goose chase to uncover my powers and bring her killer to justice. I'd decided to swing by today to offer him a shoulder to cry on and a stack of takeaway menus. Plus, I could try to bridge the gap between him and Sahil.

I walked up the driveway with Echo at my side and rang the doorbell.

Dad opened the door. His white hair hadn't seen a comb in days, and remnants of tomato sauce marred his collar. There was not a paint blotch in sight on his person or his fingers.

Things were bad.

"Oh, Dad." I held out my arms to him.

He was taller than me but came to me like a child and laid his head on my shoulder. He smelled anything but fresh.

"Where's Sahil?" I asked.

"In the attic. It can't still need tidying."

I tucked my arm through his. "Don't worry. He'll come around."

"You brought the leopard."

"You have seen better days, Joshi Verma," said Echo.

"Luckily, you still have family because friends would desert a person whose odour resembles a toilet."

I shushed Echo with a pointed look and ushered Dad into the belly of the house, past the shrine where he prayed for Mum and spent tealights showed the fervour of his prayers. I peeked into his studio facing the garden and gasped.

"Your father seems to be teetering at the abyss," the leopard said as quietly as possible.

He was right. Dad had cleared out all his joyful paintings of the animal world.

Instead, my mother's features stared back at me from the easel. Monochrome had replaced his colourful palette. In one study, he'd painted her eyes. In another, her mouth. In yet another, her profile replete with the fall of her hair when she woke in the morning.

As if in homage to each part of her. A jigsaw of love. A way to cheat the senate's erasure of Mum from pictures.

I sprinted up the stairs and called out for my brother. "Sahil, are you up there? Fancy a cuppa?"

He poked his dusty head out of the attic hatch. "Hi, sis. I'll be down in a minute."

"He needs us."

A raised eyebrow. "I've been here. Where have you been?"

I sighed and returned to the kitchen, where Dad opened the window to release some of the noxious gases from fermenting food remnants and dirty dishes. Mugs with dregs of breakfast tea littered the granite worktop.

I picked up a pair of washing-up gloves and gave Dad a grim smile. "Sahil's just finishing up. Why don't you have a hot shower while I get to grips with this lot?"

He shook his head. "I've turned into a pig. What would your mother say?"

"That you obviously miss her." I kissed his cheek. "Go on. You'll feel better in a fresh set of clothes."

"You'll be here when I get downstairs?"

How frail he'd become. "Yes, Dad."

He left with a sigh and a meandering step, stopping to look at the family photographs as he went, where Mum had faded to nothing.

My chest hurt for him.

"I will leave you now, druid, to make my mark on the once-beloved home of Rajika Verma and relive my glory days," purred Echo.

"Don't dig up the flower beds. They were Mum's pride and joy."

Echo lifted his nose into the air, his pride unmistakable. "I'm not a heathen, as you well know."

"And stay out of the pond."

"The koi will have missed me."

"Echo…"

"I will not eat them, but my frolicking and snarl may cause them to leap in fright. It is quite a show I used to perform for you in your childhood. You used to clap in delight. Especially when I nudged the stupid creatures into the pond and scared them out again."

I raised an eyebrow. "I expect I wiped it from my memory."

He pawed open the back door as if he'd done it a thousand times before and bounded into the garden, pure joy in every fibre of his body. As promised, he leapt into the pond, rolling in it as the koi leapt in fright. He pranced playfully, knocking them back in with his paw, catching them wriggling between his teeth, spitting them out into the water and repeating his antics.

Poor fish. Thankfully Dad didn't have a clue.

I got to work cleaning the kitchen. Mum had been like Mary Poppins in the kitchen, cheerfully cracking on with her tasks. I was more like King Kong, crashing about, grumpy at the enforced domesticity. But Dad needed me, and Sahil was hopeless at this sort of thing, so I pushed on until the kitchen sparkled. Then I made three portions of eggs and toast, setting Sahil's in the oven to keep warm.

Creaking wood behind me signalled someone's arrival.

"Dad," I said, turning. "You look so much better." He'd put on PJs instead of day clothes, but at least he was clean. He smelled of lemon-fresh shower gel, and that was a huge improvement.

His eyes swept the kitchen, and a red flush crept up his neck. "I would have cleaned up."

"I know, but you don't have to now." I set the plates on the table and gave thanks that he'd not yet noticed Echo taunting his prize koi. "Go ahead and eat. Sahil will come down when he's ready."

He sat at the table. "Rosalie's eggs were so fluffy."

I nodded. I couldn't compete with Mum's culinary skills, but I could make sure Dad felt loved and had a full belly. One of the perks of being middle-aged was knowing your own strengths and not taking everything personally.

"If only Rosalie's years hadn't been stolen from her. Can you imagine how the world would have changed if your mother had succeeded in yet another discovery?" He turned wounded eyes on me. "What news of bringing her killer to justice? Has the senate found its moral centre yet? All those deaths, and they dilly dally until it is too late as usual."

I bit my lip. All this time I'd hidden my real intentions from him. It would only have worried him. He didn't need to know I'd wanted to lead the charge against Ra. Especially now that my plans were dead in the water. I filled him in about Nita's death, Detective Jameson and the Shadow Squad, and the witches keen to protect humdrum lives even though the Magical Constitution prevented peculiars from meddling with the gods.

"You know, darling, you have your mother's eyes. And I still have part of her to cherish because she lives on in you and Sahil. I'm as impatient as you for that weasel god to get his due, but we have to leave it to the big shots. We are tiny players in this game, and I wouldn't forgive myself if anything happened to you."

I blew out my breath. "I've been hearing that rather a lot."

"I worry so much about you that I forget you are old enough to make your own decisions. It comforts me that Rosalie realised before her death that you would take a magical path. I can hear her voice in my ear telling me to trust everything will be okay." He sighed. "Why do you think she didn't tell me when we fell out about her releasing the lab animals at work?"

"I don't know. You know what she was like. She was so precise at managing every part of her life. Like how she made freezer meals or pruned her rose bushes or conducted her experiments. Maybe she knew you'd be upset about our family embracing the Otherworld after all these years. Maybe that's why she was so wrapped up in her project at work. My guess is she wanted to ensure our safety before telling you. To make it easier for you to accept."

He chewed his lip, deep in thought, then put down his fork. "Look at me, so caught up in myself. What is done is done. What matters is she loved us. Go on, distract an old man. I'd love to see what Ezra has been teaching you. So my daughter has power over wind currents, eh? Show me what you can do."

I smiled and cast an eye around the kitchen. Ezra had told me it would be easier for me to manipulate the breeze than indoor air currents, but I needn't have worried. The window was still open, which helped.

The pile of takeaway menus I'd brought Dad sat on the worktop.

I pursed my lips and raised a hand. The familiar tingle spread through my fingers, and the menus took flight, looped in a circle above our heads and then swooped down into a pile next to his plate.

Dad's eyes lit up. He lunged across the table to grab my face and kissed my forehead. "That is magnificent! What ease, what control! You have power over the currents. I am so proud. Prouder than when you got full marks in your Shakespeare exam in high school."

I grinned. "I'm glad you approve."

"You'll get stronger with every passing day, with every bit of practice. If only your brother would take heed. Mentoring him has been a disaster. I don't know why I expected any different. Sahil's ego is wounded, but magic can't be rushed. But you, my girl, you persevered."

I'd learned to persevere during my dead-end marriage, and it had brought nothing. It was nice when it paid off. "We should go up and speak to Sahil. I can help smooth things over."

Dad slumped. "It's no use. He's a good boy, but he's stubborn."

"He just needs time to get his head around this all. God knows, I still do. Come on." I tugged him to his feet.

We traipsed up the stairs.

He started muttering to himself. "It is rather strange for a Verma to have wind powers. I knew you weren't a painter. Anyone who saw your art attempts would know that, but I wonder whether... It didn't work with Sahil, but maybe, just maybe... I mean, the binding spell did neutralise my magic too, but if Rosalie's death broke the spell and the dormant powers of my children have been unleashed, maybe my paintings have life again."

We reached the upper landing and climbed at the wobbly ladder, Dad taking tentative steps in his bare feet and chequered pyjamas, his hair damp against his neck.

It had been years since I'd been up in the loft. A dusty bulb flickered light across the boarded space. A sun ray crept in through a damaged roof tile.

Sahil had made good progress. In one corner, he had

stacked up empty suitcases and plastic boxes full of childhood mementos. The rest of the space was an explosion of Dad's art: line drawings, canvases full of oil paint and watercolours in simple frames.

My brother, kneeling over a plastic box of trinkets, looked up. "Ah, sorry, Alisha. I got caught up."

I bent down to kiss his cheek. "More like you were avoiding confrontation."

"What do you think, Dad? It looks better, doesn't it?" said Sahil.

"It looks great, son."

Sahil chewed his lip sheepishly. "Sorry for blowing off at you yesterday. I need to get back to work, and this fishing for Otherworld talents seems to have hit the bottom of the rock pool with me."

"I didn't learn overnight either, son."

I looked from one to the other. "See, that wasn't so hard, was it?"

"Son, I want Alisha to try to animate the paintings. Like we tried with you. You wouldn't mind?"

"Why would I mind?" But his eyes carried a different message. He picked up a bear I knew from one of Dad's greeting cards and offered it to me.

Dad shook his head. "No, not that one. You don't animate a bear in a loft. You animate a bear in a field. Or in the woods. Or, if you must, in a garden. A bear in a loft causes carnage." He picked up a watercolour of a mouse nibbling on cheese and then discarded that too. "Too easy to lose up here. I don't want to introduce a mouse problem into the house."

Sahil reached for a canvas of a sloth on a tree. "How about this?"

Dad shook his head. "No, no, not for a novice animateur in suburban South London. Sloths may be sleepy, but they can be very noisy." He reached instead for a tiny canvas on a shelf. "Yes, yes...I think this is it." He handed me a painting of a frog on a lily pad. "If you manage it, we can release him into our pond."

All well and good if Echo was finished with the pond.

I held the painting, my heart thumping. The loft suffocated me, and I longed to blast my way out to clean air. I wasn't sure if I wanted this talent, but Dad's face shone with hope. "What do I do?"

His voice jittered with excitement. "Your grandmother always started by closing her eyes and thinking of a purpose for the animal. Then take a deep breath and reach for the threads of my drawing as if you're a puppet master. Then pull out the creature from the page."

"I can't—"

"But what if you can?"

A nerve throbbed in Sahil's cheek. If I succeeded, it would be hard on him.

I sighed and squeezed my eyes shut, feeling like a fool. A forty-year-old woman playing make-believe. No wonder I'd taken compassionate leave from work with all this madness around me. I silently assigned the frog a name and a purpose.

Dad hadn't mentioned a name, but I didn't want the poor thing to be born with some sort of existential crisis, and I thought a name might help. Gerry the frog's purpose would be to make friends with the traumatised koi in Dad's pond.

I opened my eyes, took and deep breath and twiddled my fingers above the drawing, resisting the urge to laugh.

I'd never felt so ridiculous in my life.

"No, not like that. Like this." Dad moved his fingers like a harpist.

I tried again, mimicking his movement.

Nothing. Nada.

"You're not putting enough belief behind it," said Dad.

"Give her a second, Dad," said Sahil.

I grimaced. "Maybe this just isn't my talent. I already have one. The universe probably doesn't want to give me two."

Dad's face crumpled. "But how can your grandmother's talent have disappeared with her? It's not fair."

"It doesn't matter." I put the painting aside and took his arm, ignoring my own pang at the evaporated link to my grandmother. "I'm so glad you showed me your work. They shouldn't be hidden away up here."

"Alisha is right," said Sahil. "We should hang them in the house."

"Maybe the senate will reconsider you exhibiting in galleries," I said.

The three of us clambered down the ladder and returned to the kitchen, where I handed Sahil his food. Through the open window, I noted Echo's sleeping form on the lawn. The dishwasher had completed its cycle, and I picked out some new cups and popped the kettle on just as my phone trilled in my pocket.

Detective Jameson's name flashed up on the screen. "Sorry, guys, I have to take this," I said. "Hello, Detective."

"I hope I'm not interrupting anything," he said. "Do you have a minute?"

I leaned against the worktop. "Yes, of course. I was going to give you a ring today. I'm afraid our deal with Lavinia won't work."

"The wolf said no."

"He did, yes."

"Actually, I was calling about something else. Are you sitting down?"

Anxiety flared inside my stomach. I pulled out a chair and sat opposite Dad and Sahil. "I am now."

"I'm sorry to tell you that at roughly seven this morning, Melissa Ramsay, your mother's colleague at EvolveTech, was killed on her way to work."

A vice clamped around my heart. "She what? What happened?"

"She flew into the third rail at Elephant and Castle. A few

dozen other commuters were further down the train, but they had their head in their phones or had headphones in. No one got to her in time. She was dead by the time paramedics arrived."

"Oh, that's terrible." I squeezed my eyes shut, picturing Melissa the last time I'd seen her. She was just a woman who liked baking and racy novels.

"If it's any consolation, my best guess is that she died quickly." Detective Jameson's voice cracked. "The CCTV was shorted, but Alisha, I have to tell you, my gut says it's him."

The noise in my head drowned him out.

Dad took the phone from my numb hands and said goodbye to the detective. There was fire in his eyes. "I heard everything."

"The woman from the memorial?" said Sahil.

I nodded. "She didn't do anything to deserve this. It's my fault she died. It's my fault for not making her a priority. If I'd acted sooner, she'd still be alive. Instead, I convinced myself that I could just walk away from you know who's killing spree. What kind of person does that make me?"

"Call me a coward, but I think you made the right call not going up against a god," said Sahil. "Some people would say that's the only call."

I clenched my fists. A grown woman didn't shy away from her problems. I had to make this right, whatever it took. I would not sit on my sorry arse while even more families were torn apart.

Even if I had to headlock Ra or turn into a banshee to make him pay.

"I know that look. It's the look of a woman about to run headfirst into enemy fire." Dad patted my arm. "You must make your own decisions. You need wit and courage to survive. You have those. But you also need allies."

He looked at my brother.

"Don't look at me," said Sahil. "I don't even have wind powers."

Dad sighed. "Don't make your grandmother's mistake, Alisha. She fell because she didn't have enough allies when it counted. Choose carefully who you trust. Betrayal is rife when power is at stake."

"Take care, Alisha," said Sahil. "And thanks for the eggs."

I hugged them both and then darted over to the open window. "Echo!"

He lumbered over, stretching out his lithe body as he came. "You called, druid? I was minded to ignore this summons, but I am in a good mood after my koi games."

"How would you like to go hunting?"

Emerald eyes sparkled with interest. "Who am I hunting?"

"A god."

22

I'd suffered from insomnia during the dark days of my divorce. The sleeplessness returned with Mum's death. Nita and Melissa's deaths only made it worse. I tossed and turned, starfished across my sheets, got up for a wee, downed water and downloaded meditation apps.

Nothing changed except my determination to act against Ra.

In the morning, I woke, put on my favourite knickers—comfy but supportive—and tried in vain to cover my dark circles with concealer. I then invited Marina over to join me on the rooftop to summon Gaia. Between my steak-eating, flat-marking, sofa-slobbering leopard and being distracted by more pressing matters, my neglected flat was in no fit state to host a goddess.

It turned out it was marginally easier to summon a magical leopard than a goddess.

There was no doubt we needed Gaia's help. An uninitiated peculiar like me was no threat to Ra. I was like an insect on his sandals. He'd crush me and not even bother disposing of my body. But with allies, I'd stand a chance.

Detective Jameson had understood that all along.

Even Lavinia, powerful as she was, needed a coven.

Marina and I had been making offerings to Gaia on the rooftop of my building for three hours straight before we realised Gaia wasn't coming. How could we hope to beat Ra without an equally weighty force on our side?

"Well, that's a bit shite," said Marina. "I was hoping to meet her. You and Ezra got all the fun last time."

"I was there too," said Echo. "She loved me best."

"That she did," I said. "Which is why I'd rather you weren't here, Echo. If she decides she wants you, we'll never see you again."

Echo put his nose in the air. "If the goddess wants me, she can have me. Who am I to stand in the way of the divine?"

"You're happy enough to stand in the way of you know who."

"That is true, but only because he is a cretinous villain and hardly worthy of god-like status."

I nodded. "Gotcha. Any further luck tracking him?"

"No, I wasn't there when Melissa was first attacked and when Nita was killed, so I don't yet have his scent. Even with a scent, it is next to impossible to track a god. I tried to track the goddess after tasting heaven at her feet. I couldn't find her either."

I chewed my lip. It would have been easier to plan our attack if we could track Ra's movements and get ahead of his next target. "In that case, we'll have to lure him to us by focusing all our attention on him, as Gaia suggested, or by making him angry enough to come and find us."

Echo inclined his magnificent head. "We need the witches, whatever the wolf says. Without them, we have no hope of gaining the upper hand, especially without Gaia beside us."

Marina grimaced. "Well, after releasing a colony of rats, a cloud of bats and a swarm of bees on this rooftop, I think we can safely say that Gaia isn't coming."

"There is someone else with information that might help,"

said Echo. "I crossed paths with the wolf on my travels. He had another lead to follow up, but he means to come here to speak with us."

My heart leapt a beat. I'd missed Ezra.

More importantly, I knew how to get what I wanted from Lavinia and to make it up to Ezra.

"But first, we must step up your training," said Echo. "We cannot wait for Wildwoods to sanction the next stage of your education. They may have assigned the wolf as your mentor, but they forget that I, Chanakya Gunbir Hredhaan of Maharashtra, have deep knowledge of my own. It was for good reason that I stood beside Rajika Verma. My beauty may turn heads, but I am powerful in my own right."

"Lighten up, dude," said Marina. "You're starting to sound like a 1990s supermodel. No need to prove how big your rod is to us. We know you're awesome."

He swished his tail. "Everyone likes others to be aware of their value, Marina Ambrose. It doesn't hurt to state it out loud sometimes. It's a good thing you brought me some rump steak this morning because otherwise, I'd think your mockery was fighting talk."

"Oh, I meant nothing of the kind, Echo. A little teasing between friends solidifies the relationship." Marina caressed him behind the ear. She was no longer nervous around him. She could sense his moods and no longer carried tranquilliser darts with her.

Her charming nature and ability to bond with all kinds of people and animals all made sense now we'd discovered she was an empath. All these years of friendship, I had pegged myself as the moon to her sun, the shade to her warmth. She had innate strengths, just like I did.

I looked around the rooftop to ensure we were still alone and rolled up the sleeves of my blouse to show I meant business. "You say I need more training. This is as good a place as any." I raised my hands and called the familiar tingling sensation to the forefront of my mind.

Echo shook his head. "No need for that, druid. I want to teach you to cast spells."

I exchanged glances with Marina. We might have been middle-aged, but something about this new life made us feel like kids in a sweet shop.

"Are you sure?" I said. "The Educator's Law states that new users of magic must be supervised until they pass the trial."

"Am I not supervising you?"

I didn't dare say that he technically didn't count as much as a person. To be honest, I preferred him to most people anyway. "Minister Willowsun said that learning spells would happen once my initial training was completed."

Echo narrowed his eyes. "Always the paper-pushers thinking they know what's best. Let me tell you, druid, there will be no completion of the initial training if you don't survive the next encounter. What will it be?"

I took a step forward. "Teach me."

"And me," said Marina. "Can I cast spells too?"

"Any peculiar can cast spells, given enough instruction and practice, so long as they have a source of power to draw on. For druids, this power is nature. For empaths, it is depth of emotion. You, Marina, must harness the strongest emotion you can muster and hold it there while you perform the spell. Alisha, you must learn to feel the currents around you. It might manifest as a vibration or a hum. Or you might learn to see them, even though they are invisible to the naked eye. Ground yourself in nature, draw on it, and your spells will rise to the occasion."

"Why have I never seen you cast a spell?" I said.

"How do you think I make the carcasses of all the animals I eat disappear? It's not like I can leave them scattered around London, leading back to me like breadcrumbs."

I gasped. "But when you stalked Milo the poodle the other night, you said you'd leave enough for burial."

"That was just a lie to make you feel better," he purred.

Marina tucked a lock of pink hair behind her ear. "I'm impressed. Let's do this. What's our first trick?"

"I'll begin by teaching you a handful of spells I think will be useful. Later, with deeper study, you may be able to create your own spells and your own manner of performing them."

Marina shuddered. "Next, he'll have us playing with voodoo dolls."

"No voodoo dolls required," said Echo. "I knew this moment would come. I have been meditating on the very choice of spells during my nightly jaunts. The taste of blood always brings me my best ideas. The first spell we will practice is Būmarēnga."

"Būmarēnga," said Marina.

"Wait, what does Būmarēnga do?" I said.

Shrewd emerald eyes shone. "That's why it's so perfect. It returns a spell to its owner. For example, if Ra turns his heat on you, act quickly, and this spell will turn his own powers against him."

Marina's eyes widened. "Will that work on a god?"

"That, I do not know," said Echo. "But it is a magnificent defence spell, and without it in this fight, you are dung beetles on your back. Now, listen closely. It is important to make the first B soft, to roll the R and to end with a soft G. Gather your emotions or ground yourself to nature, focus on the subject of the spell and say the word exactly as taught. Any discrepancy and the spell won't work, and your death will likely be swift."

"Do we need a wand?" said Marina cheerfully, completely at odds with my sombre mood.

I was starting to realise we were preparing for a battlefield.

"Do I look like I need a wand?" Echo said with the disdain of a bored king. "There are any number of tools that are used in spell casting. Some use wands. For others, a word plus a gesture suffices. Some spells call for feathers or bells. Others yet use airborne seeds or knotted ribbons. Sometimes spells use frankincense or clover or the heads of decapitated flowers. Some dark souls use blood or body parts. Spells require imagination and skill and are only as small as your ambition. I, too, take my energy from the ground I have soaked with the blood of beloved pets, roaming livestock and decorative beasts."

Marina raised an eyebrow in question.

"Don't ask," I said. "It's better not to know. So Būmarēnga then. Shall we give it a go?"

"For a language teacher, your pronunciation leaves much to be desired, druid," said Echo. "Send me a strong breeze, and I will use the spell and show you how it is done. Remember to brace yourself for the reverse blast."

"Okay." I raised my hands and braced my feet. My hands tingled, and I directed the current at him with more force than I intended.

Echo's green eyes skewered me with an intense gaze. There was a slight rocking of his head and then, "Būmarēnga," spoken with gentle determination.

The breeze reversed, hitting me full in the chest, with a force I hadn't expected. I flew backwards across the rooftop, past the drying rack with Dotty's greying underwear, past the motley assortment of chairs, past Marina, her eyes wide in shock, and towards the guard rail.

My heartbeat in my ears, I reached out to grab something, anything, but my fingers flailed.

I thudded against a hard chest. Strong arms helped me regain my balance.

"Looks like I got here just in time," said a familiar voice.

He was a sight for sore eyes in rumpled clothing, bringing

with him a rueful smile and the musky scent of mountain earth.

I disentangled myself from Ezra and scrambled over to Marina's side for safety. My legs were jelly, probably from my near-death experience, but I couldn't rule out Ezra as the cause of the butterflies in my tummy.

"Now, now, cat, what's going on here?" said Ezra.

"Just a spot of spell-casting, dog. You know, to build up the home team's arsenal. I told Alisha you were coming."

"I am indebted." Ezra bowed to him as if there had been a shift in their relationship, and respect had taken root. Brown hair flopped into grey eyes.

Marina piped up, "Hi, Ezra. Want to join us in practising Būmarēnga?"

He let out a low whistle. "So that's what you've been teaching them, cat. It's a bold move."

"Do you cast spells, wolf? You are half wizard, after all," said Echo.

"You have the upper hand there, cat. I have only a rudimentary understanding. I was brought up by the wolves, after all. I rely on my wolf side, my teleporting and my charms."

"Then I can teach you a trick or two."

"I am perfectly happy with my lot. Wolves have enough to cope with during the change without inviting more unpredictability into our lives." Just as I was starting to feel forgotten, he turned to me. "Before you continue, I have something to say to Alisha. I heard about your mother's friend, hellfire. I'm truly sorry. She seemed like a nice woman."

"She was." I held his gaze. "Where have you been?"

"I've only been gone two days. You miss me?"

"Urgh, get a room already," said Marina.

I ignored her. "You didn't answer my question, Ezra."

He shrugged. "I'm not good at conflict. I get angry. For

some wolves, that means changing to work out their anger; damn the consequences. Others run wild to iron out the rage. For me, teleporting means I get the hell out of there. I'm sorry I walked out on you."

"I'm sorry I wasn't up front."

"When I stopped smarting about our disagreement, I decided to make good on that promise I made you when we first met." He jerked his hand through his brown hair. "You did want to find the Celestial Library?"

A warm glow spread through me. He'd put me first despite being angry at me. Not even my husband had done that. "Did you find it?"

Ezra shook his head. "It should be a cinch for me to hold on to the threads of it, but it's been moving around. I can't get a grip. I teleport, and there is only residue in the slipstream like the library has moved seconds before."

Echo growled. "That only happens for one reason. The Custodian has activated the library's defences. She thinks it is under threat."

"Exactly," said Ezra. "But that's just it. Why would the Custodian feel that she is under threat? There has been no word from Aunt Lavinia that the Celestial Library is in danger, no noise in ministerial communications or mobilising of the Otherworld armies. It got me thinking we're being blindsided, and I was stupid to doubt you. That's why I came back. The right thing to do is rarely the easiest. You might be new to all of this, Alisha, but I trust your instincts. If I have to surrender a vial of my blood to my aunt, so be it."

Electricity pulsed between us.

"I won't let it come to that." I frowned, putting the pieces together. "Gaia said the gods had been weakened without prayer. At night class, the electrician said that if humans had worshipped the gods in gratitude, he wouldn't have to cause you pain."

"He hopes to trigger an outpouring of grief," said Marina.

Ezra sighed. "Grief is a more reliable basis for prayer than gratitude."

"We need to call the detective," said Marina. "And not just because I fancy him."

"We need to call Lavinia, too," I said to Ezra. "I have a plan. The question is, do you trust me?"

A frisson of static electricity sparked between us.

He nodded. "I trust you, Alisha."

"If we fail, it's possible he'll come after us."

"Let him come," said Echo. "We will be ready."

"I'm going to load up on horseshoes and four-leaf clovers and wear my grandmother's cross," said Marina. "I reckon we'll come out okay."

"We're all on the same page, then," said Ezra.

I took a deep breath and dialled Baba Yaga's Gym.

23

Lavinia Drach's singsong voice swam down the phone line into my ear. "Baba Yaga's Gymnasium. How can I help?"

I prayed I was doing the right thing. "Lavinia? It's Alisha Verma."

A pause during which I sensed her glee. "Why, hello, dear. The detective crushed my hopes of you calling."

Ezra, Marina and Echo leaned in to listen. A vein throbbed in Ezra's neck.

I blocked out their anxious faces. "I changed my mind."

"My nephew is on board?" said Lavinia.

"Yes."

A shriek of delight. "How wonderful."

"You are prepared to go against the senate to help in this matter?"

"The coven is agreed. We shall proceed to protect humdrums. It won't be the first time the Magical Constitution can be interpreted this way," said Lavinia.

"And the witches will fulfil their role steadfastly, despite the difficulties of facing this opponent? He is very powerful."

"So are my sisters and me," said Lavinia. "These meagre

gods are nothing like they once were. Our protection spells guard us well. What's the worst the electrician can do? I suppose he could pull the plug on the studio, but as I said, my little rat darlings have long seen to it that Baba Yaga's Gymnasium is self-sustaining. I take it you have a plan?"

I outlined it for her. It was a long shot, but I'd found a way for her to protect scientists. We just had to figure out how to ensure Ra didn't try this stunt again.

She listened, um-ing and aah-ing. "What an unusual approach, but yes, I think it might work. Of course, it will need a lot of focus, a pound of flesh from the electrician and maybe the third eyelids of a thousand lizards, but I can give my supplier a call."

"We will need to make sure he is neutralised and can't do harm again."

"You are asking for miracles that aren't possible, druid. We are a motley crew of peculiars facing a god. He may be diminished, but he is still a god. I cannot bind his powers. If I did, what would happen to the dawn? We can only clip his wings and make sure he is sufficiently subdued. Imprisonment may be a possibility, but I think the best we can hope for is thwarting him and escaping with our lives. Is that enough for you?"

I wanted more, but the witch was right. Without the sun, the earth would wither. "It is enough."

"After this, you will always have to look over your shoulder. I have the coven at my side. Who do you have?"

I looked from Marina to Ezra to Echo. "My friends."

"That leaves only one thing."

My throat was parched from the stress of this conversation. "What's that?"

Her laugh tinkled down the phone line. "It's time to talk terms, of course."

"I thought we could discuss that side of things at the gym. Bring the detective on board."

"The detective has nothing to trade, dear. At least, nothing of value to me. Whereas you have my nephew in the palm of your pretty hand."

I clipped my words, a tactic adopted from managing unruly kids in the classroom. "State your terms, Lavinia."

"A vial of forty millilitres of Ezra's blood then, not a drop less, to be taken by one of the coven at the conclusion of our business. No refunds, no hanky-panky. If you fall foul of these terms, the coven will forcibly take what we are owed. Do you agree to these terms, Alisha?"

How neatly she had stepped from the role of aunty to businesswoman. Ezra was right to fear her. "You promise that the threat we face will be neutralised?"

"I do."

I pressed my lips together. "Then we have a deal."

"Marvellous, dear. Heads up."

"Excuse me?" A whistling came down the line like the nearing of an aeroplane, culminating in a rush of sound and a prick on my neck. I touched my neck, bewildered.

Marina rushed over to inspect it. "There's a black dot on your neck, like a mole. It's really weird."

"Hello, empath. It's just a reminder to Alisha to honour our deal. The mole will fade when I am satisfied I have received my lot. Otherwise, it'll be a stain on her body to mirror the stain on her conscience. I was feeling kind. She's lucky it's not a nasty wart. I save those for the dodgier characters I deal with."

"Bloody brilliant." I frowned at Ezra. He could have warned me about his aunt's weird rituals. I made a mental note to zap it with my cupboard full of face creams. Time was enough of a meddler in a person's appearance without witches getting involved too.

"Shall we meet at the gym tomorrow evening to have a run-through, say six p.m. after closing?" said Lavinia. "We can strike at midnight when the humdrums are sleeping. It's

Tuesday, so with any luck, they won't be out drinking, although you never know with the Brits. Any excuse for a booze up."

"That is wise," said Ezra. "The sun god will be weakest when the night is darkest."

My heartbeat sped up. "You want to attack tomorrow?"

"Why yes, dear. We'll strike while the iron is hot. No use risking even more lives being lost to that debauched soul. I'll invite the detective to the warm-up, but he best stays away from the real fight. He's a humdrum, too, after all."

I gulped.

"Be sure to get some good rest. And maybe do some stretches in case you have to dodge any projectiles. Too late to get you to lose the extra inches, I suppose, but limbering up will help."

Charming. "Until tomorrow then, Minister."

"Until tomorrow, druid."

I hung up the phone and turned to my friends. "It's all set."

Echo broke into a rendition of Kelly Clarkson's 'Stronger (What Doesn't kill You)'.

Ezra sighed. "We have come to our moment of reckoning, and the cat is quoting song lyrics again."

"Even in the face of death, I am continuing my attempts to integrate into this culture," said Echo.

"Just for the record," said Ezra, "there's not an extra inch on you. My aunt's a little militant about fitness, that's all."

Marina nodded. "Too right. Now shall we practice Būmarēnga? I have a feeling we're going to need it."

The last of Baba Yaga's buff, Lycra-clad clientele left as my friends and I, Echo in tow, entered the gym on the dot of six p.m. I kept glancing at my watch as the minutes ticked away to when we'd face Ra. If we could lure him to the fight, that was. We sat on pink tub chairs in reception while the coven and their rat familiars cleared the gym, our mouths gaping.

Only Ezra kept his calm. He had visited his aunt's gym often enough to know what to expect.

"They look tasty," said Echo. "A rat before a hunt is like a humdrum eating olives as a starter. It's a very civilised thing to do."

"I wouldn't kid yourself," said Ezra. "They'll transform you into a bug before you have the chance."

"The witches?" said Echo, still considering it.

"The rats."

"Did you bring what I asked?" I whispered to Marina.

"Yeah. With any luck, they won't search me." She knocked on the wooden coffee table in front of us, then raised her voice a notch. "Poor Ezra was a bit of a wally about the extraction, but he'll live."

"I heard that," said Ezra.

She ignored him, fascinated by the rats at work. "Rats really are much more intelligent than I gave them credit for. Look at that one using antibacterial spray on the CrossFit. And that one over there, levitating while his teeny tiny rat hands get the smears off the mirror. Oh, and that one over there. He's my favourite. Who knew rats were strong enough to lift weights?"

"Magical rats," said Ezra. "There's a big difference."

"I'd guess magical rats are much like their humdrum counterparts. They are incontinent, of course, but with a little effort, they can be litter-trained."

"Yuck." All this talk of incontinent rodents was making me want to vomit in my mouth.

"I think they're rather magnificent. Not as magnificent as you, Echo, but much less expensive to keep. They're easy on the eye too. Look at that sweetheart over there, all snowy white with a pink nose and a flourish of whiskers. I'd quite like one of my own. Think what a help it would be after surgery. Or if I could use one to help with procedures I hate. Like squeezing anal glands," said Marina as Detective Jameson tumbled through the door.

He caught the tail end of her sentence and pulled a disgusted face. "Hello, folks. Did I miss anything? There's never a good time to talk about anal glands in public, Marina. Nice to see you've fully recovered from Ravynne's truth serum, though. I did feel guilty playing along with that."

Marina gave him a warm smile. "Nice of you to say. You must have to make tough choices as a detective."

"You have no idea." He settled into a chair and eyed the coven at work. "First time I saw this, I passed out. When I came round, I was laid out on the floor with Elvira holding smelling salts under my nose, and Lavinia had taken off my shoes to make me comfortable. That's when I knew they were a good lot. A criminal would have taken the chance to stick the boot into a vulnerable officer."

Echo honked with laughter. "The detective doesn't seem to realise the witches probably pickled parts of him while he was unconscious."

Lavinia strode over, wiping her hands on a towel.

"I'll have you know we did no such thing. Robert is one of the few men we tolerate very well. Not as well as you, of course, dear nephew." She reached up to kiss Ezra's cheek.

"Aunty, you look well," he said.

She pulled back to look at him. "You could do with a shave."

"There'll be time for that later."

"Indeed." She turned to Echo. "And you must be Rajika Verma's famed leopard."

Echo growled. "You speak as though I am a belonging, witch. Although it is true my purpose is to be of service to the Verma family line."

"Lucky them," said Lavinia. "I am honoured to meet you,

Chanakya Gunbir Hredhaan of Maharashtra. I have been looking forward to our paths crossing since Rajika Verma registered you at the Wildwoods data bank."

He purred in delight. "You took time to learn my name."

"Of course, Chanakya. It is not often that one lives in the same city as a magical leopard of historical note. Your name is hard to forget."

"I like this witch," said Echo.

Lavinia swung around to the coven and the familiars, still bustling around the gym and clapped above her head like a flamenco dancer. "Right, my dears. That's enough for today. The gym is positively sparkling."

Her coven and the rats lined up, waiting for her next command.

I waved goodbye to Elvira, the soft-spoken witch who had tended to me so kindly. She struck me as the coven member I'd most like to go for a drink with. She seemed to lack the fire and the manipulative agenda of the rest of the coven, and I liked her all the better for it.

"We'll use studio one for our planning session," said Lavinia. "Any hungry souls can make requests of the rats. Ravynne's little one is especially talented in the kitchen."

I cringed inside but kept my expression polite, just as Mum had taught me as a child. "I've eaten, thanks. Anyone else hungry?"

"Nope," said Detective Jameson.

"Nah, all good." Marina wrinkled her nose.

"I think we're all set, Aunt Lavinia," said Ezra.

Lavinia nodded. "As you wish. Let's get on with business, then. Six hours until midnight, and our success lies in how well we prepare. Come along, now. Studio one is this way."

We followed her into the studio and lined up against the walls: seven witches and their rats, a werewolf, a druid, an empath, a leopard and a humdrum. I'd hoped Lavinia would take command, but when she beckoned me into the centre of the room, I swallowed my nerves and stood by her side.

"Over to you, Alisha," she said. "You're in the driving seat."

Eighteen sets of eyes turned on me.

I'm pretty sure a trickle of wee escaped me.

My voice wavered, growing stronger as I hit my flow. "Tonight, we face the sun god. He's not going to be an easy foe. While Gaia had a hand in guiding us here today, she had not responded to my calls for aid. The electrician is one diminished being who has lost his path. A fallen god. A murderer. We are many, and we stand on the side of right. On the side of the innocent. On the side of the healers. In the next few hours, though we are strangers, we will become a team, and we will prevail."

"She's good at pep talks," said Ezra.

"You should have seen her debate at school. I'd follow her anywhere," said Marina. "She's an exceptional teacher."

I gave them a stern look. "Pay attention, you two."

Marina grinned. "See?"

"Step forward, Detective. You brought your Taser?" I said.

He nodded. "I did."

"As a humdrum, the detective will not be on the battlefield. But he will be available on the phone to coordinate the operation should anything go wrong. For now, he will play the sun god as we practice our roles. Pick a partner and make sure you have each other's backs. As soon as the electrician appears, we will surround and subdue him. It may take force, and you must be willing to use it."

Lavinia gestured to a roll of thick rubber material in the corner. "Morgan, Agatha, Ravynne, bring that here. Our goal is to wrap him in it until the deed is done. An immobilisation spell may slow him down. Maybe a lasso spell to bind him. We'll be practising on the detective shortly."

I nodded. "While the sun god is subdued, Lavinia,

Chandra and Isadora will cast the protection spell over the world's scientists. We have no hope of subduing the god after the deed is done, but the witches can fly, and Ezra can teleport the rest out of there to take stock. Objective one is to save the scientists. Objective two is to escape with our lives."

Lavinia spoke up at my side. "A nice practical approach, druid. I'd much rather be a realist than an idealist. I have gathered most of the ingredients for the spell. The third eyelids of a thousand lizards, one kilogram of rosemary, 308 grams of eucalyptus, 268 grams of Egyptian sand, eighty-one tablespoons of Himalayan salt, a dozen stethoscopes, an amethyst, an inch-wide chunk of obsidian. It is a difficult spell, given the vast coverage required, but I have checked and double-checked my calculations. The memory stick? A quite brilliant idea, Alisha, if I might say."

"Detective, do you have it?" I asked.

Detective Jameson pulled a slim silver-and-red memory stick from the pocket of his jeans. "They are all here. NHS numbers for every scientist known to the British government, together with a list of private health insurance policy numbers for international scientists. This should do the job."

Sorrow filled my voice, but I had wracked my brains and hadn't had a further lightbulb moment. "Those without health cover will fall through the cracks, but most will be protected. Unless anyone else has a better idea?"

Lavinia shrugged her bony shoulders. "All spells have their caveats. We are not gods. Beyond pulling a hair, fingernail or tooth from every living or decomposing scientist, I can't see a better way of casting such a large protection spell. Of course, protection spells don't impact natural causes and have been trialled before."

"A blanket protection spell is also used as a safety net for pupils at Wildwoods," said Elvira.

"And for much-loved rat familiars who are on missions without the protection of the coven," said Ravynne.

Lavinia steepled her fingers together. "There's just one more ingredient the spell requires. The pound of flesh we will need to take from the sun god tonight."

"You ridicule us, sister, by insisting on this folly. Taking flesh from a god is nigh on impossible," said Isadora, Ezra's red-haired aunty with the elfin cut.

Lavinia's voice was icy. "Quiet, sister. Always the dissenting voice. Always the one to rain on our parade. The diminished god is no match for a united coven nor our fleet of umbrellas." She turned her eyes to Ezra. "What we win is more than worth the risk."

"Your hubris will be the death of us, sister," said Isadora.

Lavinia stepped towards her, full of intent. "Calm yourself, Isadora. Or leave the room."

Isadora lowered her head.

Lavinia pressed on. "Aim to take a toe. That should suffice and will be far less risky than leaving his hands exposed."

"Echo, that will be your job. Your teeth will be quicker than any knife. Just ensure you don't swallow it. Ezra will be your partner. If you are in danger, he will teleport you to safety."

"You have experience summoning the gods. How will we lure the electrician to the battleground?" said Lavinia.

"Experience would be an exaggeration. I succeeded once with Gaia, but I had help."

"You sell yourself short," said Lavinia. "You are the only one in this room who has seen the gods four times in the past fortnight. I understand Gaia attended your mother's memorial, you summoned her to Wandsworth Common, you crossed paths with the electrician while saving Melissa Ramsay's life, and he killed Nita Mubarak at your night glass."

I gulped. "You are remarkably well informed."

"I told you, our rats are formidable spies."

A large rat, the size of my forearm, saluted and bowed as if claiming credit for the missions involving me.

I gave him a thumbs-up in appreciation of his skill, then addressed the room. "I have no tried-and-tested means to summon the electrician, but if I were to guess, it would mean that we acquire an offering of value to him and then clasp our hands together and focus all our attention on his name. It worked once for Gaia."

Lavinia nodded. "Then that is what we will do."

"But what is of value to the sun god?" said Marina.

"Remember, the sun god is now an electrician. How about a new set of tools?" said Detective Jameson.

"That would be fine if we wanted to bore him to death," said Lavinia.

I nodded. "An offering must inspire. We can't risk him ignoring us."

The large rat emitted a series of squeaks.

Echo honked with laughter. "The rat cannot speak."

"We understood perfectly what he said." Elvira smiled. "Those are very clever ideas, Ignacio. He suggested shares in a solar panel company or a swanky Tesla."

A smile spread across Lavinia's face, making her wrinkles seem less harsh. "That is it! Chandra, you know Elon. Call in that favour. I'm sure he can spare something from the London showroom. Maybe one of the ones with doors that open like wings."

"Consider it done," said Chandra.

"In ancient Egypt, the sun god was known to be partial to pomegranate wine. Fei Yen and Faeza sell it by the bucketload at Shanghai Moon," I said.

"I'll head down in the van to pick some up," said Marina.

I nodded. "A swanky Tesla and a bucketful of pomegranate wine. I hope this works."

"Hunting hour is almost upon us," purred Echo. "May we be victorious."

Lavinia's copper-flecked eyes glinted. "May we shed the blood of our enemies."

"Detective, are you ready for role-play? Let's have a run-through, shall we?"

He clenched his jaw, eyeing us all, and readied his Taser.

I raised my hands.

The witches picked up their umbrellas. The rats, who had been standing on two legs, braced themselves on all fours. Ezra's hand hovered above his charm necklace. Marina mouthed Būmarēnga under her breath.

Echo grinned, sensing blood. "Watch out for your toes, Detective."

"Go!" I said.

The wooden floor sprang as we launched ourselves towards him.

24

The night was cold and dreary. I'd dressed in yoga leggings and a hoodie and popped some paracetamol in advance in the hope of warding off any forthcoming pain. My courage flickered on and off like a faulty lightbulb. I hadn't told Dad the plan because his anxiety, on top of my own, would be my undoing.

The thought of burying myself under my duvet with only Netflix for company was all too tempting. Hell, I even preferred the thought of a raging argument with my ex-husband across the kitchen table.

But Mum had died at Ra's hands. What kind of daughter would turn a blind eye?

I wouldn't close my eyes. I wouldn't wish myself back into my hellish marriage. I chose to live my best life, and this was it.

For the summoning and subsequent battle, Lavinia and I settled on a dilapidated carpet warehouse in Tooting. On a road full of storage depots, sofa shops and building merchants, the area was deserted at night.

We arrived separately.

Ezra teleported, Detective Jameson had his own car, and Chandra roared up the street in the Tesla. Echo and I rode with Marina in her work van, together with the case of pomegranate wine from Shanghai Moon.

Outside the warehouse, the moon illuminated our sombre faces and the sparkling red Tesla.

Ezra reached for his moon charm. The street lamps reflected on the rain-slicked road, then flared and petered out. A hum met my ears as the coven flew through the sky in formation. The witches were dressed in matching neon gym gear, more cheerleading squad than coven.

"That is awesome," Marina whispered.

"The time is nigh." Lavinia dismounted with ease.

"Fast forward a few hours, and this will all be behind us," said Detective Jameson.

I nodded. "Time for you to take your position, Detective."

The bumps and bruises he nursed from our practice run showed the Otherworld was no place for humdrums.

"Good luck." He sprinted across the street to his car, where a vast array of laptops and mysterious phones waited. His role was to keep local police away and to be our safety net in case we messed things up.

At least someone would be able to tell Dad our fate.

"Does everyone have their heatproof gloves on? Have you applied sunscreen?" These seemed logical precautions to take against the sun god.

"Yup." Marina played nervously with her grandmother's cross. She'd gone overboard in a thick layer of Soltan and dark glasses, despite the late hour. She wore skateboarding gear with elbow and shin pads, plus a bandana pulled over her rainbow locks.

I'd been tempted to bench her like Detective Jameson. Her empath powers meant she had fewer offensive moves than the rest of us, but the truth was, I always felt safer with

Marina at my back, and I needed her here with me to help pull this heist off.

"We should limber up." Lavinia jogged on the spot, along with the rest of the coven, rats included. "At our age, it makes all the difference. Many a battle has been won or lost on the flexibility of the fighters."

"This is quite unlike Rajika Verma's battle preparations. And quite ridiculous." Echo had almost gone on strike when he'd realised the freezer steaks were all finished. A hunt was his bread and butter, and he didn't seem fazed by tonight.

Lavinia tutted. "Nevertheless, Chanakya, you should not discourage us. A leopard may not need a warm-up to progress from a sedentary position to battle mode, but the rest of us do."

"Ezra, can you get the Tesla inside?" I transferred the crate of wine to the passenger seat.

He wore his usual low-slung jeans and a T-shirt, but a stiffness radiated from his body like he was keenly aware of the stakes.

"Give me a minute to check the internal layout," he said.

Ezra vanished and reappeared seconds later next to the car. Then that, too, disappeared with him into the innards of the building.

We followed him inside and surveyed the layout. High ceilings, solid walls and the odd abandoned roll of carpet littered the concrete floor. The roof had seen better days, but holes in it allowed the airborne ones amongst us to swoop in and out. The fire-engine red Tesla stood in the middle of the space.

Behind me, Lavinia, Chandra and Isadora pulled in a wheelie bin and extracted ingredients from their satchels. I'd expected a more traditional cauldron, but by now, I'd learned the vast differences between what I had read in fairy tales and the reality of Otherworld customs.

The ingredients in the wheelie bin caldron fizzed along with my nerves.

Ezra had the roll of rubber tucked under his arm. My skin tingled as he leaned into my ear.

"Be careful," he said. "I have my own role tonight and won't be able to jump to your rescue. Make sure Elvira has your back. I'm the one who coaxed you into your first steps as a peculiar. I won't forgive myself if you get hurt."

The gentle witch Elvira and I had been paired, while Marina had inexplicably been paired with Ignacio, the fat rat. Marina didn't seem to mind, and Ignacio himself had entered a state of bliss as soon as Marina had invited him into the crook of her arm. He might have had a reputation as a master spy, but the gooey eyes he was making at Marina left me in severe doubt that he could protect her. So I'd relegated her to the outer circle of the warehouse.

I read the worry in Ezra's eyes. "You're not responsible for anything that happens tonight. I'm a grown woman. I make my own decisions. Besides, I'm as tough as old boots. I'll be fine. Just make sure you are too."

He'd be responsible for teleporting the rubber roll next to Ra before we subdued him. It took either stupidity or supreme courage to take on that role. I couldn't figure out why he'd take the risk, but I was grateful he was part of the team.

My watch showed it had gone midnight. The sun was set to rise at 5.40 a.m. Ra would be stronger then. We needed to use the window of darkness to our advantage.

"It's time, Lavinia," I said.

I sent up a prayer to the universe that we would come out of this unscathed and victorious.

Lavinia looked up from the wheelie bin. "Very well, druid."

"We work together. We stay clear of Ra's hands. We do the job cleanly. We get the hell out of there and regroup," I said.

We stood in a circle and raised our gloved hands in prayer.

It didn't matter that Dad was Hindu, Mum was Christian or that I was ambivalent about religion. Or that we had a Jew, pagans, agnostics and atheists within our number. We pressed our palms together in prayer because that was what the god wanted. His vanity would be how we lured him here.

"Ra." I rolled his name off my tongue. "We pray to you. We entreat you to appear to us."

"Ra," chanted the team. "We pray to you."

We repeated our pleas three times over. Just when we had begun to lose heart, the air stilled, and we fell silent. The goosebumps on my skin from the cold night receded.

Elvira grabbed my hand, her face white as a sheet. "He comes."

Warmth filled the room and deepened into heat. I closed my eyes to the blinding light, and my body broke out in a sweat.

The god's voice boomed. "You dare summon me, druid? What odd ensemble of worshippers have you brought me? What novel offering is this?"

I peeked through my fingers. A surreal, golden glow filled the warehouse, despite the moonlit sky.

Ra stood before us, naked from the waist up, with eyes of liquid fire in his tanned face. He had the build of a manual labourer. He was a brawler, not a talker. His black-tipped fingers sparked with heat.

Fierce pride bubbled up inside me. It had worked.

This was our chance.

I ignored the beads of perspiration that threaded down my back. I needed to keep him busy. "Mighty Ra, this electric car is for you. It will be self-sustaining with your talents."

He surveyed it with a bored expression. "The London underground quite suffices for my needs."

Gaia was right: there could be no pleasing eternal beings.

Echo bowed, showing immediate deference as he had to Gaia. "Perhaps a Tesla is not to your taste. Indian rickshaws are excellent, your godliness, if you want to feel the wind in your fur."

Amber eyes swept across us like a predator searching out his prey.

My voice jittered as I gestured to the passenger seat. "We present you also with a case of pomegranate wine."

He peered inside, his strong biceps and barrel body sending spikes of fear through me. "The wine is a welcome gesture, druid. It evokes memories of a bygone age."

With the god distracted, the witches stepped out of the circle to the wheelie bin.

The rest of us edged closer to him in pairs, bracing ourselves against the heat: Elvira and I, Ezra and Echo, plus the witches Ravynne, Agatha and Morgan clutching their umbrellas, accompanied by their rat familiars.

"Now, Ezra," I muttered under my breath.

Quick as a flash, he teleported closer and appeared behind Ra with the roll of rubber.

The god spun around, his eyes blazing gold.

We surrounded him, struggling to get the material around him. I raised my hands to call forth my powers and encircled Ra in a channel of wind, a buffer, to keep him from our vulnerable bodies. I fought instinctively to keep our team safe, pushing myself further than I had before, crying out as we held him in position.

His sparks flew at us, seeping into our skin and causing tiny welts.

Ezra teleported back and forth, evading Ra's rage, attempting to trap him as planned. We pressed Ra against the red wing door of the Tesla, and it sizzled, melting out of form. Agatha, Ravynne and Morgan chanted their immobilisation spell, but Ra broke free. His arm sent Agatha spiralling to the floor and singed her familiar, who lay belly up on the floor.

I sent a gust of wind to edge the unconscious rat out of harm's way.

"You'll pay for this!" bellowed Ra, turning up the heat.

Grunts of exertion met my ears. As the temperatures reached sauna level, I wasn't sure how long we'd last.

Agatha dragged herself to her feet, cast a look at her familiar and returned to the fold, her face a storm, her umbrella held aloft like a wand. Sparks and smoke flew from its end, but they bounced off the god.

I watched in horror as the friendly fire came my way.

"Būmarēnga," I said, but it didn't work.

Elvira shouted another unfamiliar word, and the sparks evaporated between our eyes.

There wasn't time for thank yous.

Ravynne and Morgan chanted their spell, their faces pained with concentration as they slowed him down. Their rats scuttled over the thick rubber, hot-stepping across the surface with nimble hands, but they didn't dare bite the god for fear of being burned.

Any moment, Ra would break free of the spell and tip the balance in his favour.

"We need the final ingredient, druid. Hurry," shouted Lavinia over the ruckus.

"He's too close to the car," I said, struggling to breathe. "We'll never manage it."

I leapt onto the car, followed by Elvira and then Ezra.

"No skin contact. Now!" I called.

We leapt. Elvira and Ezra shoved him with their gloved hands. My blow came a fraction of a second later: a foot jab from kickboxing class, as if all my classes had led to this moment. As if my forty years of trundling along at average speed suddenly caused me to blow a gasket, lending extra oomph to my kick and sending Ra toppling to the floor.

"Yeah!" whooped mild-mannered Elvira as I skidded

across the roof of the Tesla like a scene from *The Fast and the Furious*, feeling more badass than ever before.

The rubber of my shoes melted, and sore skin poked out.

But it was worth it. The move took the wind from his sails.

We had a brief moment to shore up our advantage and rolled him like a sausage in a blanket across the concrete until he was tightly wrapped. Ravynne turned her belt into a lasso that snaked around him to keep the rubber in place.

My heart hammered in my throat. "Echo, now!"

He hadn't played a part so far, but his paws were a disadvantage. Now was his time to shine, except he didn't look in a hurry to move. His head had dipped, and the fur on his neck lay smooth. Usually, his tail flicked in excitement in anticipation of a hunt. Right now, it lay between his legs. He neither snarled nor snapped to show his aggression.

Panic flared inside me. He was submitting to the god.

"Echo, you have to move. Just like we discussed."

He turned emerald eyes on me.

"You are in service to the Vermas. To me."

Behind me, Ra stirred. "He is in service to me now. Make her pay, leopard."

Echo growled, baring his teeth. He leapt, and his fur shimmered like I had never seen before as if he had the metallic sheen of armour.

I tensed, a rush of blood in my ears.

There was no good way to die. I would be with Mum. Dad would be okay. Ezra would get Marina out of here. At least I'd tried.

Echo leapt, and when he landed, I heard a roar and realised the roar was not his.

My leopard held the god's toe between his teeth like a trophy and ambled over to the wheelie bin, where he dropped the last ingredient into the spell.

My heart bloomed.

"There can be no good fortune for those who defy the

gods." Ra dripped with gore. Rage filled every syllable. "Humans forget how short their lives are and how expendable."

I nodded. "Perhaps, but Rosalie Verma was my mother." I needed to say her name. "And this is for her."

25

Lavinia, Chandra and Isadora rocked on the balls of their feet over the wheelie bin, their brows covered in sweat. The stench of molten plastic and garden herbs filled the room. Particles dispersed into the air, and the witches' perfectly composed demeanour evaporated. Their hair grew frizzy. Their eyes rolled back in their heads. Their bodies made jerking movements.

This was unlike the spell at the Kraglek ceremony at Wildwoods. This spell wasn't effortless. It seemed to cost them.

It cost Ra, too, judging by the milky pallor of his skin.

Finally, Lavinia came back to herself. She looked older than when she had started. "It is done. The scientists are safe. Who knows how many lives we have saved tonight? But the rubber and lasso have already begun to weaken. They will not hold him long. Hand the vial of Ezra's blood to Elvira, and we can leave."

Ra had closed his eyes.

A duo of witches, Ravynne and Morgan, watched him while their coven sister tended to the fallen familiar. I wasn't fooled. There was no way Ra would give up this easily. And I was pretty certain I didn't want to be around when he broke loose or another toe grew. That would be gross.

"We'll make the exchange elsewhere," I said.

Lavinia held my gaze, ignoring the weakened god at my feet. "No, we'll make it here."

The mole on my neck throbbed like I'd been stung by a mosquito.

Ezra bristled. "Aunty, have you no trust?"

Her tight smile did not reach her eyes. "A deal's a deal, nephew dearest."

This was all wrong. Our plan to protect Ezra hinged on us handing over the vial of his blood in a celebratory atmosphere where the witches would be distracted. But what choice did I have with the minister being so insistent?

I beckoned Marina. "Fine. Go ahead."

Marina closed the gap between us, accompanied by Ignacio. I understood now why he had been paired with her. His keen eyes followed her every move. They gave Ra a wide berth and approached Elvira at my side. Marina fished out the vial from the pocket of her skater shorts and handed the vial to Elvira.

"Thank you," said the gentle witch, uncorking the vial.

Ravynne momentarily left her post by Ra to smell the blood and clasp Ezra's wrist. "It is his."

"Then the deal is done," said Lavinia. "And the night's business is concluded. I thank you, Ezra and Alisha. It was a fair trade. Elvira, get the vial to the gym. Guard it well, child. The rest of us will destroy the evidence of this spell. Hurry, child."

I swallowed hard. Ezra hadn't wanted this. I'd failed him.

"Don't worry, druid. All will be well." Elvira walked a few steps but hesitated at a sound behind us.

A cry came from Ravynne's lips as first Morgan and then she were flung aside.

I spun around, aghast.

Ra stood tall, freed from his binding, electricity arcing from his fingertips, finding his enemies one by one.

This time, there was no element of surprise to aid us.

I turned to Marina, my chest tight with fear, and sent her and Ignacio soaring as far as I could. In the other direction, where Ezra and Echo fought side by side, a crack of bones met my ears. I swung around, fearful of whether a friend or ally had been injured, and found that Ezra had shifted. The leopard and the beautiful copper-grey wolf fought side by side, circling the god, trying to contain him.

But it was no good. As fast as they dodged his strikes, they couldn't get close enough to do enough damage. Their whimpers cut me to the core.

"Move out of the way," I said.

Echo and Ezra leapt clear.

I raised my hands, felt the familiar tingle and focused hard. A tornado unleashed from my palms and spiralled towards the roof. Great chunks of the rafters, roof tiles and chimney fell on Ra, slowing him down.

We needed a better plan.

Ra shook off the pieces of tile and wood that had fallen like rain, his eyes gleaming as if he enjoyed vengeance. As if the sun god had tired of stimulating growth. As if killing suited him better, and he could gorge himself on it.

Elvira raised her umbrella at last, a pretty travel-sized one with white polka dots on a candy-pink background.

Before she could unleash a word, she took a deep hit to her stomach.

She looked down at her wound, disbelief written on her face, and sank to the ground.

"No!" Marina rushed towards the witch, paying no heed to the vengeful god or my attempts to keep her safe.

She sank to her knees in front of Elvira just as the Drach sisters took to the air.

"Save my coven sister," called out Lavinia, swooping by.

The Drach sisters circled above Ra's head. The rest of the coven worked at ground level, sending projectiles towards the god, seeking to bury him, bringing down the building around us. Round and round went the air-bound Drach sisters, despite the heat, despite the futility of it, buying time for us to tend to Elvira.

Ra's light flooded the warehouse, but when my eyes acclimated, I saw the threads the witches had cast out, like a spider's web that trapped the god as long as they were moving.

I dropped to my knees next to Elvira.

Marina appeared to be in a trance. Her jaw was slack, and her eyes brimmed with tears. She'd removed her bandana and applied it to Elvira's wound, but the fabric was drenched in blood. Her hands rested gently on Elvira's chest.

Ignacio nuzzled the witch's hair, his eyes mournful.

I tore off my gloves and took Elvira's hand. "I didn't protect you."

Her hand was a tight fist, and her voice was barely audible. "You did what you could, druid. This isn't your fault."

I shook Marina. "Why aren't you doing something? If you can't help her, we should be calling an ambulance."

"She's taking away the pain," said Elvira, a ghost of a smile on her lips.

"I didn't know you could do that," I said.

"Neither did I," said Marina.

"Hold on, Elvira," I said as her colour drained. "Ignacio, get Lavinia. She'll know what to do."

A mere whisper from Elvira. "Stay, Ignacio, please."

The rat leaned his head against her cheek and then scurried off.

"It's too late to save me, druid." Her chest shuddered with the exertion of breathing, but there was no pain in her eyes. "I have no fear, thanks to your friend."

I glanced at the Drach sisters. They tired, circling the god.

Ignacio leapt on the floor, trying to get Lavinia's attention. Echo and Ezra fought valiantly, but they, too, were nursing wounds.

I pressed my hands together in prayer, closed my eyes and pictured the goddess. I didn't have an offering. I didn't have pretty words. But she owed me. She had set me on this path. She was the earth goddess. She could save Elvira if she wanted to; I just knew it.

"Gaia, I need you," I prayed.

The ground shuddered. "I am here, druid."

I opened my eyes, and there she was, resplendent in a sari the colour of moss, her thick, black hair loose, her cherubic face lined with worry.

"Can you save her?"

"No, but I can see to it that her essence is not lost. Life continues to flow long after mortals shed their coil." She turned to Elvira with the gentleness of a mother. "What's your favourite tree, child?"

Elvira's eyes glistened with tears. "A cherry blossom."

"It will be done," said Gaia.

Elvira's hand flopped open to reveal the vial of Ezra's blood. "Alisha, take what is yours."

My gaze darted to Lavinia, still battling to hold the god with their web. "I can't."

"You must. I have seen your path. This is the only way."

"Elvira…"

Her eyelids fluttered shut. "Tell my sisters and Ignacio I love them."

When the vial rolled off her fingers, I caught it.

A sob escaped Marina. She took Elvira's pulse and shook her head.

"She was a dear girl," said Gaia. "Like other witches, a little misguided perhaps, to use animals in servitude or as ingredients in spells. But she had a beautiful bond with her rat, so she shall have her cherry blossom."

Her graceful fingers twirled like a dancer's and coaxed a bough from a crack in the cold, grey concrete. The bough thickened as it reached up, and from its arms, cherry blossoms bloomed.

In the hiss of its growth, I heard Elvira's voice once more.

"Give me the other vial, Marina," I said.

Marina cradled Elvira's body at the foot of the cherry blossom tree. "Are you sure?"

Now was as good a time as any to make a switch. The witches were satisfied the original vial passed muster. They'd never realise this vial of wolf's blood had been prepared by Marina through her veterinary contacts. If they did, it was Ravynne who'd be in the firing line for approving the original vial.

"You heard Elvira." I prayed we'd get away with it. Lavinia wasn't one to be crossed.

I closed the dead witch's fingers around the new vial.

"Well played, druid," said Gaia. "You have the wits of Odysseus. Your grandmother would be proud. But now I must deal with Ra."

A glance at the battleground revealed that the Drach sisters had lost their grip on Ra. They retreated, along with their coven.

Morgan had sustained an arm injury, and Isadora's dress hung in threads around a wound that snaked around her torso. Echo and Ezra fought Ra still, a combination of herding and dodging that exhausted them, and they had no hope of winning the battle.

Gaia glided onto the battlefield, her hair flowing behind her.

Ra turned his blazing eyes on her, spitting the words from his bleached teeth. "Can a century pass without one god betraying another?"

Lavinia rushed over with the coven on her heels. "We need to see to our injured Elvira, and then we must all leave. When the immortals battle, mere mortals must flee."

I bowed my head. "Elvira is gone, Lavinia. I'm so sorry. Marina ensured she had no pain."

Lavinia's face crumpled.

Isadora rushed forward and knelt at Elvira's side. "I told you we'd regret this, sister. Why do you never listen?"

The coven surrounded Elvira. Their cries tore at me.

Ignacio scuttled up the fallen witch's dress and lay his body above her now still heart.

Behind us, the battle raged.

"Her last words were of her love for you all," I said.

Lavinia bent down and stroked Elvira's hair. Then she picked up Elvira's candy pink-and-white umbrella and dusted it off like a mother might tend to her daughter's things. She fought to regain her composure and addressed Marina. "Thank you, empath, for helping my fallen sister in her time of need."

Then she and the witches lifted Elvira from Marina's embrace, with Ignacio riding still on her heart.

She turned to me. "I will send a rat clean-up crew to clear the site at dawn."

The five remaining witches and rats took to the skies, holding their tender haul. They evaded the warring gods and flew up through the wrecked roof as sombre and slowly as a funeral procession.

Ra tossed out a whip of electricity, sending Echo whimpering into a corner.

I had to help.

"The leopard is under my protection. Leave him," said Gaia as vines wound around Ra.

Ra spat his words as the vines disintegrated. "You would stand here and tell me that you value these insects more than me?"

I shook Marina. "I have to get Echo and Ezra out of here before we become cannon fodder."

Marina's eyes were empty with exhaustion.

I shoved her in the direction of the door. "I'll watch your back. Get to Jameson. Meet us at the flat. We'll be right behind you."

She didn't move.

"Now!"

Marina ran out of the door, past the half-melted cauldron and abandoned gloves, into the night, where Jameson waited. The gods paid us no heed, embroiled in a war of words, energy sparking between them.

I ran to Echo and Ezra, my heart in my mouth. Both had suffered blackened flesh. Would they even be here without my insistence?

I skidded to a halt beside them. My melted rubber soles were useless. "We have to get out of here."

Echo lifted his head.

"I can't abandon the goddess," he said, bloody-minded as ever. His forelegs and neck bore Ra's impact. His beautiful coat of rosettes and white belly had been replaced by matted, bloodied fur.

The wolf nuzzled my hand. His tail had been singed, and his side charred. He, at least, seemed to agree about leaving.

I stood and raised my hands, ready to use a whirlwind to propel Echo out of the building if I had to.

Behind us, Gaia lost patience. The ground trembled. "You think this is what our father would want?"

"Our father sleeps while the world burns, Gaia. Perhaps this will wake him. Or perhaps we are on our own. Still, you simper along according to his commandments as if you have no will of your own." Ra paused. "Look at me, druid."

Heat scorched my back.

Ezra whimpered and pushed his nose against my leg, shoving me in the direction of the door.

"Look at me!" boomed Ra.

I turned in spite of myself.

His eyes held nothing but hate. "You think I'm the villain and Gaia is the heroine. How little you see. Yes, I killed your mother. But Gaia could have saved her."

Light flared from his black fingertips and rocketed in my direction.

My hands were already raised. My clever hands, which had learned to defend me in such a small, thrilling space of time.

The air moved around us as I called forth a whirlwind to surround us. Within seconds, my hair whipped around me, and both wolf and leopard struggled to remain on their feet. Their front paws lifted off the ground, and whimpers met my ears.

My heart pounded. This was the greatest show of power I had managed.

But I didn't know how long I could keep it up, and my tingling fingers were deadening.

Ra's great sparking whips of electricity wound around us, but the whirlwind acted like a shield. Gaia's vines and roots snaked up from the ground and wound around Ra, but he burned great sections away, determined to reach us. Determined to have his vengeance.

He smiled when his current sliced through and hit me.

I cried out in pain and sent one last gust from both palms at Ezra and Echo before my magic fizzled out. My efforts sent them clear of the sun god, giving them a chance to escape.

The atmosphere changed around us like the earth goddess had gone nuclear.

Or maybe it was Ra. I could barely see.

Another agonising blow tore through my body. The noise that left my mouth was alien to me. I crashed into the remnants of the Tesla. The cracking of bones filled my ears, and fire burned through me. Pain seared through every cell of my body. My legs gave way, but my fall was cushioned by something soft.

As I floated into unconsciousness, I heard Ezra's voice.

He pressed something small and cool into my palm.

"You'll be all right, I promise," he murmured into my ear. He lifted me into his arms as if I weighed nothing. "Get to the detective, cat. Tell him to arrange for the defences to be lowered at Wildwoods. I need to teleport her into the infirmary."

I leaned my head against his chest and relinquished control as the world spun.

26

Dawn rose as a pale shadow of itself. I woke tangled in bedsheets far inferior to the thread count a forty-year-old woman was used to. A stifled snore next to me frightened me into thinking I was back in bed with Alex. I jerked myself into a sitting position in an unfamiliar room, surrounded by my father, Marina, Ezra and Echo.

Ezra's snores sounded like a pig eating from a trough. He seemed to be wrapped in a bed sheet from the waist down.

Dad closed his artist's pad and came to kiss my brow. "She's awake. Thank the gods, you're okay. The shrine will be laden with offerings tonight. Why didn't you tell me your plan?"

My throat was parched. "I didn't want to worry you."

"Beta, what is a father for if not to pray for his child?"

"I hate to break it to you, Joshi," said Marina. "But the gods were responsible for this."

"The gods can be both good and bad. Surely you realise this by now, Marina?" said Dad. "I might have lost you without your friends' quick thinking. Marina sensed your distress and made the detective do a U-turn. Echo caught up with them. It was his idea to ask the Prime Sorcerer to lower the defences to allow Ezra to teleport straight here."

Echo padded over to the bed. "The dog loaned you his healing charm. If he had got you here any later, you might not have made it. He carried you in here butt naked without a thought for his own injuries."

"Is everyone else okay?" I remembered charred flesh on the battlefield and Elvira's limp body.

Marina squeezed my hand. "We're all fine."

My insides ached. I looked under the sheets, astonished to find I had nothing on except some wafer-thin hospital knickers and a barely-there gown. What had happened to my control pants?

A cursory check of my body revealed no obvious areas of concern. A map of mottled blue veins had appeared on the sorest parts of my body, but I figured I'd had a lucky escape. My skin was intact, and no bones were out of place.

I ran my hand over my head and down my neck. My hair had been combed, and the weird mole had disappeared.

Thank God. Or thank the Otherworld.

Ezra stirred. "Hi, hellfire. How are you feeling?"

"Okay, thanks to you." My face warmed as he shifted in his chair, and the sheet dipped.

Marina grinned and brought me a glass of water.

"So this is the Wildwoods infirmary?" I took a sip of the water and cast my eyes around the long dormitory-style room with eight beds.

Unlike a hospital, there was no bleeping machinery to be seen. An assortment of leaves and potions stood on a trolley nearby. Luscious tree canopies swayed outside the window. A vase of my favourite purple tulips sat on my bedside.

We'd done the unimaginable, but Ra's words ran through me like a jolt. *I killed your mother. But Gaia could have saved her.*

I didn't want to think of Gaia as anything but my ally, but

I'd made so many mistakes these past weeks. I couldn't be sure if she'd been one of them. "What happened to Gaia?"

"I don't know." Ezra glanced at the dull dawn sky. "I whisked you out of there, and we didn't look back. But the coven's rats should report back soon."

Dad left my side to tear the first page of the paper out of his artist's pad with care and handed me a watercolour. "We've been here for hours, and I've been trying to distract myself. Do you remember the childhood stories I used to make up about Tielbu the dragon?"

I nodded. "Tielbu the Magnificent."

He beamed and handed me the paper. "That's right. I painted him for you while you slept. It always helped to tell you a Tielbu story when you were scared as a child."

In my father's stories, Tielbu had always been the protector. The protector of children or villages or magical castles. Whatever the foe, there was always a happy ending.

The long-tailed blue dragon stared at me from the page. Calm, amber eyes sat within a rounded skull, just as I'd imagined him as a child. Iridescent scales covered its body. He had four slim limbs and curved talons that could do monstrous damage, along with his fiery breath and colossal wingspan.

Tears filled my eyes. "I love it, Dad."

A cough sounded and in came Phinnaeous Shine, replete in his robes despite the early hour, stepping out of the shadows along with Rayna Williamson. "How lucky you are, Miss Verma, to find yourself within these hallowed walls rather than in a grave. It seems you disobeyed the first rule: never meddle in the affairs of the gods. What makes you think you are above the law? I should have guessed as much after your shenanigans at the Kraglek ceremony. The senate would be justified in banishing you from the Otherworld before you have even attempted the trial."

Midlife Dawn

I held my breath. There was so much I still wanted to learn. I was only getting started.

"Now, hold on a minute, Prime Sorcerer. Surely you can make an exception," said Dad.

"Blame me," said Ezra. "I should have controlled her better. I'm her mentor, after all."

"You would dare blame the granddaughter of Rajika Verma for last night?" growled Echo.

I arched my eyebrow. "I knew exactly what law I was breaking, and I'd do it again."

Rayna considered me. "Maybe we shouldn't be hasty, Phinnaeous. After all, Minister Drach participated in this scheme. Would we also banish her and the coven? I would think the loss they suffered would be punishment enough. And Miss Verma managed to enlist the help of the earth goddess. By extension, Gaia is also an ally of Wildwoods. Ra poses no immediate threat after the goddess's intervention. On the contrary, Miss Verma and her merry crew appeared to have saved a great number of humdrum lives."

"At this rate, we'll be giving her the Wildwoods Medal of Honour," said the Prime Sorcerer. "And what of the destroyed warehouse in Tooting with the cherry blossom emerging from its centre? Journalists from the local paper are already sniffing around."

"Phinnaeous, you know very well it's Lavinia who must answer for disobeying the rules. Mr Neuhoff has always been her weak spot," said Rayna.

Marina nodded sagely. "The warehouse was already in a sorry state. No one will remember it tomorrow. Besides, if Alisha is banished from the Otherworld, I go too."

"And me," said Dad, who probably would have preferred that anyway.

"Not me," said Echo, "but I object all the same."

The Prime Sorcerer sighed. "You were lucky this time, but mark my words: this is a dangerous game you are playing.

While I'm inclined to leave it at a warning this time, you have won a reprieve only because of your exceptional bravery. I'll be watching you *very* closely."

Rayna approached with a wooden spatula. Her potions and hip dagger clanked on her belt. Her long, silver hair brushed my arm as she leaned over me. "Stick out your tongue."

I did as I was told and made an *aah* noise on reflex like Mum had taught me to do.

Marina stepped forward, all ears.

"The pickled beetroot, together with the bee's sting, the juice of a honeydew melon and the tears of a pony born in a southwest-facing stable seem to have done the trick. Take it easy over the next few days, Miss Verma. And be sure to pass the trial when the time comes, won't you?" She skewered Marina and me with a pointed look. "We are expecting great things from you both."

"We will train with renewed focus as soon as Alisha recovers, Minister," said Ezra.

Rayna looked down her nose at him. "You would do well to get your priorities in order, Mr Neuhoff. We have any number of peculiars willing to take up the role of seeker. Consider this a black mark on your record."

Ezra dipped his head in acknowledgement.

"Er, Minister, I don't suppose you could teach me how you healed Alisha's wounds? And Echo's and Ezra's, for that matter?" said Marina.

"The wolf and the leopard have some healing powers, although I did help things along. Alisha has no such natural defence system, but Ezra's thistle charm gave her a temporary boost. Still, it is inappropriate to ask me to share my secrets with you, empath. I am surprised you asked. A couple of training sessions in the arena and some lucky escapes from vengeful beings do not make a successful peculiar."

Marina winced. "Easy. I was doing okay until you crushed my ego."

Cool blue eyes twinkled. "No need for that, Miss Ambrose. You're quite the enigma yourself. No obvious history of magical genealogy, according to our scholars. My best guess is that you had a predisposition to empathy, and your talents were triggered by your open nature and the depth of your sisterhood with Miss Verma. Such a leap has only happened in a handful of circumstances across history. New magical lineages born overnight. It's quite exciting."

Marina beamed.

"Then we will proceed as agreed." The Prime Sorcerer sprinkled dust on me. "The dawn is weak today. It will not trouble us. Now rest, granddaughter of Rajika Verma. Your body needs to heal. Your loved ones will be here when you wake."

I fought his spell. But my eyelids didn't respond to my command, and I drifted on clouds into a deep sleep.

THE INFIRMARY WAS dark when I woke, and my loved ones had gone. I listened for other possible patients, but no breathing met my ears.

Creeping out of bed, I switched on a light and checked the other bays. Not a soul in sight, but I did spot my clothes folded on the neighbouring bed. They stank of molten rubber and burnt flesh, but they spared my modesty. The leggings had a tear just below the bottom, and the hoodie was missing an arm, but I whooped when I found my control pants and sports bra.

A few minutes later, I had dressed, picked up my father's drawing of Tielbu the dragon and plotted my escape. Walking through Crystal Palace Park and onto the tube barefoot would probably raise some eyebrows. I didn't care.

I missed home.

I missed Marina and Echo.

I missed Ezra.

I wanted a proper reunion without the big shots from Wildwoods cramping our style.

Outside the window, the tree canopies shuddered with such magnitude that I thought a storm had erupted just in time to prevent my getaway. I pressed my forehead to the window, exhausted from the past twenty-four hours. My reflection showed huge eyebags and a pasty complexion, but it was nothing a powder puff and a slick of lipstick wouldn't fix. I let the cool glass take the edge off my fuzzy head.

A movement in the window reflection sent a shiver of panic up my spine.

"I am pleased to see you survived, Alisha, granddaughter of Rajika Verma."

The storm outside petered out.

The tulips in the vase on the nightstand bowed their heads in her presence.

"Gaia." I swung around, and my father's drawing slipped from my fingers.

She wore a sequinned, burnt orange sari, chosen perhaps to taunt Ra. Her hair no longer flew wild about her shoulders. A benign smile shone from her cherubic face. She looked harmless. In the humdrum world, this Gaia was simply an old woman. But my eyes had been opened.

I remembered Ra's words, and my anger swelled at her betrayal. But I swallowed it. I had learned to choose wisely before spitting in the face of the gods, and I didn't want Rayna Willowsun to find me in a puddle on the Wildwoods floor.

Gaia smiled. "It takes years for a druid to master their talents. I know this because I have known many druids across the ages. I have found them natural allies. Their talents have been varied: potions, plants, communicating with god's creatures, and transformation abilities. As such, we have much in common. I'm relieved I don't need to lower myself to fraternising with vampires or goblins." She shuddered. "It is my job to love all creatures, but there, I draw the line. A druid, however, is a worthy ally and a sweet-smelling one."

To be honest, I had smelled better. I took a step back and tried to slow my breathing.

"You have no need to fear me, druid. We are on the same side."

In her eyes, I saw the turning of the Earth. I blinked, wondering if Rayna's medicines had hallucinatory properties. I quite fancied asking for more.

"Are we on the same side, though?" I said, my heart thumping. "Ra said you could have saved my mother. You chose not to."

"There was a breath's instant to make the decision." Gaia paused. "A daughter is always a child until her mother dies. You wouldn't have taken the steps you did without the impetus of your mother's death. You wouldn't have discovered your place in the Otherworld."

I couldn't imagine going back to my old life.

But I would give it all up to have Mum back.

"It was you who filled the car with her favourite flowers, wasn't it?" The penny had dropped when I'd seen the cherry blossom push through the concrete. It all made sense now how the detective had found flowers growing out of metal.

Who else but Gaia had that power?

Gaia nodded. "She didn't smell death or the burnt electrics in the car. She didn't see the twisted metal or her broken body. The garden of Gallic roses grew around her. Their scent filled her nose, and her pride for her family filled her heart."

"For that, I thank you."

Her wrinkles deepened with a frown. "It occurred to me

that I may not have been entirely fair to you. You are lucky not to have lost an eye or your life. I have a gift for you."

I bit my lip. Gifts rarely came without expectations. Hell, Alex had expected a lifetime of bondage in return for my wedding ring. How else could I explain the amount of time I'd spent at the kitchen sink, the stove or the washing machine?

"There is no need for a gift, goddess," I said. "I managed just as well without one."

She eyed my torn clothes and wan face. "The evidence says otherwise. Would you refuse me, druid? Am I not the giver of gifts? Would you risk failing at your task because of pride or mistrust?"

I searched her face. That sounded scarily like my task wasn't over. I definitely hadn't signed up for a rematch. "Will Ra return?"

Gaia shrugged. "Perhaps, one day. For now, he has skulked off with his tail between his legs. May his retreat be long-lived. Yesterday took its toll on both of us. Still, immortal beings can never be entirely vanquished. Mortals, on the other hand…" She pulled out a sword from the folds of her sari. "You will accept this gift if you hope to survive. Next time won't be so easy."

I stared open-mouthed at the sword. It looked like something that belonged in a museum. It had a slender, black blade. The hilt was ivory, smooth and unadorned, except for a small, deep-set blue jasper.

"The sword was given to me by Death when we were lovers. Its blade, once translucent, was made from a heavenly cloud. When Death blessed it, the blade became obsidian black. In mortal hands, it is only as strong as the bearer's magical lineage, and you can channel your ancestors through it. If the strike is true, an ancestral thrust can add power and disrupt the mind of the attacker. Its name is Transcender."

"Goddess, I can't accept it." My voice quivered.

Her eyes flashed. "You would say no to me? Would you refuse an abundant supply of food or the gift of children or a place in paradise?"

"When you put it that way... It's just I'm afraid of not meeting your expectations."

"Mortals rarely meet my expectations, druid, but once in a while, they surpass them. Would you take that chance?"

I gulped.

"Besides, it is a meagre weapon in my hands. It is lightweight and double-edged, perfect for an untested swordswoman. I never cared for it. Death never paid attention to my likes, even when we were lovers. She was utterly inattentive and more interested in corpses than pillow talk. The sword's hilt is made from mammoth tusk. What kind of fool offers the earth goddess a gift made from a creature? Still, in the right hands, Transcender is capable of doing much good. Beware of listening too carefully to the voices when you hold it. They are often more of a distraction than a help."

She handed me the sword.

"Thank you." A rush of sounds filled my head like the wind-laden voices on a carousel. I dropped the sword like a hot potato.

Gaia sighed. "Be careful with that, druid. Perhaps put it down until you have regained your strength."

I laid the sword on the bed.

The voices disappeared like someone had lifted the stylus from a record player. Pretty freaky gift, if you asked me. I much preferred Dad's painting.

Gaia pointed to the floor, where I had dropped the painting of Tielbu. "That is one of your father's inkings?"

I nodded. "A dragon."

She smiled. "One of the earth's most magnificent creatures. Have you such disdain for art? Pick it up, druid."

"I dropped it in fright when you arrived."

"No doubt a sneezing ant would also frighten you. Centre your mind, druid. Match my breathing." She inhaled to a count of three and then exhaled. "That's it. Match the breath of the universe, and when you are ready, rest your fingers gently on the inking of the dragon and draw them back. Not so hesitant now. With belief."

I focussed on the image of Tielbu. It was easy. I knew his stories. I loved his face.

My breathing came steadily, at one with the earth goddess's. My fingers caressed the painting, and when I drew them back, I sensed the dimensions in the paper. Not two or three but many more. I sensed blood and veins and cells. I sensed danger and friendship and hot, burning flames as if the painting wasn't a page but an ocean, and I could coax the dragon from deep inside.

The blue lines of the Tielbu swam before me, lifting off the page. Smoke filled my nose, and reptilian skin danced beneath my fingertips.

I jerked my hand away from the page and let the watercolour plummet to the cold floor, breaking the connection. The dragon became cold and lifeless on the page once more.

This was madness. I wasn't ready.

I stumbled, dizzy, and blackness crept in from the corners of my eyes.

Gaia laughed. "You didn't think that wind was all you could do?"

Soft hands coaxed my trembling body into bed—a feather-light kiss on my brow, like the ones Mum used to give.

"Rest now, druid." The goddess's voice was a lullaby. "Your body tells you to sleep. All will be well. Be sure to give the leopard my regards when you wake."

27

After my run-in with Gaia, I slept like a stone. When I eventually made it out of the infirmary the next day and over the Wildwoods rope bridges, I half expected Ezra to appear, toss me over his shoulder in a fireman's lift and whisk me home. That would have been hot, but it turned out he wasn't that protective of me.

I missed him, but he didn't owe me anything.

Besides, I was an independent woman. I didn't need him to rescue me. I hailed a cab home, squelchy bare feet and all.

Over the next week, Dad and Marina did their best to nurse me back to full health. They even managed to restock the freezer with premium salmon and steak for Echo. Surf 'n' turf, just like he liked it. I breathed a sigh of relief at not having to worry about any poodles, Labradors or deer he might get his claws into.

Processing what had happened was harder than my physical recovery. I didn't regret putting myself in the fight. I was proud of myself, and I was proud of my friends. We had avenged Mum. We'd faced a fearsome enemy and won, despite only just getting our training wheels in the

Otherworld. Turned out an old pony could learn new tricks. What was more, not blowing my own trumpet or anything, but the earth goddess seemed to like me. She didn't have to give me the sword. She didn't have to show me that my druidry extended to more than the wind.

I was an animator too. That was if I ever got the hang of it.

On the morning of Nita's funeral, I woke with an aching heart. I knew I had to go, despite my pangs of guilt for putting her in danger and not saving her. Her family didn't blame me for her death. Detective Jameson had informed them that the intruder at night class had compressed Nita's windpipe.

"It's easier that way. They don't need to know the truth," he said on the telephone. "A loss is hard enough without distorting their view of reality. Some things are on a need-to-know basis. Otherwise, the world would descend into chaos."

Who was I to argue? The Founder's Law, too, stated that peculiars must hide the existence of the Otherworld from humdrums.

I arrived at Streatham Cemetery early to pay my respects at Mum's grave and Melissa's.

Then I joined the mourners at Nita's funeral under a cloud-heavy sky. Her parents stood bowed at the graveside as the priest spoke his words. Ashes to ashes. Dust to dust.

My night class students had turned up in full—Tomás and Santiago in matching suits; Farzad handing out spare hankies; Nagma dabbing her eyes with the scarf of her salwar kameez; Ethan, Hassan and Marek, whispering hello and their regrets. All readily accepted the detective's explanation, with the exception of Fei Yen and Faeza.

"We won't say a word," said Fei Yen under her breath.

"Not a word." Faeza gave me a thumbs-up.

I still hadn't unravelled their place in the Otherworld. This wasn't the place.

Afterwards, when the service had concluded and we had

thrown handfuls of dirt onto Nita's coffin, I hugged her parents, murmured my condolences, and then walked away past mounds of fresh earth, weeping angel statues and weathered gravestones.

Suddenly, Ezra materialised next to me. Like the universe had told him I was in need.

I jumped three feet high.

His damp hair and skin had the tang of the sea like he'd taste of sun and salt. "Hey, Alisha."

I ignored the butterflies dancing in my belly and swatted him. "Hey, yourself. Are you *ever* going to make a normal entrance?"

"Surprises are the spice of life. Haven't you learned that by now?" Grey eyes locked on mine as he turned serious. "I'm glad you're safe."

"Thanks to you."

"Thank you for not forgetting your promise about the vial. It takes a gutsy druid to cross a witch. I won't forget it."

"How did you find me?"

He smiled. "I'm a seeker. It's what I do. But this time, a leopard told me you might need me."

I swallowed hard. "I don't need you."

"You don't? Are you sure?" He cupped the small of my back and leaned down to kiss me.

Heat travelled all the way to my toes. I leaned into him, closed my eyes and returned the gentle pressure of his lips.

Energy pulsed between us like static electricity.

The ground moved, and I travelled through time and space in his arms.

He pulled away, and we were back on the path leading out of the cemetery.

"There's something about you that makes me want more," he said. "Do you feel it too?"

My heart raced. I let my lashes shield my desire. There was no doubt I wanted him. I looked up at him and smiled.

"Tease." He cupped my cheek and pulled me closer again, this time with more force. "I have some werewolf business to tie up. It shouldn't take more than a few days. It's about time we go on a date, don't you think?"

Then he was gone, leaving just the hint of his presence on my skin.

I ARRANGED an afternoon picnic in the park with Dad, Sahil, Marina and Echo. The fresh air with family and friends was exactly what I needed to clear my head after a week of being cooped up in the flat.

I poured out some lemonade. "I visited Mum's and Melissa's graves before the funeral this morning."

"How thoughtful of you," said Dad. "The flowers I planted seem to like it there."

I nodded. "Melissa's grave was empty, but I brought along a racy Jilly Cooper novel I found in a charity shop and left it there for someone to discover. She would have liked that."

"The book will turn into sludge in the London rain," purred Echo. "It would have been better to leave a deer carcass. That would have made a real statement and would have had the dual purpose of making wandering creatures happy."

Dad laughed, and it did my heart good to see him smile. "You may be centuries old, but you still have much to learn, Echo."

"That might be true, Joshi, but did you hear? The goddess sent me her regards," the leopard said.

"Hooray for you, Echo." Dad rolled his eyes. "My wife dies, my daughter allows herself to be a pawn of the gods, and I've not had so much as a hello. She could have at least let me witness Alisha bringing Tielbu to life."

"No need to be sour about it," purred Echo. "You may be

past your prime, but your time may yet come. Especially now that Alisha has inherited Rajika's talents. Animator and painter pairings are blessed by the heavens."

"Actually, you two, I barely lifted him off the page. What I don't understand is why it didn't work for the frog in Dad's attic."

"Well, darling, you probably weren't giving it any oomph," said Dad.

Sahil rolled his eyes. "See how he blames a lack of magical talent on us instead of our genes?" He swallowed a chocolate-covered strawberry and offered me one. "You're lucky, sis. I'd be happy with one, but the peculiar gene seems to have skipped me. Even Marina ended up with empath gifts. It's not fair I'm the odd one out. Who can a man speak to about getting an upgrade on peculiar talents?"

Echo paused from chasing butterflies. "The man-child is jealous."

"Do you blame me? I mean, the goddess even gave Alisha a sword." He eyed me warily like I'd snuck it out underneath my vest top. "Where is it anyway?"

"In my knicker drawer. I figured any thieves brave enough to put their hand in there would be welcome to it." It called to me in the dead of the night when all I wanted was sleep. Part of me wished Gaia had never given it to me.

"Seriously?" laughed Marina. "I reckon that's the best place for it. You know, Sahil, I could help you unblock your talents."

Sahil waggled his eyebrows. "You just want to get me flat on my back."

Marina groaned. "Unlikely. Afraid these days I'm sharing pillow talk with Robert Jameson."

Dad coughed to hide his embarrassment. Indian Dads weren't great with this level of sexual honesty.

Marina took pity on him. "I'm so glad Rosalie's pictures are back, Joshi. That must be a relief."

"My heart sang when I saw them," said Dad. "She had such a beautiful face. I was afraid I would forget it. Now I don't have to paint her features individually. It had rather a frightening effect when I walked into my studio. We've been through so much. Your mum would be proud of us all."

I believed it. It had taken forty years to understand my own worth.

I cleared up the remnants of our jam sandwiches and lemonade, then stood up. "How about a game of humdrum Frisbee? Four players, two teams. Echo doubles as referee and ball boy. Dad, you're with me. Sahil, you're with Marina."

"Game on." Sahil sprang to his feet. He put his arm around me. "You look trim. Are you on the stinky cabbage diet again?"

Marina guffawed. "More like she's pining for Ezra. Not that my radar says she should worry."

The mottled blue veins on my skin were receding, and although I wasn't quite bikini-ready, bumps and bruises aside, I was slimmer than I'd been in my life. I almost didn't need my control pants. I put my weight loss down to grief and running hell for leather from crazy gods. I'd accidentally found a new exercise fad. Some women would kill for that knowledge.

I chucked my flip-flop at Marina. "Actually, I saw him this morning."

She grinned and nibbled on a sandwich. "You sly fox! Tell us all the details."

"Later, I promise." I couldn't wait to fill her in on all the details when we were alone, but they weren't for Dad's ears. "But first, I'm going to whoop your arse at Frisbee."

Sahil grinned at Marina. "We're going to make a great team, Ambrose."

Echo picked up the Frisbee between his teeth and tossed it at my feet. "Everyone feeling good? That's a Nina Simone lyric." He honked with laughter. "No peculiar powers allowed. Take your places. Begin!"

I felt a tingle in my fingers, the druid gift that was becoming as familiar to me as my own skin.

What else were rules for, if not to be broken?

ACKNOWLEDGMENTS

This pandemic year has been the perfect time to write Alisha's story. Escaping into fantasy is a way to soothe spirits and right wrongs when the world is troubling.

My deep thanks to the thirteen authors who founded this genre for magic-wielding heroines over forty. It's a joy to write about wise women with life experience who kick arse.

I'm so grateful to my beta readers, Debbie, Sherry and Jen, for your book instincts and wisdom. To Bianca, your support and keen eye mean so much. Thank you to my editors Jeni and Toni, and my cover artist Maria for making this story shine.

Thanks to our daughter Hana for dropping what you were doing every time I asked you to read and for not pulling your punches when giving critiques. To our son Raiyan, you keep me on track with your word count demands, and your interest in my workday makes me melt. To our little one, Noah, your cuddles lift me, and yes, you can have a snack.

The biggest thanks goes to my husband, Jan, for always being in my corner, being my first reader and letting me warm my cold feet on you.

And thank you, dear reader, for taking a chance on this story. I hope you stay for the ride.

SHARE YOUR READER LOVE

I hope you enjoyed *Midlife Dawn*. Please take a few moments to leave a review online. Reviews are so appreciated. They tell authors which stories resonate and help readers discover our work.

In the next book in the series, *Midlife Tremors*, Alisha faces a magical trial at Wildwoods, gets flirty with Ezra and must overcome a new threat. Read on to enjoy the first chapter.

If you are a book blogger and would like to feature my books, please get in touch at www.NilluNasser.com.

N. Z. Nasser

xoxo

STAY IN TOUCH & GRAB YOUR SHORT STORY

Come and be part of my tribe and join my facebook reader group at Nasser's Book Nymphs.

To receive the short stories in the Druid Heir world and keep up to date with my news, sign up for my fantasy newsletter at www.nillunasser.com.

For a close lens into my world, you can get early access to work-in-progress chapters and other goodies by joining my exclusive community: https://reamstories.com/nznasser.

Here's a coupon for the first time you make a purchase in my online store (it's so pretty!) at www.nillunasser.com: NILLU15.

MIDLIFE TREMORS: DRUID HEIR BOOK 2

My friends and I might have saved the day against a vengeful god, but I still don't know the first thing about the Otherworld. There's training sessions with my mentor Ezra, history lessons with the vampire Orpheus, plus my haunting dragon dreams. It's not easy to stay on track, especially given how distracted I am by Ezra's crinkly eyes and hot bod. Who knew that a new love at forty would give me dewy skin and a renewed zest for life?

When a series of earthquakes hits London, the Prime Sorcerer advises me to focus on my upcoming magical trial at Wildwoods. But I'm my own woman, and my instincts tell me to dig deeper even before the goddess Gaia invites me to tea. It's not like I'm going to pass the trial anyway. I've already made enough enemies in the Otherworld to fill a granny annex.

To find my place in the Otherworld, all I have to do is gather my allies and trust myself. How hard could that be?

If you're a fan of Paranormal Women's Fiction and magic-wielding heroines over forty, grab Druid Heir Book 2 today.

ALSO BY N. Z. NASSER

DRUID HEIR

Midlife Dawn, Book 1

Midlife Tremors, Book 2

Midlife News, Book 3

Midlife Drift, Book 4

Midlife Portals, Book 5

Midlife Eclipse, Book 6

Midlife Battle, Book 7

Druid Heir Collections

MAJESTIC MIDLIFE WITCH

To Save a Sister, Book 1

To Curse a Rival, Book 2

To Trick a Raja, Book 3

To Hunt a Foe, Book 4

NEWSLETTER EXCLUSIVES

The Magical Grandmother, Druid Heir Short Story 0.5

A First Date in Paris, Druid Heir Short Story 1.5

Midlife Battle, Druid Heir 7 Bonus Epilogue

To Become a Witch, Majestic Midlife Short Story 0.5

Biryani Junction, a Majestic Midlife Witch Cookbook

ABOUT THE AUTHOR

N. Z. Nasser is a writer of fantasy fiction. Her stories are about women who change the world, filled with magic and rooted in friendship.

A lover of barefoot walks along the beach, she is glad to have left behind her career in the civil service and to never wear heels again. Whether she is writing in her garden office or wrangling laundry, she is happiest with a cup of tea at her side.

She lives in London with her husband, three children, two cats and a fox-mad dog.